100 DRESSES

The Starlight Slippers

100 DRESSES

100 DRESSES

The Starlight Slippers

③

Susan Maupin Schmid

Illustrations by Lissy Marlin

A Yearling Book

Text copyright © 2018 by Susan Maupin Schmid
Cover art copyright © 2018 by Melissa Manwill
Interior illustrations copyright © 2018 by Lissy Marlin

All rights reserved. Published in the United States by Yearling, an imprint of Random House Children's Books, a division of Penguin Random House LLC, New York. Originally published in hardcover in the United States by Random House Children's Books, New York, in 2018.

Yearling and the jumping horse design are registered trademarks of Penguin Random House LLC.

Visit us on the Web! rhcbooks.com

Educators and librarians, for a variety of teaching tools, visit us at RHTeachersLibrarians.com

The Library of Congress has cataloged the hardcover edition of this work as follows:
Names: Schmid, Susan Maupin, author. | Marlin, Lissy, illustrator.
Title: The starlight slippers / Susan Maupin Schmid ; Illustrations by Lissy Marlin.
Description: First edition. | New York : Random House, [2018] | Series: 100 dresses ; 3 | Summary: Darling and her friends locate Queen Candace's wedding slippers, which Princess Mariposa wants to wear on her own wedding day, unaware that they are laced with magic.
Identifiers: LCCN 2017006199 | ISBN 978-0-553-53377-4 (hardcover) | ISBN 978-0-553-53379-8 (ebook)
Subjects: | CYAC: Fairy tales. | Courts and courtiers—Fiction. | Magic—Fiction. | Clothing and dress—Fiction. | Orphans—Fiction. | Shoes—Fiction.
Classification: LCC PZ8.S2835 St 2018 | DDC [Fic]—dc23

ISBN 978-0-553-53380-4 (pbk.)

Printed in the United States of America
10 9 8 7 6 5 4 3 2 1
First Yearling Edition 2019

For the Hanleys: Jennifer, Dave,
Devan, Shaylynn, and Brienne

1

Fog wrapped the castle. Not the cloudy vapor of an early-spring morning, but the fog of forgetfulness. It became as though thoughts of the past slipped through people's fingers. Oh, not that they couldn't remember when they tried, but more that they lost the desire to keep those memories.

I knew the dragons were to blame, because they were what people forgot the most. I'd mention them and receive a blank stare in response.

"Dragons?" they'd gasp, blinking in astonishment. "There is no such thing as dragons!"

How quickly they forgot. When my father, Magnificent Wray, had collared those dragons, they'd celebrated. When he'd set the dragons to build the Star Castle, they'd cheered. But when he passed away, the dragons became a myth in a matter of months. A foggy, uncertain idea that was best left unthought. Only a few *people retained the memories of those days. A handful held the precious trickle of thoughts: vital notions of dragons, magic, and danger.*

I am one of the few.

—*Lady Amber DeVere,* My Father, Magnificent Wray

The key burned a hole in my apron pocket. It was small and silver, with a starburst inscribed on its bow. And although dozens of keys hung in the Head Steward's office, they were ordinary. None had a starburst. *This* key had once belonged to Magnificent Wray, my ancestor and the architect who had designed the castle. A man of mystery and magic. The starburst was his emblem, and that made this one special.

The bow held the smallest spark of magic. I hadn't noticed it until I pressed my thumb down hard, but it was there. Which made me wonder: Did the lock it fit hold a greater magic? A stronger, more powerful force? What would happen when the two met? And what lay behind that lock?

Did *this* key unlock a treasure?

That question fired my imagination with possibilities.

"Gold? Jewels? A magic ring?" I mumbled under my breath. "Magnificent Wray's secret workshop? *What?*"

"Quiet," Gillian whispered, peeking around the corner ahead of us.

I rolled my eyes. We were pressed against a wall outside the corridor to the Princess's suite. It was early, and everyone in the castle was busy getting ready for the day. Our chances of running into someone were small. But the past weeks of slinking around together looking for the keyhole had given Gillian a taste for stealth. She made each search an ordeal of hand signals, tiptoeing, hiding behind curtains, and flattening ourselves against walls.

It had gotten a bit ridiculous. But every keyhole beckoned, *Try me.*

Each chance we got, we hightailed it to the next tantalizing lock. One of us would be the lookout while the other tried the key. So far we hadn't had any luck. But Roger, the First Stable Boy, was right: it was too small to open doors. And we'd discovered it was too big to open jewel cases.

We were no closer to finding out what the key *did* open than we'd been when we started. There were at least a million locks in the Star Castle. We'd given the key to Roger, and he'd tried every keyhole in the stables and the outbuildings. Nothing. But it had to open *something,* and we planned to keep searching until we found out what.

Ahead of me, Gillian braced herself to sprint for the

next lock. Her dark curls were swept back with a ribbon, her brow furrowed in concentration, her brown eyes fastened on the prize.

"On the count of three," she whispered. "One—"

"Three," I said, eager to arrive at the next lock.

I bounded around the corner and down the corridor. Past the ornate doors of the Princess's suite and straight to the double doors leading to the soon-to-be King's suite. It had been closed up since the death of Princess Mariposa's father, years earlier. Until now.

Gillian hurried to catch up with me.

"Darling, wait!" she called.

The doors to the King's suite were painted to resemble a view from a window. The painting portrayed Eliora by the White Sea, this very kingdom. The details were stunning. A mountain rose above the sea. Birds soared. Ships drifted in the harbor. The city sat nestled in its cove. And the Star Castle crested a rise that climbed to the mountain's top. I squinted at the brushstrokes: every leaf and stone was executed so that you felt you could reach out and touch it.

"It's a special kind of painting," Gillian said, panting a little. "Trumpet oil, Baroness Azure called it. I think that's a kind of paint. Anyway, it's supposed to fool you into thinking it's real."

Gillian had the habit of repeating what the Baroness told her. Although not necessarily correctly.

"Trompe l'oeil," I said. "It's a style, not a paint."

"Sure," she agreed affably.

She reached out and turned the castle, which rotated because it was actually the doorknob. The enameled metal piece fit so neatly into the painting that you didn't suspect it was there. She pulled the door open and walked inside.

"The Baroness said," she began, "that the Princess's suite used to be the Queen's suite when there was a queen. But now the Princess uses it, since she's like a queen. Only not. But she will be."

Princess Mariposa had stayed a princess since her parents' death because her father's will stated that she could be queen only upon her marriage. In a matter of weeks, there would be a wedding, a coronation, and a ball! The entire castle was abuzz over the upcoming events.

"I hope the Baroness said something we don't already know," I replied.

"She says lots of stuff." Gillian paused a moment to admire the suite's anteroom, with its three doors. "The King's suite is a mirror image of the Princess's."

A forest flowed around me, holding the walls, the floor, and the ceiling in its painted leafy embrace. The doors nearly melted into the walls. A bluethroat eyed me from its perch in a tree. The sun dappled its little brown head and the white-tufted blue patch under its beak. A rabbit hid in a hollow.

"The fastest way is to go straight through the bedroom," Gillian added.

She opened the center door, breaking the illusion, and stepped through. I followed her into a room devoid of furniture, where the scents of turpentine and lemon oil tickled my nose. The walls glistened with fresh paint: royal blue, Prince Sterling's favorite color. The carved crown moldings glinted with gold. The marble floor gleamed.

"It's being redecorated for Prince Sterling," Gillian explained, gesturing at the ladders and buckets scattered about the room. "New furniture, drapes, carpet. Well, all except for the reading room, of course."

"Uh-huh," I said.

"Prince Sterling declared that it was already perfect. He said don't change anything but the drapes," she continued, following me. "Mind your step."

I nearly stumbled over a rolled-up carpet. Gillian caught me with a grin. Threading our way around buckets and ladders, we reached the next door. Beyond it was a lounge. A partially finished mural wrapped the walls, but Gillian didn't waste time admiring it. She raced to the last door and threw it open.

"Here it is," she announced, as if I wouldn't grasp where I was. "The reading room!"

The King's reading room was a symphony of woods: maple, walnut, cherry, and mahogany. Polished parquet graced the floor. Carved panels braced the walls. Bare windows stared, wide-eyed without their draperies. A plush throne-sized chair sat next to a marble-topped table in the center, and a wonder of built-in bookcases and cabinets circled the room.

Silver keyholes winked at me from every door and drawer. *Untried* keyholes. The King's reading room: what better place to hide Magnificent Wray's treasure? My hand crept into my apron pocket and fastened around the key.

"Don't you want to curl up in that chair and read?" Gillian asked. "Well, I mean you would if the Prince's books were on the shelves. They will be soon—"

"Sure," I said, making a beeline to the nearest lock. "Watch the door."

I slid the key in and jiggled it. Nothing. I tried the next lock, and then another.

"Argh!" I exclaimed, shaking my fist at the cabinet. "One of you has *got* to open!"

Diving from lock to lock in a frenzy, I searched until I felt Gillian's hand on my elbow.

"My turn," she said with a smile that brought out her dimples.

I blinked, the key clutched in my fist. I was halfway around the room from where I had started.

"You look like a Laundress with a stubborn stain." She giggled.

I felt my face heat up. "Sorry," I said, handing her the key. "I got carried away."

"That's okay," she replied. "We do need to hurry. There are a lot more locks in here than I thought there'd be."

"Yes," I said a bit sheepishly.

"I'm starting to sympathize with Cherice," Gillian said.

Cherice, the former Wardrobe Mistress, had dropped the key when she was captured. She'd been hiding in the cellar, lurking in the castle's secret passages, so she'd had months—and before that maybe even *years*—to look. If finding the keyhole that fit the starburst key were easy, she'd have found it ages ago.

"It's got to be here," I said.

"If it is, we'll find it," Gillian replied.

I went to stand guard as she wielded the key like a piece of fine crystal, gingerly testing it keyhole by keyhole.

"Hurry," I reminded her.

She nodded and teased the key into another lock.

The reading room windows grew brighter. Time was slipping away. Sweat broke out on my forehead. We did not want to get caught fumbling around in here where

Princess's Girls had no business being. And there were a number of keyholes left to try.

"Gillian—" I growled.

Through the door, I heard the muffled sound of voices. Someone had come into the suite. I lunged forward and grabbed her.

"Someone's coming!" I hissed in her ear.

We looked at each other and then around the reading room. There was no place to hide.

"We are in so much troub—" she began.

I didn't wait to hear more. I dragged her out of there and into the empty lounge. I scanned the walls, ignoring the mural. The castle was riddled with secret passages that Roger and I had discovered. Since then, Roger had been walking through them, sketching a map. And although we hadn't stumbled on a passage to this part of the castle, there had to be one. Cherice had used one. If I could just find the hidden door—

"A quick peek at your progress, gentlemen," a voice said, "and then I will leave you to your work."

Prince Sterling!

Gillian went white. Footsteps echoed on the marble floor beyond the door. Up on the mural, a waterfall glimmered. I yanked Gillian in front of it.

"Say something about the mural," I said.

9

She tottered for a moment but then recovered herself. She snapped back her curls, conjured up a smile, and exclaimed in a loud voice, "Oh my!"

"It's so pretty!" I sang out just as the lounge door opened.

Prince Sterling walked in with a couple of Painters at his heels.

"Good morning, Girls," the Prince said with a sparkle in his warm brown eyes. "Admiring my mural?"

"Oh yes!" I said. "We couldn't resist taking a peek."

"We hope you're not angry," Gillian said.

"Angry?" The Prince laughed, and then he noticed Gillian's hand. "What's that key you have?"

Gillian and I looked down at the starburst key still clenched between her fingers. Both our hearts skipped a beat. We couldn't lose that key!

"Um . . . ," she said.

"It belongs to Marci," I said.

"Yes, we have an errand," Gillian gasped. "We ought to be going."

The Prince eyed us with a quizzical look. "It's early for errands."

"It is," Gillian stupidly agreed.

"Yes, well," I said, putting on my best servant's face and dredging up the one indisputable excuse I could think of, "we—all of us servants—want everything to be perfect for the wedding. Everything. Perfect." I punctuated my statement with nods.

"All of us," Gillian echoed. "Perfect."

"And yet you've made a detour into my lounge," the Prince pointed out.

"Ah," I said forlornly. "We did."

You couldn't accuse Gillian of being a coward. Armed with only a fork, she had once faced down a gryphon. And now that same courage rose up in her. She winked at the Prince and wagged her finger at him.

"Now, now, you know how it is," she said. "Just because Marci wants something doesn't mean the other servants are available. We were buying time." She gave him her most dazzling smile. "You won't tell on us, will you?"

He ran a hand through his brown hair, considering. "No," he said with a chuckle. "Run along."

We bobbed quick curtsies and escaped before he could ask any more questions. We raced back through the bedroom and ducked into the hall beyond.

Smack-dab into Francesca, the Head Girl.

2

"**W**here have you two been?" Francesca demanded, planting a fist on her hip. Her tone was as crisp as her silver-gray dress and white apron. Even the embroidered silver-gray butterfly on her apron pocket appeared stiff.

As the Head Girl, she was in charge of all the Princess's Girls. But Gillian and I were special cases. I reported to Marci, the Wardrobe Mistress. Gillian took orders from Lindy, the Head Presser. But as far as Francesca was concerned, *every* Girl was accountable to her.

And she had the power to make our lives miserable.

"Oh," Gillian said, batting Francesca's question aside, "His Highness showed us his new mural! So lovely. Didn't you think so, Darling?"

"Yes!" I exclaimed. "Gorgeous."

Francesca chewed on the likelihood of that. "Really? And what is it a mural of?"

I drew a blank. I'd been too busy getting out of trouble to pay attention to the actual painting. All I could recall was the glimmer of a waterfall. But Francesca wasn't allowed in the King's suite either, so I doubted she'd seen it.

"Scenery," I said, shrugging as if all murals were scenery.

"Mountains. Trees. That sort of thing," Gillian added.

Francesca's gray eyes narrowed. She didn't believe us. But she was one to pick her battles wisely, so she snapped her fingers. "Marci wants both of you. In the wardrobe hall. Now," Francesca said. And then she broke into an uncharacteristic grin. "We're getting new uniforms."

I stood in the wardrobe hall as regrets rumbled around in my head. If only we'd gotten up a few minutes earlier. If only we'd had time to try all the locks in the reading room. If only we had some hint, some clue as to what kind of lock the key fit.

At that moment, the key lay beyond my reach, concealed in my clothes, which were neatly folded on a chair across the wardrobe hall. My apron topped the pile, the pocket carefully tucked underneath so that the lump it made wasn't visible.

Twisting at the waist, I glanced over my shoulder.

"Hold still," Rose, the Head Seamstress, admonished.

"Sorry," I said.

I stood in my stocking feet, wearing only my camisole, my bloomers, and my locket. The locket was silver and inscribed with the same starburst as the one on the key. It had been handed down through the Wray family to my mother and then to me.

"Arms straight, please," Rose said.

I held my arms out while she tightened the measuring tape around my middle. I struggled with the urge to sneak another look at my clothes. My shoulders twitched.

"Young lady," Rose said, tilting her head to one side and blinking owlishly, "if you don't hold still, you will be the only Girl wearing an ill-fitting dress."

Marci, the Wardrobe Mistress, cleared her throat. She was enthroned behind her desk, eyeing me.

I stiffened into a statue. The measuring tape squeezed my hips. I hoped that the Head Seamstress's idea of a well-fitting dress allowed for things like bending over and breathing.

Rose squinted at the tape and then scribbled in her notebook. Her bristly black hair was sprinkled with gray and lay twisted in a knot at the nape of her neck. Heavy black eyebrows accented her flat, broad face. She wasn't pretty, but she was striking. Everything about her was clearly defined. Her shoulders squared off. Her black eyes snapped with interest. Her chin thrust out like she meant business.

And she did. She'd measured her way through the roomful of Princess's Girls like the Head Cook whipping up a meringue. Girl after Girl had whisked through Rose's measuring tape. Well, we were only the Princess's Girls for a few more weeks. When the royal wedding day dawned, we would be the Queen's Girls. New title, new uniforms.

"Which one are you again?" Rose asked, tapping her notebook.

"Darling—" I began.

"Dimple," Marci said.

"Fortune," I said at the same time.

"Which is it, Dimple or Fortune?" Rose asked.

"It's Fortune." Marci sighed apologetically. "Sorry, Darling."

I'd been called Darling Dimple for so long that people often forgot it wasn't my real name. Actually, I was Darling *Wray* Fortune, heir to Magnificent Wray and the very last Wray of all. At least I thought I was the last. Cherice had claimed she was. But I had no particular reason to believe her.

"Assistant Wardrobe Mistress," I finished, standing a little taller.

"Under-assistant to the Wardrobe Mistress," Marci corrected.

I shrugged; that was too much of a mouthful. I'd short-ened it. It amounted to the same thing. Princess Mari-posa had given me the title as a reward for apprehending Cherice.

"Ah," Rose said, ticking off my name on her list. "Thank you. You may go."

I scurried to the chair and snatched up my clothes. Francesca and the other Girls had already left, eager to be about their chores. Only Dulcie, the youngest Girl, and Gillian remained. Gillian, already having been measured, dressed slowly and deliberately. When she was finished, a perfect bow would grace her back. Her sleeves would puff just so. I yanked on my clothes. The faster, the better.

Once dressed, I patted my pocket, just to be sure the key was safe.

"Dulcie," Marci warned, "the Head Seamstress is waiting."

Dulcie planted herself, fully dressed, before Rose. Arms crossed tightly over her chest. A stubborn frown on her face. She scuffed her toe into the carpet.

"You are . . . ?" Rose asked her.

Dulcie clamped her lips together.

"This is Dulcie," Marci said. "Dulcie, take off your apron and dress."

Dulcie shook her head, red braids flying. A stray curl slid over her forehead.

Rose reached into the satchel at her feet and pulled out a drawing.

"Young lady, you must cooperate or you will not be wearing this," Rose said, flourishing the picture under her nose.

Dulcie's cheeks pinked with pleasure. I scrambled over to see for myself. Gillian followed, leaning over my shoulder.

The drawing was of a Girl wearing a sky-blue dress with a lace pinafore that had ruffles over the shoulders and a heart-shaped pocket. She wore white stockings and shiny black shoes with straps. Two squares of fabric samples were pinned to the paper: a sky-blue silk and a delicate white lace. *Lace! Ruffles! Silk! Shoes!*

Could this be our new uniform?

"Oh my," Gillian said.

"Is that what we'll be wearing?" I gasped, imagining my boots gone and the shiny black shoes in their place.

"That is what the Queen's Girls will wear to the royal wedding," Rose said. "Stubborn children who will not be measured will not attend."

"*Only* to the wedding," Marci said. "You'll have more serviceable clothes for every day."

I didn't care; I'd wear all the serviceable clothes they gave me just for the chance to wear a silk gown and a lace pinafore.

"Did you draw this?" Gillian asked Rose. "It's beautiful."

"Oh, no." She shook her head. "I only sew what the Royal Dress Designer dreams up."

The Royal Dress Designer! My heart quickened.

"Who is the Royal Dress Designer?" I said.

"Madame Zerlina Trinket."

"I've never heard of her. Does she live in the castle?" I asked.

"Gracious, no, child, she has a grand salon in the city."

A grand salon.

"Oh." I imagined gold-trimmed doors atop a sweep of marble steps. DARLING WRAY FORTUNE, ROYAL DRESS DESIGNER, a brass plate on the door read. Behind the door lay acres of marvelously thick carpet and scores of fabulous gowns. Just like Queen Candace's closet, only these dresses would be mine. *Darling's Gorgeous Gowns.* I liked the sound of that.

"Dulcie, did you wear your camisole or your petticoat today?" Marci asked.

Dulcie turned scarlet. I glanced down at her suspiciously flat skirt.

Marci let out a prodigious sigh that said her patience was worn to its last thread.

"Go get properly dressed, and make it quick," she ordered. "Before I have to have a talk with Mrs. Pepperwhistle."

At the mention of the Head Housekeeper, Dulcie dashed off.

"She'll only be a moment," I told Rose, who tucked the drawing back into her satchel.

"She's really fast," Gillian agreed.

Just then, the door swung open and Princess Mariposa swept in. Her movement set the ruffles on her violet skirt dancing. Her ebony tresses bounced. Her changeable sea-blue eyes sparkled like sapphires. The blue-diamond engagement ring on her hand flashed as she waved a yellowing paper.

Marci and Rose stood up at the Princess's approach.

"Marci—" Princess Mariposa cried, and then stopped. "Good morning, Rose."

"Good morning, Your Highness," the Head Seamstress replied.

"Are the Girls measured?" the Princess asked.

"All but one, a Miss Dulcie," Rose said.

"She'll be here in a minute," Marci told the Princess. "May I help you with something?"

"I've discovered an old letter of my grandmother's." Princess Mariposa flourished the paper in her hand. "Marci, I *must* have the starlight slippers!"

3

"I shall dance all night," Princess Mariposa cried, waltzing across the carpet. The paper flapped as she moved. "I shall wear a beautiful gown with the starlight slippers twinkling on my toes. My wedding ball will be the most wonderful—the most romantic—evening of all!"

"The starlight slippers?" Marci echoed with an odd frown.

Princess Mariposa stopped twirling so quickly that her skirts twisted around her like a funnel. She shook her skirts loose and held the paper up.

"They are mentioned in this letter written by Magnificent Wray. I found it when I was reviewing some old correspondence. The slippers sound wonderful. Just listen." The Princess cleared her throat and read: *"Wedding slippers crafted of leather and lace and bejeweled with starlight opals. Slippers that reflect the starlight itself. Memorable shoes for an unforgettable evening."*

With a flourish, she folded the letter and tucked it in her sash.

"They sound dreamy," Gillian breathed.

"Indeed they do," Marci said. "But I have never seen such a pair."

"Never?" The Princess's brow creased. "They were made for Queen Candace's wedding."

"They sound marvelous, Your Highness," Rose said. "But shoes aren't like dresses; they can't be altered. If you had them, they would probably be too big or too small."

"Are you sure?" the Princess asked. "A little padding or a little loosening . . ."

"It's the lasts, you see," Rose said. "They are carved the exact width and length of the person's foot."

"But the Royal Cobbler could—" the Princess said.

"You could pad them if they were too long, but they would be difficult to dance in," Rose continued. "A shoe that is too short?" She shook her head. "Cut off the front of the shoe? Lop off one's toes?"

Gillian shuddered.

"Well, I won't know until I try them on," Princess Mariposa said. "I shall just have to find them and see."

"Do you know where your grandmother kept them?"

Marci asked, tugging at the scarf knotted under her collar as if something were bothering her.

"Surely they are still in the Queen's closet," Princess Mariposa replied.

My stomach clenched. I glanced at Marci.

"I don't know," Marci said slowly. "I'll look and see."

Closets lined both sides of the wardrobe hall. One through six held the Princess's clothes, and the seventh contained Queen Candace's dresses. All one hundred of them. Nobody wore them anymore. And nobody went into her closet.

Well, no one but me.

It wasn't your average closet; Queen Candace's dresses weren't ordinary gowns. They were filled with magic. Just by trying one on, I could become someone else in the castle. The Princess never, *ever* went in there.

"Hand me the key," the Princess said.

"The closet isn't kept locked; the key is missing," Marci said, bustling toward the door. "I'll take a quick look."

"Missing?" Princess Mariposa exclaimed. "When did that happen?"

Marci stopped in her tracks. "Long before I was the Wardrobe Mistress," she said. "Baroness Azure talked about having a new key cast, but so far as I know, that hasn't been done."

Gillian and I caught each other's eyes. My hand

dropped to my apron pocket, and my fingers curled around the starburst key. Could the solution to my mystery be that simple? I'd been so busy looking for the right lock, I'd forgotten all about the missing closet key. I squinted; the closet's lock seemed a little smaller than the locks on the other doors.

"Oh, let's not bother about that," Princess Mariposa said, waving the matter away. "Let's look."

"I'll—" Marci began. But before she could move a muscle, the Princess darted over, flung the door open, and flew inside.

Marci's mouth hung open. Gillian gasped. What would happen when the Princess touched those dresses? My knees knocked together.

"Oh!" the Princess cried from the closet.

I raced in after her, with Marci and Gillian at my heels.

Sunlight flooded the long, narrow room, splashing over the rose-patterned carpet and shimmering on the dresses themselves. The stained-glass canary set in the great peaked-arch window glinted at me. Beneath it, on a small table, sat a gilded birdcage in which a real canary fluttered on a gold perch.

"Oooh," Princess Mariposa crooned, leaning over the cage. She poked her finger inside the wires and stroked the canary on his head. "My widdle precious birdums, Sir Goldie Sweetie."

I gaped; I'd never heard the Princess talk like that to *anyone* before. I squirmed with embarrassment. But the bird, whose real name was Lyric, closed his eyes and arched into the Princess's ministrations.

"I was just keeping him here where he'd be close by. So I could look after him," I said.

Lyric's birdcage usually hung from a stand in the Princess's dressing room. But lately, having a million wedding-related decisions to make, the Princess found that his singing irritated her and she wished him out of her sight. She never said where we should keep him. And I never volunteered that I'd put him in the closet.

"You be good for Darling, birdie boy," the Princess cooed.

Gillian tugged on my sleeve. "Sir Goldie Sweetie?" she whispered, fighting back a chuckle.

I wrung my hands, aware of the dresses on their silver hangers with the numbered gold badges. They hung as stiffly as icicles. A frosty glaze covered the normal sparkle of jewels and glimmers of lace. If dresses could hold their breaths, then these were puffed up and turning blue.

Marci coughed behind me.

Princess Mariposa straightened and looked around.

"I'd forgotten how beautiful they are," she exclaimed, petting a nearby sleeve.

I winced. Would she notice anything unusual about them? Pick one up?

The dresses obviously heard her, because the next thing I knew, they had thawed enough to recklessly flash a few crystals and wiggle a few ribbons at her. I glared at them. Were they crazy? Did they want the Princess to *know* about them?

After I'd worked so hard to keep their secret?

But, no, Princess Mariposa was too caught up in admiring them to notice anything out of the ordinary. I tweaked the ruffle on the one nearest me. A silent warning.

"The Queen's wedding dress is here at the back," Marci said. She padded over to One Hundred, a white satin gown embroidered with doves and roses, speckled with crystals, and frothing with lace. Marci unceremoniously pulled up the train and peered beneath.

"They're not here," she said. "I'm sorry."

"But there are shoes under some of these," Princess Mariposa remarked, rifling through the dresses.

"We'll check under all of them for you," Gillian exclaimed, pulling me down to the floor.

I knew it was a waste of time, but I made a show of crawling around on the carpet with Gillian, peeking under every dress. Gillian held up the flame-colored slippers that sat under Eighty-Two.

"These are pretty," she said.

"You could try them on for size," Rose offered from her post at the door. "That way you can decide if the search is worth the trouble."

"That's an excellent idea," Princess Mariposa said, taking the slippers.

She placed them on the floor. Then she slipped out of her shoes and wiggled into the bright orangey-scarlet pair.

"A perfect fit!" she announced, holding out her foot for us to see.

"Oh my, how lovely," Rose said. "Perhaps the wedding dress fits as well?"

I felt like someone had wound my nerves around the bristles of a brush. The dresses couldn't be left off their hangers. If they were—

"Oh, I don't know, Your Highness," Marci began. "These dresses are old, fragile—"

But the Princess was already pulling One Hundred off the hanger.

"Nonsense," she said. "They look like new."

And they did. But they only remained as bright and fresh as the day they'd been hung in the closet when the rules were followed. If someone took the wedding dress off its hanger and left it off—it would age into rags overnight.

"Unbutton me, please," the Princess told Marci.

My heart thudded painfully as Princess Mariposa slipped out of her violet gown and into Queen Candace's wedding dress. *Please don't fit.*

And—miraculously—it didn't.

The shoulders pinched, the waist puckered, and the sleeves hung askew. The fit couldn't have been more off-kilter if it had been made for a sea serpent. And then my pulse slowed. The dress was doing it on purpose!

"My goodness," Princess Mariposa said, eyeing the left sleeve trailing over her hand.

"Hmm," Rose said, walking over to her with an intense stare. "It seems rather . . . odd in the construction. But maybe"—she examined the too-short right sleeve—"it could be altered."

Princess Mariposa's eyes lightened with interest. "Do you think so?"

"We could remove the sleeves, refashion the bodice, rework the train," Rose mused, circling the Princess and studying the gown from every angle.

Every dress in the closet shrank in horror. One Hundred's train contracted as though it already felt the bite of scissors slicing into it.

"No," I blurted out. "You can't cut up Queen Candace's dress!"

The shocked expression on the Princess's face told me I'd gone too far.

"I mean, um, I think, it's just that . . . ," I mumbled, red-faced.

"What Darling means is—" Marci paused and gave me a warning glance to be quiet. "Madame Zerlina Trinket will be *crushed* if you don't choose one of her latest designs for the royal wedding. *Crushed!*" she repeated.

"Oh." The Princess thought a moment. "That's true."

She took the dress off and handed it to Marci, who put it back where it belonged. The dresses sagged in relief. Rose helped a disappointed Princess back into her violet gown.

"I did so want those slippers," she said with a sigh.

"There are six more closets, Your Highness," Gillian pointed out.

"There are!" Princess Mariposa exclaimed.

"It can't hurt to look," Rose said. "You've plenty of time to order a pair if you don't find them."

Marci jangled the keys on her chatelaine. She glanced back and forth between the Princess and Rose. Her stance reminded me of a Kitchen Maid with two impossible tasks to complete at the same time.

"Darling and I will search them all," Marci said finally, but she looked less than thrilled at the prospect.

"Yes! Do!" Princess Mariposa cried.

"We'll find the slippers!" I piped up.

"We'll start immediately," Marci agreed with an insincere smile.

I frowned at Marci; every servant in the castle was determined that *this* wedding would be perfect. *So* perfect that it would erase every memory of the other—failed—wedding to Dudley, the fake Prince Baltazar. I shuddered to think what would have happened if I hadn't put a stop to it by exposing that imposter! And up till now, Marci had been just as determined that *this* wedding would be everything that the first one hadn't been. What was wrong with her?

She was probably just tired, I decided. Between dressing the Princess and maintaining the closets, Marci had a lot of demands on her time. She hardly ever sat down.

That had to be it. Because what harm could there be in a pair of slippers?

4

I remember sitting on Father's knee while he sketched.

"It's in the line," he explained as his charcoal flew over the paper. "It begins nowhere and ends nowhere. It thickens"—he paused to demonstrate—"and thins, creating the illusion of space. Weight. Motion."

I nodded, although I didn't really understand at that age.

Illusions, he told me, were the building blocks of perception. He went on to draw one marvelous structure after another. I thought the line was the page's prisoner, that it escaped from the charcoal only to be captured by the paper. Because it fled to my fingers when I yielded to temptation and touched it.

It was only when he took me to watch the men building that it began to make sense. His drawings weren't merely pictures. They were houses and palaces and the great cathedral rising in the city. On paper they were silent. Out in the town they were sound—hammering, banging, clanging—and height, taller and taller monuments of wood and stone sailing to the clouds.

"You have to see it in your mind," Father said, offering me a charcoal of my own, "before you'll see it in the landscape."

I thought about how the line had stretched and become the building—and it came out of the shiny black stick in my fist. It looked like licorice, so I tasted the charcoal. It tasted like dead wood and fire. The tang puckered my mouth.

My lips felt sooty. I rubbed at them. Black dissolved on my hand. I tried cleaning it off on my pinafore.

"What are you doing?" I felt Father's hand on the back of my head.

"The line got all over me," I said.

"Amber," Father said, pulling out his handkerchief to wipe off my mouth, "lines can't be tasted."

"You could use a bath," Roger told me at supper.

Gillian sat next to me, her dinner already eaten. She wrinkled her nose, but she didn't comment.

I'd spent the day crawling through all six of the Princess's closets, going shelf by shelf, hatbox by hatbox, and drawer by drawer. Marci and I had discovered any number of interesting and forgotten items, but not the starlight slippers. Normally, the Head Cook expected us to tidy ourselves before appearing in her kitchens. But disheveled as I was, it had been so late when I finished that I hadn't wanted to risk missing dinner. So I had snuck in, hoping no one would notice.

Beneath the brim of his First Stable Boy's leather cap, Roger's brow furrowed in concern. He'd been promoted from Second Boy to First over the winter and put in charge of Lady Marguerite's horses. Thanks to me.

"You got a smudge here," he said, wiping his freckled chin to show me where.

"Some of us work late."

"And your ribbon is slipping," he replied.

I reached up, snatched the aquamarine ribbon from its precarious perch on my dandelion-fluff hair, and stuffed it in my pocket. Steam rose off the plate before me. My stomach growled. I decided to ignore Roger and eat.

"We didn't find *anything*," Gillian said with a sigh. We tried to be as cryptic as possible in the crowded kitchens.

"I did." Roger pushed his plate aside.

"What?" Gillian asked.

Roger glanced at the closest table, where a couple of Dusters were just finishing up.

"A passage from the ballroom to a certain *interesting* location," he whispered. "I'll show you after supper."

"How interesting?" I asked.

Just then, Dulcie landed on the bench next to me with

a bounce. She folded her hands on the table and blinked at me expectantly.

"What are you doing?" she asked.

"Eating," I replied.

Her left eyebrow quirked. "No, you're doing something," she said. "Every night you three vanish. *Poof.*" She snapped her fingers. "Like that."

Roger and Gillian eyed each other.

Dulcie waited, a hopeful look in her wide blue eyes.

"Run along and play," I said.

Her lower lip quivered.

"Don't cry," Roger said, glancing over his shoulder.

"Dulcie, we just talk," Gillian said, "about stuff that would bore you. Really."

"Oh-kay," she hiccupped. "I'll go ask Francesca what you're up to."

At *Francesca,* Gillian and I froze. Francesca had been so busy bustling about as if the royal wedding depended on *her* that she hadn't paid much attention to us. But then she'd caught us outside the King's suite that morning. It would be impossible for us to hunt for the keyhole if she became too concerned with our activities.

"Francesca doesn't have any say-so over our free time," Gillian said.

"Nope, she doesn't," Dulcie agreed. "But she might have a say-so about your *poofing.*"

"*Poofing* ain't a word," Roger said.

"Maybe not," Dulcie said with a grin, "but I'll ask Francesca, just to be sure."

"You're bluffing," I said.

Dulcie's grin widened.

No one spoke. Roger scratched his ear. Gillian crumpled her napkin. I was about to remind Dulcie that I'd rescued her from being sent to the orphanage, when she curled her hand companionably around my forearm and gazed admiringly up at me.

Like I was her hero. I, Darling, Champion of Orphans.

Do something, Roger's expression demanded.

"We'll show you if you swear not to tell another living soul," I told her.

Dulcie's eyes grew round.

"I swear!" she said.

"Darling, are you crazy?" Roger said as we walked through the main hall.

We'd told Dulcie that we all had to take a different route to avoid raising suspicion. So we'd sent her around the long way to the ballroom while we took a shortcut.

"We'll just show her this," I said. "We won't tell her about anything else."

"She's bound to keep following us if we don't," Gillian said.

"Girls!" Roger said, rolling his eyes.

Gillian punched him in the arm. "Don't think Francesca can't make your life hard too," she told him. "All she has to do is talk to Daddy."

"Daddy?" I asked, surprised. I'd have expected Gillian to mention Francesca's mother, Mrs. Pepperwhistle, the Head Housekeeper.

"The Stable Master, silly," Gillian said.

"Huh?"

"Do you ever pay attention?" Roger said. "Or have all those stories you're always dreaming up damaged your brain?"

I bristled at that. I told great stories.

"I have an excellent brain, thank you," I retorted.

"Mrs. Pepperwhistle is married to the Stable Master," Gillian said, as if everybody knew this.

But nobody called the Stable Master Mr. Pepperwhistle. They called him Sir or Master Derek. And Underservants like me knew better than to address him at all. He was right up there in importance with Marsdon, the Head Steward, or Esteban, the Head Footman, or Mrs. Pepperwhistle herself.

"How come Francesca never mentions him?" I said.

"Does she ever tell you anything?" Gillian asked.

She had a point there.

"The Pepperwhistles don't see eye to eye," Roger said.

"Some feud about those girls. She wants them to run the castle, and he wants them to marry well."

"Can't they do both?" I said.

"Not according to Mrs. Pepperwhistle," Gillian explained.

"Oh-kay," I said. Maybe being an orphan had its sunny side: I could chart my own destiny.

The entrance to the ballroom rose before us in gilded grandeur, a hint at the splendor beyond. Dulcie stood in front of it, hopping anxiously from foot to foot. I warned her with a finger to my lips while Roger pushed open the door. The four of us crept in on tiptoe.

Moonlight danced across the unlit ballroom. Patterned marble tiles gavotted across the floor. Velvet curtains sashayed at the tall windows. Gilded carvings traipsed across the walls. Crystal prisms on the candelabras and chandeliers sparkled in the evening light, waiting for their tall ivory candles to be lit. The high ceiling vault glowed like the inside of a pearl.

Dulcie gaped, turning around and around to see it all.

"Imagine: dancing, candlelight, beautiful gowns," Gillian breathed. "So romantic."

"Dancing is for sissies," Roger told her.

"You don't have a romantic bone in your body," Gillian snapped.

"Got lucky there," Roger said.

"Well, where is it?" I asked, eager to skip past the romance and get straight to the adventure.

"Over here," Roger said, leading the way.

We followed him to the far corner, where a series of gilded screens stood. There were doors behind most of them, servants' entrances that allowed the Footmen to whisk in and out without being intrusive. But the last door concealed a narrow circular staircase.

I stared up the twisting steps into the darkness above.

"Musicians' gallery," Roger explained. "Nothing up there but chairs and music stands."

"Well, where is it?" I asked, eager to see where Roger had found his newest secret entrance.

With a grin, Roger slid behind the staircase and wiggled the toe of his boot into the baseboard. The wall moved aside, revealing a black hole. A lantern waited behind the wall.

"I left it here for tonight," Roger said, digging a matchstick out of his pocket.

"Gosh," Dulcie breathed. "How did you know that was there?"

Roger just smirked.

"Where does it go?" Gillian asked, poking her head inside.

The match flared as Roger lit the lantern. "You'll have to climb up and see," he said.

"Up?" I said.

Dulcie nudged me, pointing.

Just then, I saw the hint of a spiral stair as lantern light illuminated the opening.

"Last one up is a rotten egg," Roger said, and raced up the steps.

"No you don't," Gillian exclaimed, bounding after him.

"It's *dark* in there," Dulcie began.

I didn't stop to argue. I grabbed her hand and plunged in after them. Round and round, up and up, we climbed until we reached a landing. There we stopped to catch our breath. Halfway down the dim hall, Gillian and Roger walked in a pool of light.

"R-Rog, we didn't close the door," I called, panting.

They stopped and turned around. A flush colored Gillian's face; a sparkle lit her eye. "Catch up," she said.

"We're going right back down in a minute," Roger said.

"Keep going," she told him, prodding him in the back.

Flashing a grin, Roger motioned to us. Dulcie and I hurried to catch up, galloping past wooden beams and plastered walls. Our footsteps rang on the floorboards.

Roger and Gillian stood at a fork in the passage. White chalk numbers and letters marked both entrances. I knew they corresponded to the map Roger was making, but I had no idea what they meant.

"Okay," Roger said, pointing left, "that way leads to the western tower."

"Is that *interesting*?" I asked.

"This one," he said with a wink, "goes someplace nobody goes."

"Do you think there are spiders?" Dulcie asked, peering into the darkness above.

"No, just cobwebs," I said, squeezing her fingers.

Her brow puckered as she thought that over. "But—" she began as a sharp scent wafted through the air. She sniffed. "Resin."

"More like varnish," Gillian said.

"Tree sap," Roger explained. "Most of the beams in these passages are oak, but these here—" He thumped the nearest. "Pine."

"Resin *is* tree sap," Dulcie said.

"So is varnish," he retorted.

"None of which is interesting," I said.

"And cedar," Roger continued as if I hadn't spoken. "The closer we get to the interesting part, the stronger the smell."

"Show us already," Gillian said.

"This way," Roger said, ducking through the right-hand doorway.

This passage was unlike any of the others I'd been in.

Empty candle sconces hung from the walls every few feet. Floor polish gleamed through the dust glazing the boards. And as the passage rose up at a steep angle, the scent of cedar tickled my nose.

"Cedar is very expensive," Gillian said. "And those candleholders are gold. Who hides stuff like this in a secret passage?"

"A King?" Dulcie guessed.

As if to agree with her, a royal crest marked a set of stairs at the passage's end. Slowly, awed by our surroundings, we tiptoed up the stairs to a small wedge-shaped landing. A dead end. Guarding the back wall was a large chair, upholstered in dust-covered tapestry, with gilding on the arms and back. A King's chair. We crowded the small space.

On either wall of the landing were carved doorframes. Roger thumped the one on the left.

"The Princess's dressing room," he said.

"No!" I exclaimed.

"Yep, and that one is the Princess's bedroom."

I squeezed past him to the other door. A royal crest hung on it. I squinted at the squiggles painted there. Roger held up the lantern so that I could see the gilded letters: *CVAC*.

"CVAC?" Gillian cast a longing glance at the dressing room door.

"They're initials," Dulcie said, pleased with herself.

"I know that, but they aren't Princess Mariposa's," Gillian said.

"They're Queen Candace's; this wasn't put here for a King. It was put here for her," I said.

"This explains how Cherice stole that pin and ransacked the Princess's bedroom," Gillian said.

"Nope, you can't go in the bedroom," Roger said.

"He's right," I told Gillian. I pulled open the door, and a dark, solid mass stood just inside.

"What's that?" Gillian said in a hushed tone.

She'd never been in the Princess's bedroom, but I had. "It's the headboard of her bed," I said, studying it. "Cherice would have gone through the dressing room and into the bedroom."

"Who would block a door with a great hulking bed?" Gillian asked.

"Someone who didn't know the hidden door was there when the Princess moved into the suite," I murmured.

"Or somebody who didn't want anybody to find it," Dulcie piped up.

She had a point. A series of tiny holes dotted the carving. A shiver crawled down my spine. This was how Cherice had spied on Francesca and me last winter. Thinking about it gave me the willies, and I was glad she was safely locked away in the asylum.

I pressed my eye to one of the holes and squinted.

"Do you see anything?" Dulcie breathed in my ear.

I did. Glimmering in the light of an upheld candlestick, a slight woman with dark braided hair cocked her head as if listening. I'd know that silhouette anywhere. As she turned, I caught sight of the gleam in her gray eyes. Stifling a gasp, I stumbled backward.

"What?" Roger said.

"Quiet," I whispered, and motioned to Gillian to shut the door.

"Was it the Princess?" Gillian mouthed.

I shook my head.

"Mrs. Pepperwhistle," I said. "She's in there listening."

Gillian snatched her hand back from the latch as if a monster lurked behind the door she'd just closed. Roger held his breath. Dulcie gripped my arm. The four of us stood there like statues for a long, long time before we gathered the courage to creep back down the stair.

Hours later in bed, I still couldn't shake the expression I'd glimpsed on Mrs. Pepperwhistle's face. I'd glimpsed the same narrowing of the eyes and pressing together of the lips on Captain Bryce's face when he sent his men to hunt for Cherice. It was a grimace that said, *I'll find you wherever you hide.*

5

First thing the next morning, Gillian and I headed to Queen Candace's closet.

"This is it! I just know it," Gillian said, dancing with excitement.

"Right here all along," I said, snapping the key into the lock.

I held my breath. My stomach churned. If the key opened the lock, then we'd have solved the mystery. But was this all there was to it? The closet was wonderful; the dresses were amazing. But deep down I knew *this* key opened an even greater treasure. A jewel that granted wishes or a talisman that transported one across the sea or a scepter that—

Gillian nudged me. I turned my wrist, but the key refused to budge.

"Maybe it's stuck; jiggle it," Gillian said.

I twisted the key until I was afraid it would break. Nothing.

Inside the closet, Lyric whistled sharply.

"It's the wrong one," Gillian said with a sigh. "Again."

"Uh-huh." The search would continue! I tucked the key back into my apron pocket.

At that moment, Lindy walked into the wardrobe hall, humming.

"Pack of work," she said to Gillian.

"Yes, ma'am," Gillian replied with a face that said, *Work never ends.*

I went inside the closet. Lyric sat on his perch, preening his tail feathers. I walked over, pulled out his food tray, and filled it.

"Sir Goldie Sweetie, eh?" I said.

Lyric eyed me like a flea infesting his plumage. I laughed at him.

"Your secret is safe with me." I slid the tray back into the cage. "And you, ladies," I said to the dresses, "showing off for Her Highness?"

The dresses sashayed on their hangers. An apricot gown gave me a saucy bounce to let me know they weren't sorry for their behavior. A scarlet ribbon caught my hand and tugged longingly. It belonged to Sixty.

"I can't wear you right now," I told the dress.

But I wished I could. Between trying keyholes and searching for hidden passages, I hadn't worn one of the dresses since I'd shown Gillian the closet, weeks before. And then I'd tried on Nine, Twenty-Six, and Fifty-Seven. Gillian had kept begging me to show her one more, just one more. It had been hard to stop at three.

But the dresses weren't playthings. They were endowed with the same magic that laced the castle walls—magic created from the distilled wisdom, courage, joy, and tenacity of the Wrays, my ancestors. Magnificent Wray had plundered them to fashion his great work—a magic that would bind the dragons to the roof and protect the castle.

I wasn't sure how I felt about what Magnificent had done. Excited? Angry? Afraid?

I felt the vibration of magic in the scarlet ribbon wound around my palm. For a moment, I closed my eyes and soaked it in. The magic in the dresses had a lighter, more playful note than that in the castle walls or the books in the King's library. A trilling joy soared through my hand and tugged on my heart.

The dresses danced on their hangers. Jewels flashing. Ruffles flailing. They wanted my company as much as I wanted theirs. The urge to try this one on grew until I could scarcely breathe.

"I have to get to work," I said with a sob.

I unwound the ribbon, breaking the magic's bond. The

dresses deflated on their hangers. I left them, stifling the urge to glance back over my shoulder. I wasn't sure I could resist a second time. I closed the closet door firmly behind me.

And squeaked with surprise.

A tall woman strolled about the wardrobe hall. She was handsome, from her lustrous brown eyes to her close-clipped hair to the color of her skin, dark like the Princess's black pearls. She wore a fitted purple jacket and a lavender skirt, drawn up on one side to reveal an underskirt the color of a melting sunset. Yellow leather gloves covered her hands. A strand of pearls wound around her long neck and fell to her waist.

A mouselike girl dressed entirely in brown tottered after her, weighed down by an enormous yellow portfolio.

"What bones!" the lady exclaimed, sweeping forward to grab my chin.

She turned my face this way and that, studying me.

"You can always see a woman's beauty in her bones," she told me. "You'll grow up to be very attractive." She released my face and stepped back, frowning. She ran a gloved hand over my dandelion-fluff hair. "Grow this out. Shoulder length at least."

"Why shoulder length?" I asked. She spoke so authoritatively that I didn't stop to question her right to order me about.

"Because," she said, pulling off her gloves, "hair like yours requires weight; grow it out, and this"—she flicked her dark fingers at my head—"flyaway nonsense will be tamed."

"Oh," I said, touching my hair involuntarily. I imagined it replaced with disciplined tresses.

"Now then, tell Her Highness that Madame Zerlina has arrived!" She gestured grandly at herself.

Then she snapped her fingers and pointed. The girl scurried forward, plopped the portfolio down on Marci's desk, and proceeded to pull out a series of sketches and spread them across the surface.

I slipped inside the lavender dressing room with its white-and-gold trim. Princess Mariposa stood before her mirror, admiring her newest gown, a shimmering jade satin. Marci stood behind the Princess, lacing her up. Lady Kaye, Baroness Azure, sat in her accustomed chair, gripping the silver knob of the cane I was pretty sure she didn't need. Her upswept white-streaked dark hair sparkled with diamond clips.

"I'm more than happy to help with all the little details, my dear," Lady Kaye said in a tone that implied there was no such thing as a *little* detail.

"Thank you," Princess Mariposa said. "I've a great deal of correspondence to answer and a number of petitions to review."

I curtsied.

"Yes, Darling?" Marci said.

"Madame Zerlina is here," I announced.

"Tell her I'll be out in a moment," Princess Mariposa said.

"I'll entertain her until you are ready," Lady Kaye offered, rising. "Come along, Darling," she added, motioning with her cane.

I jumped aside as she sailed out the door. The Princess was stepping into a pair of embroidered slippers as I hurried to catch up. The Baroness was already greeting the Royal Dress Designer when the dressing room door swung shut behind me.

"Madame Zerlina Trinket," Lady Kaye said. "Here you are! *Early.*"

Madame Zerlina stared at her as if it were not possible that *she* could be early. The mousy girl had taken up a position in a corner, standing with her hands folded and her head bowed. But I noticed that her cheek twitched at the Baroness's comment, as if she were fighting off the urge to smile.

"I see you've brought drawings of your wonderful creations," the Baroness continued.

She advanced to the desk and selected a drawing to examine. The designs were all wedding gowns, elaborate symphonies of bows, ruffles, lace, and ribbons. Except for one simple gown that drew my eye. Before I had a chance to study it, Princess Mariposa arrived with Marci.

At the Princess's appearance, Madame Zerlina swooned into a curtsy so low her nose nearly scraped the carpet. Then, just as quickly, she rose.

"Your Highness! You glow! You sparkle! And with my creations you will shine on your day of days!" Madame Zerlina exclaimed, holding out her hands.

"I have no doubt that one of your gowns will accomplish just that," Princess Mariposa said, squeezing her hands. "I can't wait to see."

The Royal Dress Designer gestured at the desk.

"This one," she said, scooping up a sketch to show the Princess, "is a special favorite of mine."

The dress featured a fitted bodice caught up on the shoulder in an enormous bow. The overskirt puffed up, held by more bows, over a tulle underskirt. A tiny crease formed in the Princess's brow.

"This might be a bit ..." Princess Mariposa paused as if hunting for just the right word.

"Overwhelming," Lady Kaye supplied, holding out the sketch she had. "This is interesting."

This gown had big puffed sleeves and a slender skirt with a long train.

"There are so many to choose from," Princess Mariposa said, eyeing the desk.

"There is this," Madame Zerlina said, flourishing another sketch.

This one featured an elegant gown made entirely of lace.

"Very beautiful," the Princess said, "but I couldn't wear lace . . . again." She blushed.

She'd worn a lace dress when she almost married that imposter Dudley the previous fall.

"We shall not speak of that!" Madame Zerlina tore the paper in two and threw it aside.

"Actually, Madame Zerlina," Princess Mariposa said, "I was hoping to find something that would match the starlight slippers."

"What slippers?" Madame Zerlina asked.

"Darling, fetch that letter from my bedside table," Princess Mariposa told me.

I hurried to the Princess's bedroom as she explained to Madame Zerlina about her search for the perfect shoes. I ducked through the dressing room, pausing a minute to glance at the walls. There were three doors in the room: one led back to the wardrobe hall, one led to the pressing room, and one went into the Princess's bedroom. The doorway to the bedroom appeared to be no wider than the others. I couldn't see how the hidden passage sat where it did, until I walked into the bedroom. And there, beyond the Princess's massive canopied bed, the curve in the exterior was visible.

The Princess's suite sat next to the wardrobe hall in the western tower. From the inside, most of the rooms appeared square or rectangular, but the tower was not. It was a semicircle. And the dressing room had been set at an angle to the bedroom, creating an open wedge between them. You didn't notice from the doorway because there you were standing at the point of the hidden triangle. Clever.

Satisfied, I hurried to the bedside table and picked up the folded letter. It flopped open in my hand. And then I did something I knew I shouldn't. I read the letter.

Dearest Candace, Princess (Most) Royal,

It has been my honor to serve you as my Sovereign! Ever I have endeavored to create greater works on your behalf. And now I have fostered a new kind of work, one of which I am sure you will approve, for the occasion of your marriage to Prince Richard. Wedding slippers crafted of leather and lace and bejeweled with starlight opals. Slippers that reflect the starlight itself. Memorable shoes for an unforgettable evening.

Shoes, my most treasured Princess, created
by the Royal Cobbler that embody something
new, different, strange, and wonderful. Shoes
that can truly be appreciated only when seen
by starlight. I am having them sent directly
from the city to you. It will be my great
pleasure to explain more fully when I arrive.

Your Most Humble, Obedient Servant, M

Prince Richard! I'd always thought that Richard was
a mighty king who married a beautiful princess named
Candace. But it was the other way around. No wonder the
hidden passageway went to the Queen's suite! This entire castle had been built for her. Everything Magnificent
Wray had done to create the magic, he'd done for her.

I tucked the letter into my pocket and walked back to
the wardrobe hall, where Princess Mariposa, Lady Kaye,
Marci, and Madame Zerlina were still examining sketches.

"Note the details. Exquisite embroidery. Chiffon
sleeves." Madame Zerlina pointed to the sketch in the
Princess's hands.

"The neckline is rather low," Lady Kaye replied.

"A trifle, perhaps, but that can be adjusted," Madame
Zerlina said.

"That is true of any design," Marci said, gesturing to

the pile. "If something isn't exactly what you're looking for, I'm sure Madame Zerlina can make changes."

"True, Your Highness! So true," Madame Zerlina agreed.

As Princess Mariposa considered this, I picked up the sketch that had caught my eye earlier. It was a simple gown with a lace-trimmed bodice and a full skirt. Scattered jewels sparkled across the front, and lace rippled along the skirt's hem. Lace butterflies graced the waist and settled along the train. I could picture Princess Mariposa wearing this dress and kissing Prince Sterling.

"*This* is perfect," I exclaimed.

A startled Madame Zerlina grabbed the paper from me. "All my designs are perfect!" She gave me an assessing glance. "That one especially so. You have a good eye."

"Darling, what have you found?" Princess Mariposa asked.

"This is something I think you will like," Madame Zerlina said, presenting the design.

I rolled my eyes, but Princess Mariposa squeezed my shoulder as she admired the dress.

"This is perfect. I shall wear this *and* the starlight slippers!" she said, holding out her hand for the letter. And she proceeded to read the description she'd read to us the day before.

"They sound exquisite," Lady Kaye said.

"Hmm." Madame Zerlina's brow furrowed. "May I see these slippers?"

"We haven't found them yet," Princess Mariposa admitted.

"I cannot match a dress with shoes I have not seen!" Madame Zerlina said. She gestured to the letter. "Are there instructions for their manufacture? Perhaps the Royal Cobbler can copy them."

"No," the Princess said. "There aren't, and I've never *seen* the slippers. I just want my wedding to be special." She handed the letter to Marci with an air of regret.

"In that case, my dear," Lady Kaye said, taking hold of the Princess's arm, "let's go see these slippers. Queen Candace's wedding portrait hangs in the green salon. That's the first place to look."

6

arci skimmed the letter as Lady
Kaye escorted Princess Mariposa out of the wardrobe hall. Madame
Zerlina trailed behind them, exclaiming
about her designs. The mousy girl stuffed the sketches
back into the portfolio and tottered after them.

Marci chewed her lower lip, thinking. I got out my
sewing basket.

"Darling," Marci said, "these slippers sound like
trouble."

"They do?" I set the basket down. "I thought they
sounded pretty."

"Get a dress and follow them. Find out what's going
on," she said, folding the letter.

I blinked in surprise. Was Marci *ordering* me to wear
one of the dresses?

"Are you sure?" I asked.

"My grandmother, the Wardrobe Mistress, talked about something that Queen Candace had," Marci began uncertainly. "Something that Grandmother believed lured the dragons out of the mountains."

"She probably meant one of the tiaras," I replied. "Dragons love gold and jewels."

Marci shook her head. "No, it was something else. Grandmother described it as something strange and different. . . ." Marci paused. "And these slippers fit that description."

"Surely dragons aren't attracted to shoes?" I scoffed. Not the castle's dragons. They were murdering, pilfering agents of evil, intent on wreaking havoc. I couldn't believe they'd waste their time on slippers, no matter how sparkly. Besides, dragons couldn't even *wear* shoes.

"They might be if the shoes were filled with magic!" Marci waved the letter under my nose. "Read!"

But I didn't have to. I remembered reading the words in the letter: *new, different, strange, and wonderful*. The starlight slippers had been cobbled before the old castle burned down and the dragons were captured. Were the starlight slippers *magic*?

I shivered at the possibility.

"Hurry up," Marci roared. "Take the back stairs so you can reach the green salon before they do. Run!"

Startled, I raced into the closet. Lyric trilled happily at me. The dresses shivered with excitement. I grabbed Sixty.

"I'm wearing you after all," I told the dress as I shimmied into it. "I need to go to the green salon."

The gold chiffon bodice squeezed me. The rippling gold skirt swirled about me. The trailing scarlet ribbons danced as the dress instantly conformed to my size. In the mirror on the back of the closet door, I saw a lady in a blue-and-white-striped gown. Stripes were all the rage at court that spring. Everyone wore them except Lady Kaye; *she* sneered at stripes. The lady in the mirror had dazzling blue eyes, chestnut-brown hair, and an hourglass figure. Stripes suited her.

I dashed off, through the wardrobe hall, along the corridor, and down the back stair. The Princess used the wide marble stairs that wound down the center of the castle and up and down all four corners. Servants had several back stairs, concealed by walls, which allowed them to move quickly from place to place.

Halfway down, I realized I didn't know where I was going and stopped short. A Footman passed, tray in hand, studiously avoiding me. Of course, he didn't see *me*, Darling Wray Fortune, at all. He saw the lady from the mirror. Ladies ought not to use the servants' stair. But the Footman was too well trained to take notice. I smiled sheepishly and waited for him to disappear from view.

"Where is the green salon?" I whispered to Sixty.

Sixty whirled around me, pulling me forward. The ruby ribbons strained, guiding me. I raced down stairs and along corridors, leaving a startled gaggle of Dusters and Sweepers in my wake. No doubt this lady's unseemly behavior would be the talk of the kitchens later.

I arrived at the main gallery, gasping for breath. A series of beautiful gilded doors rose around me. I'd been in most of these rooms when I was younger, and the Guards had good-naturedly looked the other way as I ogled at their grandeur. I didn't remember one of them being green. Sixty chose the doors that led to the gold receiving room, and hustled me inside.

"Green, not gold," I told the dress.

But it paid me no heed. It dragged me across the room to another door, which was closed. There it swished impatiently around my hips. I opened the door to a salon I'd never seen: a gorgeous room decorated in shades of green, from the leaf-colored wallpaper to the forest-green draperies to the fern-colored carpets. White furniture with gold trim and apple-colored cushions finished the décor. And between a pair of tall, twisty golden candlesticks hung the portrait of a young woman in a wedding dress. It had to be Queen Candace; I'd recognize One Hundred, the dress in the picture, anywhere.

I heard voices and snatched up a book someone had discarded on a table.

"Lady Seraphina," Princess Mariposa said as she came into the room. "Enjoying the view?"

Lady Kaye and Madame Zerlina were with her. The mousy girl clung to the shadows behind them as if she were afraid she'd be seen.

For a moment I was at a loss; then I spied the castle's rose gardens through the window.

"Yes, Your Highness," I said, curtsying. "It's distracted me from my reading."

"Seraphina," the Baroness greeted me with a nod.

"Countess Carioca, you are marvelous in stripes," Madame Zerlina said.

"Thank you," I murmured.

"Don't let us disturb you," the Princess said, and headed straight for the portrait.

I followed along with the others, careful not to get close enough to touch them. I might have *looked* like Countess Carioca, but my body *felt* like an eleven-year-old girl's. I had to be careful or I could get caught.

Queen Candace smiled out from her portrait as if she knew secrets the rest of us could only guess at. She was beautiful. Her ebony locks resembled the Princess's. But while the Princess's eyes were a changeable sea blue, the

Queen's eyes were emerald green. She stood in a garden, one hand holding up her skirt. A lace slipper peeked out from under her hem. Milk-colored gems blazed on the instep.

"The starlight slippers!" Princess Mariposa said, pointing. "You can see them in the portrait. I never noticed that before."

"You weren't looking for them," Lady Kaye said.

I leaned closer to the canvas; rose, blue, and gold twinkled like stars in the milky sky of the gems. The rest of the shoe was obscured by painted shadows. The starlight slippers didn't appear particularly magical. But could you tell that from a picture?

"You catch only a glimpse here, but it should give you an idea," Lady Kaye told the Royal Dress Designer.

"Lace slippers; terribly impractical. And starlight opals! The rarest jewels of all. I have seen one only once, long ago in a brooch worn by—" Madame Zerlina waved the thought aside. "The Royal Cobbler could make similar shoes —and decorate them with paste gems!"

"But then they wouldn't be starlight opals," Princess Mariposa said.

"My dear Mariposa, if you require starlight opals, then I shall obtain them," Lady Kaye said, patting her arm. "Of course, it may delay the wedding. . . . Oh, but not more than a year or two."

"So long?" Princess Mariposa cried.

"Starlight opals come from the farthest east," Madame Zerlina agreed sadly. "And you'd need several to trim both shoes."

The Princess twisted her fingers together.

I studied the tall, narrow portrait. It seemed odd to me that it pictured Queen Candace in her wedding dress . . . but no King Richard.

"Do you think the portrait was larger once?" I wondered out loud.

"Larger?" Madame Zerlina echoed.

"When the d-*disaster* occurred," I sputtered, catching myself just short of saying *dragon*. Most people in the castle didn't remember the dragons, let alone believe that the creatures were real. They hadn't seen them up close on the roof, like I had. "When the castle burned down."

"Seraphina, you astound me," Lady Kaye exclaimed. "That's brilliant! Ring for a Footman." She pointed to the bell pull.

I tugged on it. Straightaway, two Footmen came running into the salon.

"Take down the Queen's portrait," Lady Kaye commanded, "and turn it around so that Her Highness may see what lies behind it."

A bemused Princess Mariposa waited as the Footmen hurried to do the Baroness's bidding. They struggled to lift the heavy painting down from its hooks. Once accomplished, the Footmen rested its base on the soft carpet and slowly rotated it. On the back of the canvas, you could see the discoloration caused by smoke and a trace of burned edges.

"It was damaged in the fire," Princess Mariposa agreed. "How sad. I wonder what the original looked like."

"See if there's anything written on the back," Lady Kaye said, nudging me. "People used to write secrets on the backs of paintings sometimes."

"Secrets?" Madame Zerlina wondered aloud.

"The location of family heirlooms," Lady Kaye assured her. "People snoop through letters—"

I felt a twinge of guilt.

"But nobody thinks to look on the backs of paintings," Lady Kaye concluded. "Maybe Candace left us a hint as to what she did with those shoes."

I knelt down and looked, but if there had been anything there, it was obscured by the damage.

"Nothing," I said, shaking my head.

"But don't you think we can find the slippers ourselves?" Princess Mariposa asked Lady Kaye. "The wedding dress is still in Candace's closet. It didn't perish in the fire. Surely the slippers must be somewhere?"

"You can search the castle from the rafters to the

cellars if you wish to find these shoes," Madame Zerlina said. "Or you could wear a lovely pair of—"

Princess Mariposa's eyes welled up with disappointment.

"Or," Lady Kaye said, pounding the carpet with her cane, "we can search the storage trunks in the attic."

"Exactly!" Madame Zerlina said. "That is what I meant!"

7

M agic held a special fascination for Father. The King believed that Father discovered it to ensnare the dragons, but really, he'd known about it long before, holding its secret close to his heart. From the time I was a little girl, he'd searched, certain that not only did magic exist but that it could be harnessed like a team of horses. And reined in by his desire.

Where and how he found it, he would never say. And the evening before he died, I found him in his study, kneeling before the fireplace. His white hair waved around his head in the blasting heat as he frantically shoveled books and manuscripts into the flames.

He frightened me. His red face shone with perspiration. Soot marred his snow-white beard. His aquamarine eyes blazed bright with fever.

"They mustn't tamper with it," he'd warned me as I urged

him to retire and rest. "They don't understand. They don't real-ize what it is."

I pleaded with him to stop, but he thrust me away. With a strength he'd not possessed in years, he ejected me from his rooms and locked the door behind me. I went away sobbing, cer-tain that he had gone mad.

The next day, when we could not raise him, we broke down his bedroom door. He lay on his bed, hands folded over his best gold-embroidered silver robes, hair and beard combed clean—dead. In his study, smoke hung in the air. His bookshelves were empty. Only the small cache of papers he'd left in his desk survived.

The wealth of what he'd known and what he'd discovered lay in a mound of ashes that overflowed the hearth and littered the singed rug.

I pulled the crate stamped ARTICHOKES out from under my bed. Marci had given it to me long ago to keep my treasures in. At that time, I hadn't any, but I'd clung to the box like a Gardener clutching his last tulip bulb. And now the crate was no longer empty.

I slid back the lid. My mice friends lay curled up on the mittens and socks Jane had made. Painfully nearsighted, Jane had first knit only for me. But when the Head Cook saw Jane's fine work, she asked for a hood and mittens. They created such a stir that now Mrs. Pepperwhistle kept Jane knitting for all the servants.

That suited Jane. She spent her days by the hearth, needles clicking away, a basket of yarn by her side. If she hadn't been worried about my toes being cold, she'd still be working with the Pickers. I told her how much I loved the socks and mittens, but I didn't tell her that the chief beneficiaries of her talent were five little white mice.

Iago opened his eyes and blinked at me. He gave me a warning twitch of his whiskers—he didn't want his children disturbed. It was too early in the evening for them to be up.

I nodded, reached in, and gingerly slid my book out. Iago's ears drooped. His tail curled in a corkscrew. He seemed . . . sad.

"Is something wrong?" I asked him.

He shook his head and snuggled back down next to his children. I bit my lip. I'd never seen him downcast before. Did he need more cheese? Another pair of socks or a scarf, perhaps? Something more challenging to do than keep tabs on the dragons for me?

"Are you sure everything's all right?" I asked him.

His tiny brow creased. He burrowed deeper into the lavender wool. One of his children rolled over in his sleep—and off his mitten. His eyes popped open when he felt the rough wood. He sat up and stared at me. His tiny eyes grew round.

I suppose I was quite the giant to someone his size. But after a minute, he overcame his shock and scampered to the side of the box.

"How do you do?" I asked, and received a string of squeaks in reply.

Now, try as I might, I had never mastered Mouse. Iago communicated with me through pantomime. But if Jane had taught me one thing, it was manners.

"Good evening," I said. "I'm Darling."

He squeaked louder, something like *Eeckabonbon,* which I assumed was his name. Or rather *her* name, now that I looked closer. Her eyes were blue, and she had the most delicate pink ears.

"What a nice name," I said politely, not wanting to admit I couldn't pronounce it. "Shall I call you Bonbon?"

The little mouse wriggled with delight.

"And I'll call your siblings . . . Éclair, Flan, and Anise!"

Iago opened one eye. Obviously, those weren't the names he'd chosen for his children, but after a moment's reflection, he nodded and went back to sleep.

I put my hand down, and Bonbon hopped aboard. I held her up where I could talk to her without disturbing the others. She chittered away as if telling me a mighty tale of woe. I listened, wondering what had her so excited. Finally, she yawned so hard that her eyes disappeared in her furry face. I bid her good night and put her back on my mitten. Then I pulled the lid closed and pushed the box back where it belonged.

I settled on my bed and ran my thumb down the spine of the slim gray book. *My Father, Magnificent Wray, by Lady Amber DeVere*, it read. Gillian had asked Lady Kaye if she had any books on the Wrays. And Lady Kaye had given her this.

It told me only so much and no more. Lady Amber neglected to mention the starburst key—or the starbursts at all, for that matter. Instead, she wrote about her father's life. It was interesting, sure. But it didn't help me figure out what Cherice's inheritance had been or how it fit into the magic. I kept revisiting the book in case I'd missed some clue. But if one was there, I hadn't found it.

"You disappeared after supper," Gillian said, plopping down on the bed next to mine.

"I didn't want Dulcie to follow me," I said.

"Are you going to waste the evening reading?" She leaned forward with a mischievous grin. "Or are you going to have an adventure with me?"

"What kind of adventure?"

"A dress kind," she said, arching an eyebrow.

"We can't risk Dulcie finding out about that." I studied the closed cover of the book.

"The Icers are rolling fondant roses for the wedding

cake," Gillian said. "They have hundreds to make. So they're starting now."

"And? You need a dress to swipe one?"

"No, goose. Dulcie dear is helping them. You know—filling bags, mixing colors, the easy stuff. She begged until they gave in."

"Really?" I set the book down.

"They'll be at it for hours," Gillian replied. "Roger had some"—she rolled her eyes—"*whatever* to do in the stables. And I heard that Mrs. Pepperwhistle volunteered Francesca to help address the invitations. Apparently, she has nice penmanship." Gillian shrugged as if even Francesca had to have *one* talent.

I was up and out of the dormitory before Gillian could blink. I raced down the corridor. She ran behind me, laughing. We bolted through the wardrobe hall and into the closet. Our arrival stirred up a drowsy Lyric and caused the dresses to flutter expectantly on their hangers.

The dresses vied for my attention, bouncing and flashing away. Until they spied Gillian. While the dresses had given Roger the cold shoulder, they had taken to Gillian like a long-lost friend.

"Good evening," she purred, tidying a bow here, a flounce there. "You're looking lovely." The dresses swelled under her touch. "Where shall we search next?"

The dresses rustled on their hangers, but I knew she

wasn't asking them. She was talking to me. We'd taken turns sneaking back into the King's reading room to try the key. We'd had to go at lunchtime when we were sure Dulcie was elsewhere. But we'd found nothing. So where to go next?

"The kitchens are a waste of time—there isn't a lock there that hasn't been opened a million times," I said.

"True," she replied. "Do you remember you told me that Cherice kept mumbling about six and seven?"

"Yes, but six and seven could mean anything."

"I've been thinking." Gillian feathered a ruffle with her fingers. "What if she was counting, like six of one thing and then seven of another?"

"Okay, but six and seven of what?" I asked.

"What about the library? Shelves of books. Six across, seven down. Or the sixth book in the seventh bookcase—"

"There are a million books in there! How would we ever guess which one?" I argued. "Besides, you don't need a key to open a book."

"Maybe there's more in the library than books?" Gillian said.

"Oh!" I said. "The King's special collection sits inside a locked cabinet. *Magnificent Reflections*, that book written by Magnificent Wray, was on one of those shelves."

The dresses shivered with delight; the library books were *full* of magic. Not exactly the same flavor as in the dresses, but it was magic all the same. And I'd only ever gotten a glimpse of the library. The Royal Librarian wasn't fond of me since I'd been found with a book from the library. He'd lent it to me—but I'd been wearing one of the dresses, so he hadn't known it was me. Which made it impossible to explain how the book had gotten into my hands.

"Master Varick won't exactly welcome us," I said.

"Silly," Gillian said.

Eighty-One flashed a sequin at her.

"Not you, lovey—Darling," she told it. She poked me. "You will distract the Librarian while I—" She twisted her fist as if she held an imaginary key.

Eighty-One caressed my arm with a gossamer sleeve. The deep purple dress had shoulders and sleeves made of chiffon as sheer as a spiderweb. Crystals and sequins twinkled over the shoulders and met in the center of the satin bodice to form a *V*. Below a girdle of crystals and sequins, the skirt billowed out in layers of chiffon. Matching slippers sat on the rose-patterned carpet beneath it.

"Eighty-One agrees with me," Gillian said. "Let's go."

I handed her the key and took Eighty-One off the hanger. I slithered into it. The crystals and sequins blazed as the dress gave me a welcoming squeeze. Then, in a purple flurry, it transformed into my size.

"I know you," Gillian said. "You're Lady Kaye's daughter Lorna, the Duchess of Umber!"

"Really?" I asked, turning to see myself in the mirror. A tall, hazel-eyed lady with brown hair piled atop her head regarded me from the glass. She wore a spectacular ruby necklace and a dress that might have come from one of the Princess's closets. "How do you know her?" I asked.

"I don't *know* her," Gillian said, "but I've seen her with the Baroness. Lady Kaye talks about her all the time." Gillian clasped a pretend cane. Then she threw her head back and eyed me down her nose. " 'She has iron in her bones,' " she said, imitating the Baroness. " 'Iron, I tell you!' "

"Then no mere Librarian will stop her," I said, chuckling. "Good work, Eighty-One."

A sequin winked at me.

"Let's look at books!" I cried.

"Wait," Gillian said, grabbing my arm. "Why don't you wear the shoes, too?"

Most of the hundred dresses didn't have matching shoes, but if one did, I'd never worn them.

"They won't fit," I said with a laugh, remembering the orangey-scarlet shoe on the Princess's foot.

"Shouldn't they work like the dresses?" Gillian arched an eyebrow.

I pondered that. Eighty-One's skirt swayed in the direction of the matching shoes. I'd never considered wearing them before. But what Gillian said made sense. And they *were* gorgeous.

I unlaced my boots and set them aside. Then I slid my feet into the purple slippers. The crystals and sequins across the insteps flashed brilliantly. Magic bubbled under my toes, tickling them.

And then something strange happened.

My bones grew hollow. My ears rang. Sparks flew before my eyes. My vision blurred until the image in the mirror grew watery. I felt myself thinning, flattening, and *stretching*.

8

"Are you all right?" Gillian asked, grabbing my arm as I swayed. Then she dropped it with a little shriek.

I looked down at her. I was slightly tall for my age, but Gillian was almost my height. I blinked and looked down at her again. I squeezed my eyes shut. Counted to ten.

But when I opened them, I was still looking down. She was shorter than me. Much shorter.

"You shrank," I said, my mouth dry.

"You grew," she gasped. She reached up and brushed my shoulder with a fingertip. Then she stood on tiptoe and touched my hair. *"Amazing."*

The closet around me had also shrunk. The ceiling was closer, but—weirdly—the carpet was farther away. The sequins on the purple slippers sparkled beneath Eighty-One's hem.

"The shoes did this!" I pointed to the Duchess in the mirror. "They made me *her* size."

"Do you feel—" Gillian groped for the right word. "Big or wide or fat?"

"She's not fat," I said. "Just tall and, um, ladylike." I blushed. I didn't feel at all ladylike, just rubbery and thin, like a piece of the Head Cook's taffy. "The dresses never did this to me."

"Well, you never wore a dress *and* its shoes before." Gillian patted her arm as if making sure *she* was unchanged. "But it's a good thing, right?"

"I guess so."

Eighty-One no longer had to shrink to fit me; I was its size. The dresses tinkled their hangers together as if applauding. No one would suspect it was really me. Even if they touched my hand or took my arm.

"What now?" I asked the dresses.

A ripple ran through their skirts, leading toward the door.

"Let's go," Gillian said.

That's when it hit me—I wore an impenetrable disguise! The only way I could get caught was to take off the dress. Or run into the real Duchess. Otherwise I was invincible. I put my nose in the air and marched out of the closet.

"Come along, missy, keep up," I called over my shoulder in my most aristocratic-sounding voice.

Gillian giggled as she followed me. Through the castle we sailed. I nodded regally at everyone we met, and she pranced along at my heels like a well-trained Maid. And just like the time I'd appeared to everyone as Lady Kaye, courtiers and servants scrambled to bow and curtsy as I passed.

It was exhilarating to go from being the one taking orders to being someone who could give them. I passed a Guard lounging at his post. The moment he saw me, he snapped to attention. I was tempted to scold him—just for fun. But the less I said and did as Lady Lorna, the better. I didn't want anyone carrying tales to the *real* Duchess later. I smiled generously and strolled on.

When I reached the west wing, I turned into the corridor where the King's library waited behind great carved doors. As Gillian trailed me down the hall, the doors swung open. The Stable Master walked out with Francesca at his heels. She wore a plain green dress without an apron and a sulky expression on her face.

I faltered in midstride. I could bluff my way past them. Duchesses didn't explain themselves to servants, but

Gillian needed a good excuse for being there—and fast. Eighty-One billowed around my knees. For a moment, I was tempted to tell Gillian to crawl under the skirt and hide.

But Gillian trod on my heels and then jumped back with a yelp.

Francesca's head whipped in our direction. A ball of ice surrounded my heart. I took one step back, but the Stable Master had already seen us.

"Good evening, Your Grace," he boomed, galloping down the hall toward me. "A pleasure to see you."

Francesca padded after him, braids bobbing and her mouth in a crease.

"Good evening," I replied, noticing the book in his hand. "Did you find something interesting to read?" I hoped to steer their attention away from the wayward Princess's Girl behind me.

"'Deed I did," he said, and bowed gallantly.

The Stable Master was tall, taller even than the Duchess. With wavy dark hair, brown eyes, and the squarest shoulders I'd ever seen, he cut an imposing figure in his leather version of the palace livery. I had seen him march through the stables, riding crop in hand, barking orders. He was strict with the Stable Boys and Grooms but easy on the horses. He carried apples and carrots in his pockets and referred to the horses as his *little darlings,* a nickname that caused Roger to snicker every time he heard it.

I'd never thought it was that funny.

"Might I present my daughter Tina?" he asked, gesturing to the girl I had taken for Francesca.

"Faustine!" I squawked, startling them both. "I-I-I've heard that's your name."

This was the very Girl whom the Princess had fired, leading Lindy to pick me as her replacement! Faustine was the reason that Francesca had never liked me. She thought I'd stolen her sister's job. But it hadn't been my fault! It was Faustine's own carelessness.

Faustine curtsied. Gillian gripped my arm, straining to get a look at her.

"They're *twins,*" Gillian gasped, forgetting herself.

"Yes, miss, my daughters are i-den-ti-cal twins," the Stable Master answered with pride.

Gillian pinked with embarrassment and bobbed a quick curtsy.

"I'm sure you're very, er, *pleased* to have two such pretty daughters," I said, figuring that the Duchess would make some such remark. As for myself, I studied Faustine like a pirate with a treasure map. From head to toe, she was Francesca's double except for her mouth. Francesca always smiled at adults. This girl kept her lips taut, as if she were frightened something would escape. So I was surprised when she opened them.

"Our little sister, Faye, doesn't look anything like us," Faustine said. "She's fair, but none of the rest of us are fair." She shrugged. "She's six; she likes parties."

"Really," I said. I liked Faye already, and I hadn't met her.

"Enjoy your evening," the Stable Master said, collaring Faustine. She shot him a look that said she wasn't finished talking. "We'd best be going."

I murmured a polite good-night as they walked on down the corridor. Just before they reached the stairs, Faustine looked over her shoulder. Her gray-eyed stare drilled through me as if she knew I wasn't the Duchess. And then she disappeared from view.

"Whew," Gillian said. "No wonder she got fired. She'd curdle sour cream."

"Good thing she's not a Girl anymore," I agreed with a shudder. "Imagine having to deal with both of them."

"Don't say any more," Gillian said. "You'll give me nightmares."

We strolled on to the big doors with their snarling lion's-head doorknobs and opened them. The library exhaled its fragrance of paper, leather, and lemon oil. The warm glow of candles lit the parquet floor. Volumes bound in red and green leather gleamed with gold lettering from shelves that rose tier after tier toward a ceiling lost in darkness.

"Look at all the books," Gillian said. "Oh, shelf after shelf of *stories*!"

"I'll tell you a story later," I said absently.

But I wasn't thinking about making up tales at that moment. A deep *throb* of magic reached out to greet me. Not the light, playful touch in the dresses. No. A hungry, anxious throb like the gong of a deep-sounding bell. It echoed through me, rattling the sequins on Eighty-One.

Gillian was oblivious. She flitted from shelf to shelf, reading titles and exclaiming.

"*A History of the Wars of the Dragons*," she cried.

That sounded interesting.

"Oh, no, look. Look. *Poems of Lost Love! The Adventures of Hurlstone the Troll!*"

Before I could blink, she had darted to another shelf.

"Oh my. *A History of the Queens of Eliora.*"

I started to ask where she'd found that one, but her attention had shifted again.

"Oh. Oh. OH! *The Ghosts of Umber,*" she gasped, holding a book out. "Do you think there are really ghosts in—in—" She blanched with a gulp.

"What are you doing in here annoying the Duchess, moppet?" a voice demanded.

"Umber," she squeaked.

I whirled around. Master Varick, the Royal Librarian, stood behind me, glowering at Gillian. If he hadn't spoken, I wouldn't have seen him standing there in his patched, multicolored coat.

"Good evening, Master Varick," I said. "It's all right. She's with me."

"I see." He pushed aside the thatch of white hair that hung before his sharp blue eyes.

Gillian curtsied, dimples deepening in her cheeks. Her dark curls tumbled around her shoulders. She batted her eyelashes and gave him her winningest smile.

"Are *you* the Librarian?" she asked, clasping *The Ghosts of Umber* to her chest.

"Who else?" Master Varick pulled on the lapels of his coat, making his stooped, thin frame even more skeletal.

"Our little servant girl here likes stories," I said with a reassuring smile. "Put the book back now, dear."

Gillian held the book closer.

"It sounds so interesting," she said.

A spark glowed in Master Varick's sharp eyes. He reached a gnarled hand out for the book, which Gillian reluctantly handed over.

"There are stories in here," he said, opening the book, "that would scare the wave out of those curls. Tales of revenge, murder, phantoms, and graveyards."

Gillian's eyes grew round. Eighty-One crept sideways.

I felt the books lean in on the shelves, rapt with attention. The throb of the magic deepened to a growl.

Master Varick caressed the open page, warming to his topic. "Why, the ghosts of Castle Umber are among the worst blood-soaked villains—"

"Master Varick!" I cried, aghast.

He slammed the book shut. "Begging your pardon, Your Grace," he said. "It's not the sort of book you'd enjoy."

"No, I should think not." I turned around, eyeing books and searching for something to say next. "I think perhaps I'll just look around."

"I insist on being of service," Master Varick said. "I could show you a nice book with colored plates of owls?"

"Her Grace prefers something inspiring," Gillian offered.

The Librarian tucked *The Ghosts of Umber* back on its shelf.

"Ah," he said, "follow me." He offered me his arm.

I darted a glance at Gillian. She smiled, the picture of innocence, and patted her apron pocket that held the key.

"Wait here, Girl," I said for the Librarian's benefit, and took his arm with a suppressed sigh. While it was only fair that Gillian had her chance to use the key, I wanted to be there when the key found the right lock.

Master Varick led me to a section of the library I hadn't

been to before. Narrow circular staircases snaked up to an overhead balcony, where bookshelves lurked.

"I always find mysteries inspiring—the case is solved, the criminal caught, justice served," Master Varick said, pulling out a thin purple volume. "Now, this is especially good. *The Mystery of Sea Echo Point.*"

"Hmm," I murmured, taking the book while he searched for another.

A wrought-iron banister curled across the balcony. More iron curls decorated the balcony's shelves and traced what looked like a pipe organ. I squinted. That wasn't any musical instrument—it was a desk! With a glance to be sure the Librarian was occupied, I drifted in that direction.

The massive desk sat like an elephant crouched under a rainbow of books. A candle burned on the desktop, illuminating stacks of papers. The back of the desk—what I had mistaken for organ pipes—was a row of rounded drawers with silver keyholes. And a silver plate etched with the entwined letters *M* and *W* decorated the center drawer. I caught my breath. I craned my neck. If I had been any shorter—my size, not Lady Lorna's—I wouldn't have been able to see the letters.

But there they were: Magnificent Wray's initials. And drawers—my mouth fell open—six up and seven across.

"Now, this is quite enjoyable," Master Varick said,

cradling a thick volume. "I think poetry is inspiring. And calming," he added, staring at me.

"What are those books up there?" I pointed to the balcony.

"Old records—housekeeping mostly," he replied.

"That's quite an unusual desk." I figured the Duchess could get away with being nosy. "What's in all the drawers?"

"Haven't the foggiest," Master Varick said. "Don't have the keys."

"Thank you for your time," I said, handing him back the mystery. "But I'm just not sure what I'm looking for. I'll have to come again another day."

He took the mystery, a startled look on his face. "I assure you we haven't exhausted the possibilities!" he exclaimed.

"No," I said with a smile, "I'm sure we haven't. I'll just have to search harder next time."

And *next* time, I, Darling Wray Fortune, Solver of Enigmas, would have the starburst key in my fist.

"Good job, Eighty-One," I murmured, patting the dress as I went to fetch Gillian.

"Whew," I said, wiping my brow. The Princess's Girls had spent the better part of the day in the high attic, emptying trunks, examining all the items, and stacking them in a pile. When we reached a trunk's bottom, we packed it all back inside, and then Marci marked each finished trunk with a chalked X.

It was fun for a while. A buzz of excitement accompanied the lifting of each lid. We'd exclaimed over gloves, fans, miniatures, and all manner of odds and ends. One Girl had even found a battered sword with a gem-encrusted handle. And shoes! Every kind from baby booties to riding boots. But no starlight slippers.

"Are you sure Lady Kaye didn't say anything else?" Marci asked me for the tenth time.

She stood over me, fiddling with the keys on her chatelaine. She'd volunteered to lead the hunt. The Princess had been touched, but I knew Marci had her reasons. She was certain there was something sinister about the slippers.

"Positive," I said, pulling another item out of a large brass-bound trunk. "I've told you everything she said. And the slippers looked like . . . slippers."

"Let's hope that's all they are," she said.

I'd neglected to mention what had happened when I wore both a dress and slippers—and I couldn't explain now and risk being overheard by the other Girls. But it didn't matter. Did it? If the starlight slippers *were* magical, they wouldn't change the Princess's size, because she was already grown up.

And I doubted we'd find them anyway. If the Baroness— as old as she was—hadn't ever seen them, then they had to be lost for good.

"A-a-choo!" Ann, the eldest Girl, grimaced and dug her handkerchief out of her pocket. A small cloud of dust accompanied the movement. "Ugh, this place is disgusting."

The high attic wasn't anything like the upper-attic, where the Girls' dormitory was, all fresh, clean, and homey. No. These rooms hunkered under the great rafters that supported the castle roof. We'd opened the dormer windows to let in some air. It helped a little, but the high attic had sat closed up for a long, long time.

A chorus of Girls agreed. "Nasty." "Horrid." "Foul."

"You should have listened to me," Marci said, unimpressed. She'd offered to borrow the brown dresses and canvas aprons worn in the under-cellar, but only Gillian, Dulcie, and I had taken her up on it.

Grime covered my hands and knees, but the heavy canvas protected the rest of me. The other Girls' clothes— once silvery gray and sparkling white—looked as if they'd been worn to muck out the stables. It was a good thing we were getting new uniforms.

"Keep digging!" Francesca growled. She'd plunged into the job as if finding the slippers were her personal responsibility.

"We don't have shovels," I remarked.

Francesca favored me with a glare, banged down the lid of the trunk she'd just searched, and moved on to the next one.

"Is it time for supper?" Dulcie asked, rubbing a stray lock out of her eyes and smudging her forehead.

"Fifty-two trunks to go," Marci said. "Then you can have supper."

"I need a drink of water," Kate, the tallest Girl, said.

"And I need a long, hot bath," Ann chimed in.

"A cup of tea." "A nap." "A day off!"

"Girls!" Marci said. "I'm surprised at you!"

"I found them!" Francesca cried, jumping up and waving a pair of shoes in the air. "I found them!"

A cheer rang through the attic.

"Excellent, Francesca. Hand them here," Marci said.

Francesca shook her head. "I'm going to take them to Her Highness," she said.

"Don't be ridiculous," Marci snapped. "Give them to me."

"No!" Francesca hugged the shoes to her chest. A fire lit her eyes. Radiating determination, she looked like she'd die before she'd hand over those slippers.

Several Girls fidgeted. We all knew Francesca wasn't one to cross, but we'd never seen her be anything but polite to her superiors. And I'd never known her to disobey a direct order.

Ann plopped down on the lid of her trunk, causing everyone to jump. "Just *give* them to her," she said.

Francesca glowered at Ann. "I should be the one to take them to Her Highness," Francesca said. "I found them."

"Fair enough," Marci said. "Show them to me first. So I know they're the right shoes."

Francesca held out the slippers as if she meant to snatch them back at the slightest movement. Triplets of starlight opals sparkled on the dingy lace pumps. Had it not been for the gems, the shoes would have been entirely ordinary.

I felt relieved and disappointed all at the same time.

"Very well, then," Marci replied, satisfied. "We'll go down together."

"I'll carry them," Francesca said, squeezing the slippers tight.

"The rest of you go wash up," Marci said.

But we were already lining up behind Francesca. Not one of us wanted to miss out. It wasn't every day you saw Francesca clutch a pair of slippers like a dragon with a golden chalice.

"You found them!" Princess Mariposa cried. She stood with Prince Sterling in the gold room. Lady Kaye had commandeered the closest comfortable chair.

We crowded behind Francesca as she presented the slippers to the Princess.

"Yes, Your Majesty," Francesca said. "*I* found them."

"How can I ever thank you?" the Princess said.

"All the Girls searched, Your Highness," Marci put in.

"Indeed," Prince Sterling said, looking especially handsome in his blue-and-silver coat, garnet-colored sash, and tall, polished boots. He rewarded us with a bow. "Good job, all of you."

Ann and Kate nearly swooned. Several Girls giggled nervously. Dulcie smoothed her unruly braids, smearing more dust through her hair. Gillian beamed. I sighed.

"Now your wedding will be perfect," Francesca added, annoyed at the Prince's acknowledging all of us.

"They're filthy," Lady Kaye commented. "Not that I'm not pleased you've found them," she hastened to add. "But still, Mariposa, you can't mean to wear them?"

The Princess turned the slippers over in her hand. "They do appear as if they could use a good washing," she said.

"I could send them down to the Head Laundress," Marci said, as if *that* were the last thing she wanted to do.

"Try them on," the Prince urged. "Allow me." He held out his hand for the slippers. Then he knelt at her feet.

Marci grabbed my arm. I held my breath as the Princess stepped out of her shoes and Prince Sterling helped her into the slippers.

They fit as though they'd been made for her.

I waited, twisting my hands together. Marci's grip bit into my arm. But nothing else happened. The Princess was herself. The slippers were ordinary shoes. I exhaled and pulled against Marci's hand. Marci blinked and let me go.

Princess Mariposa twisted her foot this way and that.

"See the starlight opals!" she exclaimed. "They're beautiful."

"Posy," Prince Sterling said, gazing up at her, "no jewel can compete with you."

Posy!

A collective gasp escaped the Girls. I choked. Even Marci turned crimson. Lady Kaye cleared her throat, but the Prince smiled at the Princess as if she were the only person in the room.

"Thank you," the Princess said, blushing. Then she took a gold ring off her little finger and held it out to Francesca. "For you," she said.

An awestruck Francesca took the ring.

Next to me, Ann tossed her hair.

"Princess's pet," she muttered under her breath.

10

My father's papers were precious to me. They scintillated with hints of magic and flashes of his great mind at work. One torn page gave me a frightening glimpse of what he meant when he'd told me, "They don't realize what it is." He'd poured the magic into the castle, and we'd all assumed that it was safe there. Fixed. Contained. But as the fog descended and people's memories blurred, I wondered. Did I understand this magic at all?

Did I know what it could do?

Was it really safe? Was it truly contained?

At the King's request, I collected the papers from Father's desk and bound them in a book.

Francesca paraded the ring through the castle. We Girls trailed after her with a despondent shuffle.

"We're *all* getting new uniforms," Gloria whispered,

"because we're all just as important as she is." Gloria kept peppermints hidden in her pillowcase. Francesca called her Sugar Baby.

"She only opened that trunk by dumb luck," another Girl said.

"If she'd been a little slower emptying the one before—" Kate agreed.

"Or we'd been a little faster—" a third added.

"One of *us* would have found the slippers," Ann finished.

They nodded in miserable agreement.

"It's only gold," I said. "There isn't even a jewel on it."

"None of us has a gold ring," Gillian said, twisting a curl around her finger. "I don't even have a locket like you do."

The other Girls eyed me suspiciously. My hand crept guiltily toward my chain.

"I have a bracelet with a pearl on it," Ann said. "And Darling got that from her mother."

"That makes it okay, I guess," Kate said.

"The worst of it isn't that Francesca got that ring," Gloria said. "It's that she'll never let us forget it."

Francesca flounced along ahead of us, showing the ring to everyone we met. Flashing it under noses. Announcing where it had come from. Polishing it on her sleeve.

Ann rolled her eyes so many times, I thought they'd fly out of their sockets.

At last, just when we'd reached the end of the main hall and arrived at the juncture to the servants' back stair, Francesca saw her mother and called out to her.

Mrs. Pepperwhistle stood at the bottom of the main staircase. As always, she was neat and contained, from her high, tight collar to the ebony braids coiled at the nape of her neck to the self-composed gleam in her gray eyes. Her slender fingers sorted through the keys on her silver chatelaine.

"Look!" Francesca crowed. "It's the Princess's very own!" She bounded over to her mother, waving her hand in the air.

We trooped after her as Mrs. Pepperwhistle examined the ring closely.

"A reward for finding the starlight slippers," Francesca said, as if she were the only who'd looked for them.

"Yes, it's very nice to be noticed by Her Highness," Mrs. Pepperwhistle said. "But if you'd had your wits about you, you would have asked for a promotion."

Francesca's face fell.

"You should be more forward-thinking," Mrs. Pepperwhistle added, rubbing the marcasite butterfly pinned at her throat. Her gaze traveled across us, noting our grubby appearance with a frown. "All of you ought to be making the most of your opportunities." Her gaze settled on me. "*One* of you has."

They stared at me like a fly that had landed in their porridge.

If I'd wondered whether the Head Housekeeper was pleased by my promotion, I didn't any longer. Dulcie inched closer to me, fists balled.

"But Marci helped Darling! Just because she's her friend," Ann protested.

"Then be more selective in your choice of friends," Mrs. Pepperwhistle replied.

Francesca twisted the ring on her finger. A tear trembled on her lashes, but she held her chin up.

"Gillian has been," Gloria said. "She's friends with the Baroness."

They all turned to glare at Gillian.

"I haven't done anything wrong," Gillian protested.

"No, she hasn't," I agreed. "The Baroness knows quality when she sees it."

That earned me a calculating glance from Mrs. Pepperwhistle. I held her gaze. She pursed her lips as if she were about to reprimand me, but then she turned back to Gloria.

"Really, Girls, you'll never be important to the Princess if you fail to exert yourselves."

"We work hard," Kate argued. "We do everything we're asked to."

"The choice is yours," Mrs. Pepperwhistle replied,

dismissing us with a wave of her hand. "Make what you will of it."

"How are we going to get back into the library, climb those stairs, and try all those locks without getting caught?" I asked Gillian later that evening.

We were sitting cross-legged on the carpet in the closet, hiding from Dulcie. Roger had been right; showing her the hidden passage had only roused her appetite for more. Roger refused to show her anything else on the grounds that she was a nosy little twerp and therefore apt to get—as he put it—"caught or hurt or *poofed*."

"Well . . . ," Gillian began.

The dresses leaned in as if interested in her reply.

"Can you help us?" she asked them. "Another nice visit to the library? One that involves avoiding the Librarian? Snooping?"

Ribbons dropped. Flounces fell. Collars flattened.

"What do they mean by that?" she asked me.

"I suppose there isn't anybody in the castle who can get away with all that," I told her.

A jet button winked at me.

Lady Kaye could get away with anything, but I'd been her with one of the dresses already. The dresses didn't do repeats. Which also meant that I couldn't be the Duchess again either.

"I know you'd help if you could," Gillian told them. She dug a piece of toffee out of her apron pocket. "Want one?"

"Sure," I said, taking it.

I knew she had a source in the kitchen who slipped her candy every now and then. But I'd never figured out who it was. I pulled the wax paper off the sticky sweet and popped it into my mouth.

"Where does Gloria get her peppermints?" I asked.

"Her mother sends them in parcels, hidden in socks," Gillian answered. "Kate told me."

I waited for her to volunteer where her treats came from, but she didn't.

"Do you think that desk really belonged to that Magnificent guy?" she said instead.

"It's old, his initials are on it, it's got lots of locks, it fits Cherice's six-and-seven thing," I said, ticking the items off on my hand. "And the keys are missing."

"I've been thinking about inheritances," Gillian said. "Lots of time they're property—like a farm or a house. Cherice could have meant a deed. You could roll that up and stash it in one of those drawers."

"Yeah?" I said. That hadn't occurred to me.

"Or a mansion," she continued. "Maybe that's it."

"Hmm," I replied. "Cherice kept going on about being royalty. Maybe—"

"A castle," Gillian exclaimed, sitting up straight. "What

if she meant *this* castle? What if she was secretly some long-lost princess?"

"No," I said, my chest contracting with a breathless squeeze. An ache bloomed under my rib cage. The Star Castle belonged to Princess Mariposa. And I wouldn't let anyone take it away from her. After all, Magnificent Wray wouldn't have shielded the castle with magic for Queen Candace if it had really belonged to *his* heirs. Would he?

I shook my head, suddenly dizzy. "Cherice said she is the last Wray, not some princess."

"You are the last Wray, though," Gillian insisted. "So maybe she got it all wrong and it's really your inheritance. Maybe you're royalty. Maybe you've got a castle; maybe *you* are a long-lost princess."

For a moment I could see it, rising like a soap bubble above the scrubbing-room mist. Me, Princess Darling, long-lost heir to a shining castle tucked in a forest like a cherry in a bonbon. Then the dream bubble burst.

I was the Under-assistant to the Wardrobe Mistress. And fortunate to be that. Cherice was simply crazy.

"Even a little cottage in the woods would be a nice in-heritance," Gillian continued. "Somewhere you could live with Jane."

I winced at the thought of Jane; for weeks I'd been too busy to spend time with her. Poor, loyal Jane had never had a home of her own. She'd raised me in the castle kitchens.

"She could keep a couple of chickens. Maybe a cow . . . ," I said. I thought about living far away from the castle with nobody but Jane for company. Far away from the Princess. And the dresses. "Wouldn't Jane be kind of lonely in the woods?" I said, not wanting to admit that it was me I was worried about.

"You could sell it." Gillian dug out another toffee for herself. "And give Jane the money."

"True," I said, relieved to be rescued from the woods.

I leaned back into the velvety folds of the dress behind me. Daydreams were all well and good, but we'd never know what Cherice meant by her "inheritance" unless we found a way to use the key.

The hem of the dress lifted, and Bonbon peeked out. Gillian was unwrapping her candy; I shook my head at Bonbon, shooing her away with my hand. Gillian looked up.

"I was thinking," I said, and twisted the wax paper from my toffee around my finger to distract her from looking down. "Servants can't use the library without permission. After I borrowed that book last winter . . . ," I trailed off.

"You're afraid to ask," Gillian finished. "So?"

"What if *you* could get permission?"

"You want me to ask the Princess if *I* can use the royal library?" Gillian said.

"It gives you an excuse to be in there. It's a start."

Gillian clicked her toffee against her teeth, mulling

that over. "It would have to be the right moment," she said, offering me another candy. "When Her Highness was in just the right mood."

"She's been so busy, I've hardly seen her," I said.

"And I see her even less than you do," Gillian replied.

"If we don't find the right moment before the wedding, we'll have to wait until after she returns from the honeymoon," I said.

"She'll be gone for months." Gillian sighed.

"There has to be a faster way." Finding the right keyhole was so close; I could feel the key turning in my grip.

"I know!" Gillian said. "Roger!"

"You want Roger to ask her?"

"Silly," Gillian said, swatting my knee. "Wouldn't that be funny? No. Roger's been making all those maps. What if there's a passage into the library?"

A shiver went down my spine. The idea was so clever, I wished I'd thought of it.

"We could sneak in late at night when Master Varick is snoring away!" I said.

"Now we just need to get Roger in a good mood," Gillian replied, fishing out another toffee.

"Wait," I said, holding out a hand to stop her. "Save that candy. It's Roger bait!"

Gillian grinned in agreement. She dangled the wax paper rectangle in the air. "Here, fishy, fishy," she said.

We giggled together. We were about to unlock the greatest secret in the realm.

The next morning, a storm of wedding preparations swept the castle, catching Gillian and me in its wake. Lindy loaded mountains of napkins and tablecloths onto Gillian's already monstrous pile of ironing. And Rose, the Head Seamstress, appeared at Marci's desk with a bundle of sky-blue silk.

"I've heard what a deft hand with a needle Darling has proved to be," Rose said. She had the tone of someone who wouldn't take no for an answer.

"Yes?" Marci said, looking up from scribbling in one of the wardrobe logs.

I parked my needle in the hem I was stitching.

"We're rather overwhelmed in the sewing rooms," Rose said. "The Princess has ordered new clothes for all the head servants, new coats for the Footmen, new vests for the Messenger Boys, and new clothes for her own Girls. It's a wonder she hasn't wanted new aprons for all the kitchen staff." Rose broke off with a blush. "And for heaven's sake, Marci, don't suggest that to her!"

"I wouldn't dream of meddling in the affairs of the Under-servants," Marci said drily, blotting her writing. "I take it that you've come for a little help."

"I have. I've never asked before, and I know you're

swamped with the Princess's wedding clothes and what-not." Rose paused to catch her breath. "But Darling—" Rose cast a pleading glance in my direction.

"I can help," I said. "If it's all right with Marci."

"Would you mind terribly if she did?" Rose said.

"Did what exactly?" Marci asked.

Rose plunked her bundle on the desk. "Piecing bodices together. Straight seams. I've marked all the pieces with chalk; two goes with two, three goes with three. Simple as pie."

A silk piece labeled *six* in white chalk sat on top of the pile, along with three spools of sky-blue thread.

"Are these the Girls' dresses?" I said, admiring the fabric.

"They are. And we're in a rush to finish them," Rose said. "They're needed for the wedding. And on top of this"—she poked the bundle—"we've all the lace aprons *and* an entire set of new work clothes to sew for the Girls. We've worn our fingers to the bone, and we aren't half-done yet."

"You'll have to finish your regular chores first," Marci said to me.

"Yes, ma'am." I draped a piece of the glossy silk over my hand. It was as soft and light as a spring day. I could already picture myself twirling down the corridors in a sky-blue dress. "Whatever you say, Marci."

"If you're sure," Marci said pointedly.

"I'm sure," I said.

"Thank you," Rose breathed as if she'd been holding her breath for hours. "I'll owe you a favor, Darling, and you too, Marci."

"As you wish," Marci replied.

Once Rose had left and I was sorting the pieces in the pile by number, Marci tapped me on the shoulder. "I hope you know what you've gotten yourself into."

"What do you mean?" I asked, still picturing myself waltzing about the castle. "Rose said it's just straight seams."

"It isn't the sewing that concerns me," Marci said. "It's who will be wearing those dresses once they're made. That's a great deal of extra work. You'd better be careful to do a good job—or you'll have a whole crew of angry Girls to contend with."

The image of me in my new dress vanished, replaced by an outraged Francesca in a sky-blue disaster.

11

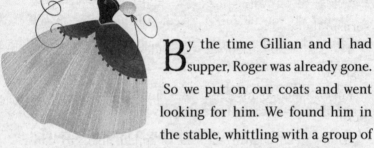

By the time Gillian and I had supper, Roger was already gone. So we put on our coats and went looking for him. We found him in the stable, whittling with a group of Stable Boys. The sweet smell of hay mingled with the scent of wood chips and the aroma of growing grass carried in on the chilly breeze. I pulled my coat closer as we walked over to him.

"What are you up to?" Roger said, flicking a wood curl at our feet.

He sounded cool—not harsh, but not exactly friendly either. The other Stable Boys toyed with their pocket-knives as if waiting for something to happen.

"We're going fishing," I said with a grin.

"We have a big fish to catch," Gillian added, eyes glowing.

"Which one's your girlfriend, Roger?" a skinny Boy named Corley asked.

Roger's face burned so bright a shade of red that his freckles caught fire.

"He'd choose that dark-haired one if he's smart," Eric said, as if they hadn't all known us for years.

"Or a can of worms for fishing—if he's *really* smart," Norman quipped.

The Stable Boys slapped their sides and howled with laughter.

Roger snapped his knife shut and shoved it into a pocket.

"Don't need a girlfriend," he snapped. "No girl can hold a candle to Lady Marguerite's horses."

The Stable Boys laughed harder.

My cheeks blazed. My fists curled. How dare he imply that a *horse* was better than me?

Not that I was his girlfriend. Or wanted to be. And I was just about to tell him so when Gillian spoke up.

"It's too bad you Boys are stuck out here with the horse manure," she said with a sigh, and dug a toffee out of her pocket. "You must miss out on so much." She peeled back the wax paper on the candy. Then she parked the toffee between her teeth while she folded the paper in a neat square and tucked it in her pocket.

Every Boy's eyes were on her as she popped the candy into her mouth and chewed.

"You have toffee?" Corley asked.

"Only for my friends." She flashed her most dazzling smile. "Let's go, Darl," she said, turning on her heel.

"Bye, guys," I said, taking my cue from her and waving.

Gillian and I strolled off arm in arm as if the Stable Boys didn't exist. Once outside, Gillian pulled me into the bushes. Overhead, the stars burned crisply against the blue-velvet evening.

"We'll wait here," Gillian said, parting the bush just enough to see through.

I was about to ask what we were waiting for when Roger came walking out of the stable, whistling. He saw us but kept right on going. Gillian counted to twenty under her breath, and then she hauled me off after him.

We found him on a bench around the corner.

"What do you want?" he asked, crossing his arms.

Gillian settled next to him and handed him a toffee.

"Information," I said, sitting down on his other side.

I hadn't exactly forgiven him yet, but the breeze had sharpened. I wanted a quick answer so I could get back to the warm kitchens.

"We need a secret passage into the library," Gillian said. "What have you got?"

"I don't think there is one," he said. He pulled off his leather cap and dug a wad of papers out of the lining. He spread them on his knee. And then he fished a match out of his pocket and struck it on his boot heel. "See here," he said, holding the flame over a series of squiggles. "This is the stuff I've found on the second floor so far."

Gillian studied the paper. "That's not even close," she said.

"Nope, it's not, but these here circles," he said, showing her, "are passages I haven't mapped yet."

"Why not?" I asked.

"Haven't had time," he replied. "Got any more?"

Gillian dug out a couple more toffees for him. Then she pointed to a jumble of lines. "Do you have a compass? What if you went back here and looked for a branch that headed west?"

"I don't promise anything, but—" Roger began.

Right then a shadow blotted out the stars. We looked up in unison.

"Good evening, ladies, gentleman," the Stable Master said. "What have we here?"

Roger scrunched the papers in his free hand, speechless.

"Nothing," Gillian said, smiling. "Just some drawings."

But either it was too dark or the smile was wasted on the Stable Master.

"Allow me," he said, holding out his hand. "I like a good drawing, same as the next man."

Miserably, Roger handed over the papers. The Stable Master held them up to the starlight to study. Then he said, "I think this requires an explanation, Roger, me lad."

The matchstick in Roger's fist snapped in two. The match head dropped to the ground. He hurried to stamp it out.

"It's a treasure map," I said quickly. "Sir."

The Stable Master's eyes widened. "Do tell."

"Not a real one," I said, wondering what possessed me to say something so stupid. "A make-believe one."

The Stable Master stared at me.

"It's just a game we were playing," I finished in a small voice.

"I see," the Stable Master said, folding the papers and tucking them into his jacket. "If you have time to play, then you have time to work. Go on in, Girls. Young Roger here has business to attend to."

Roger shot me a dirty look as Gillian and I made a hasty retreat.

I was woken by a tickling on the end of my nose. Bonbon blinked at me from her position on my pillow. A button sparkled in her paws.

"Where did you get that?" I asked.

She wiggled her nose at me.

"From the dresses?" I guessed.

She shook her head and scampered to the end of the bed.

"Are you going somewhere?" I whispered, conscious of the roomful of sleeping Girls around me.

Bonbon slid down the counterpane and dropped to the rug below.

I threw back my covers. Maybe Iago needed me. But when I knelt to pull the crate out from under my bed, Bonbon leaped up and down excitedly.

I paused, hand outstretched.

"Does your dad know where you are?" I asked.

She screwed up her whiskers, considering.

"Tell me the truth."

She shook her head. Then she held up the button with a hopeful gaze.

"Do you want me to follow you?"

At that, Bonbon scurried off across the room. I hurried after her, but I lost her in the corridor when she squeezed under a baseboard.

"Hey!" I called in a loud whisper. "I can't fit in there."

Nothing.

I hunched down and knocked softly on the wood. Silence. I waited awhile, but it was still early enough in the spring that the cold crept into the soles of my feet. Yawning, I got up and went back to bed.

In the morning, I'd ask the dresses if there was a button missing.

But when the morning broke out in a sunny spring glow and windows all over the castle flew open to take advantage of the weather, the Princess took it into her head to breakfast in the dew-drenched gardens. Which threw the Upper-servants into disarray.

Mrs. Pepperwhistle took charge of us Girls and sent us scurrying. Hampers had to be packed. Clogs dug out. Pillows and rugs and trays assembled. Parasols unfurled. A group of hastily attired Footmen stood ready to escort it all outside.

The only thing missing was the Princess.

Marci was beside herself, running from closet to closet.

"What on *earth* do Princesses *wear* for much-too-early-in-the-morning meals *out* of doors?" she exclaimed.

I trotted at her heels, a pile of shawls, sashes, and stockings over one arm. "Something green?" I suggested. "Or yellow? For spring?" I added when she scowled at me.

"Something floral!" she proclaimed, and flung open the door to closet number four, where the Princess's day dresses were kept.

Madame Zerlina had designed three new spring gowns: the shimmering jade that Princess Mariposa had worn a few days earlier; a pink-and-white-striped dress; and a watercolor floral, a jacquard of misty flowers strewn across a pale blue background. It had the most delicate lace trim and two rows of enameled buttons at the waist, three on each side.

"Excellent idea," Marci said, whipping it off its hanger.

Which was when I noticed the thread hanging off the front.

"What's that?" I asked.

Marci gaped at the dress—one of the enamel buttons was missing.

"Madame Zerlina!" she cried. "What does she mean by this?"

"It had all six buttons when it arrived." I was certain because I'd been fascinated by the tiny ladies painted on them.

"How could this happen? Mariposa hasn't even worn it yet!"

I'd never heard Marci forget herself to the extent that she neglected to give the Princess her proper title.

"Um," I said, remembering Bonbon, "mice?"

"Mice!" Marci shrieked. "Where?" She hopped from foot to foot as if besieged by an army of the creatures.

"I didn't mean there were any *here*," I said, surprised. I'd never known Marci to be frightened by anything.

She staggered to a stop.

"But one might have gotten in. Like late at night or something," I said.

"Do you think they could get in *all* the closets?" Marci swayed on her feet.

"Oh, no. Of course not," I said, prying the dress out of her hands. "That daisy-sprigged cotton will do nicely."

Distracted from the ongoing threat of mice, Marci peered at the dress in question.

"Oh," she said, and pulled it out. "Good work. Let's go."

I trailed after her, pausing just long enough to lay the watercolor dress across her desk. I was going to have a word with Bonbon the first free minute I had.

12

Roger was still sore at lunch. "Can't ride today," he said, clutching his cap in a white-knuckled grip, "'cause I got to clean out the stable attic."

"At least you won't have to shovel anything," Gillian told him.

"*Girls,*" he retorted, making girls sound suspiciously like snakes, "who cost a fellow hours of extra work—not to mention their map—are no friends of mine."

I pretended I hadn't heard him as I sliced my roast beef. He took himself off to eat with the Messenger Boys.

"*Boys,*" I said after he'd gone.

"He's just doing that to prove to the other Boys that he doesn't like you," Gillian said.

"Thanks," I said, buttering my bread.

"Because he really does," she added. "Like you, I mean. Lots. Gobs. Kissy-kissy bunches," she added with a smirk.

I was just about to tell her what a load of nonsense that was when Dulcie piped up.

"He's cute. I like his freckles," she said.

If she hadn't looked at me with that admiring, wide-eyed gaze, I'd have dumped the gravy over her head.

Selma, the Head Laundress, came stalking into the kitchens and cornered the Head Cook, who was busy assembling a platter for the Princess.

"You should have seen those aprons!" Selma complained. "We send them upstairs pure white—spotless! Oh, the amount of scrubbing that requires!"

"I can imagine. Nut?" the Head Cook said, holding out the bowl she kept handy. With her other hand she garnished the platter with a spring of parsley. "Cora, take this up!"

Cora swept the platter off the table and raced off to the Footmen's station, because only the Footmen were allowed to serve the Princess directly.

"Obliged to you," Selma replied, selecting a walnut. "And we got those pretty whites back in such a state." She paused to crunch. "My Laundresses woulda kept 'em cleaner. And you know how hard they work. And ooh— that miss, that smug little piece . . . what's her name—"

"Francesca?" the Head Cook guessed.

Gillian perked up.

"Yes, Francesca! She waved a ring under my nose and said—"

"I suspect she's just excited. It's a nice little ring," the Head Cook said. "No doubt her mother was quite pleased to see her noticed by the Princess like that."

"Indeed," a voice as mellow as an oboe replied. "A signal honor. Of course, it's only what Francesca deserves."

That voice sent shivers down my spine. I glanced up at Mrs. Pepperwhistle, who stood right behind me.

"D-deserves?" Selma sputtered.

"And," Mrs. Pepperwhistle continued, "if you have complaints, Selma, you should address them to Marci. She's responsible. I thought she had better sense. The idea of sending the *Girls* to the high attic."

Selma choked on her nut.

"It's a messy job, no matter what. Who would you have sent?" the Head Cook inquired, pounding Selma on the back.

Mrs. Pepperwhistle glanced down and caught my eye. She had a dilemma. If she said that some of the Underservants should have gone, she'd be accused of playing favorites. If she said the Sweepers or the Dusters, then she'd be asked why she hadn't volunteered their services in the first place.

Instead, she patted me on the head.

"As I was saying," she continued, "three of my Girls had the sense not to wear their white aprons. Marci should have insisted that the others do likewise."

I knew she hadn't been saying that at all, but Selma grunted in agreement. "Order extra lye; we're running low," she said.

"I'll do so," Mrs. Pepperwhistle replied. "Eat your lunch, Girls. There is work to do."

We nodded and ate faster.

Mrs. Pepperwhistle turned to the Head Cook. "It has come to my attention that the Baroness has taken a bit of chill after this morning's outing. Please see that a tray is sent to her rooms."

"What?" the Head Cook said, brandishing a sprig of parsley under the Head Housekeeper's nose. "Haven't I enough to do? See these platters? The lot of them have to be filled and garnished for Her Highness's table. When will I have time to make up something special for the Baroness? And which of my kitchen staff has time to take it all the way across the castle when they're all needed here?"

"We'll do it," Gillian said. "We're almost finished. And we have to go back upstairs anyway. We'd be glad to help." She poked me. "Right, Darling?"

"Sure," I said, massaging my ribs. "Glad."

"That's settled, then," Mrs. Pepperwhistle said. And she almost smiled.

"Thanks a lot," I said, lugging a tea tray up seven million steps to the Baroness's rooms in the west wing.

"You can thank me later," Gillian said, balancing a covered soup tureen. A bread basket swung on her arm.

The Head Cook had outdone herself. She'd loaded us down with enough luncheon for six Baronesses.

We turned into a peach-colored corridor with white wainscoting. A frieze of plaster mice lined the wall. They were alive inside the castle's magic. I knew because Iago and his children had come out of the wall.

"I like this wing," Dulcie said, bringing up the rear. She carried napkins folded over her arm as if they were royal tapestries. "It has lots of nice mouseys."

"That's *mice*," I said. I'd meant to take a quick trip back to the dormitory after lunch to pounce on Bonbon for the whereabouts of that button. But now I'd have to wait until after everyone was asleep.

"Here we are," Gillian said. "Knock, Dulcie."

Dulcie used her free hand to rap on the door, which flew open to reveal the Baroness's Maid, Aster.

"About time," she said, fussing with her ruffled collar.

"We hurried," Gillian said, pushing past her into the suite. "And this is heavy."

Aster gave herself airs; she believed that being a Baroness's Maid elevated her above the castle's servants. I wanted to retort that *she* might have done the fetching herself, but the Baroness called from another room.

"Is that the Girls I hear?" Lady Kaye cried. "Send them in."

Aster screwed her lips into a frown but motioned us to follow her. She led us into a spacious bedroom done in pastel pink, ruffles, and lace and dotted with bows. I couldn't have imagined a less Baroness-like décor if I'd tried.

"You brought me a feast," Lady Kaye said. She wore a quilted pink satin bed jacket that matched the room, ruffles, bows, and all. She appeared almost grandmotherly—almost, had it not been for her sharp gaze. "Evidently, the Head Cook believes I am in imminent danger of starving."

"She thinks that food cheers people up," I said, setting down my tray on the table Aster pointed to.

"Oh? Did you bring dessert, then?" Lady Kaye inquired.

"No, ma'am," Dulcie said. "Just soup and bread and jam and tea and—"

"I get the idea; thank you, dear," Lady Kaye said.

"What a pretty room," Gillian said.

Beside the pink-canopied bed stood a dressing table. There were three wardrobes, and numerous jewel cases were scattered everywhere—everything from small leather cases to carved chests to fancy armoires on spindly legs.

"What lovely cases," I added. "Azure must have a great lot of jewels."

"Oh, those." Lady Kaye waved them away. "They are locked away in Castle Azure. My husband's family had poor taste when it came to jewels. These are the DeVere jewels."

"Her Ladyship was a DeVere," Aster said, wielding a breakfast tray she'd set with the Baroness's lunch. "Now then, you may—"

"Like Lady Amber DeVere, Magnificent Wray's daughter?" I burst out. Was I related to the Baroness, too?

"The same family, yes," Lady Kaye said, "but she was an aunt, married to Father's stepbrother."

Aster gave me a pained look as she set the tray on the Baroness's bed.

"Did you know her?" I asked.

"Slightly," Lady Kaye said, adding sugar to her cup. "I didn't see her often."

"What was she like?" Gillian said.

"Crazy, mostly." Lady Kaye took a sip of tea. "That armoire over there—the one with the swans painted on the lid? That was hers. Half the keys are lost. Probably buried under the rhododendrons. She liked to hide things. But she was old, poor dear."

"Older than you?" Dulcie asked.

"Older even than me," the Baroness replied with a sparkle in her eye.

"It was ever so kind of you to give Darling that book," Gillian said. "Books are such a comfort."

"Hmm," Lady Kaye said, salting her soup. "Are you in need of another, Darling?"

"No, ma'am," I said, sizing up the painted armoire.

"You tell such wonderful stories. But seeing as how you aren't feeling all that well . . ." Gillian paused to look properly concerned. "I thought you might write a note for me to the Royal Librarian."

I tensed; Gillian was piling it on a bit thick. And then I realized what she was up to.

"Have an eye on his books now, do you?" Lady Kaye said with a keen-eyed glance that showed she wasn't fooled.

"Maybe. There's such a lot of them." Gillian sighed wistfully.

"You are a glutton for stories," Lady Kaye scolded. "But *after* lunch I will send a note down for you."

"Oh, you are too kind," Gillian said.

"Master Varick detests children. You enter his domain at your *own* peril," Lady Kaye remarked. "Don't say I didn't warn you."

"Her Ladyship is tired," Aster said pointedly, grabbing Gillian and me by the collars.

"Good-bye, Baroness," Dulcie said as we were hustled away.

"Good afternoon, Girls," Lady Kaye called.

I glanced over my shoulder, catching one last glimpse of Lady Amber's armoire, glistening with little silver keyholes: six across and seven down.

13

He held my hand as we watched the stars burning in the night sky.

"Can you count them?" he asked me.

"No, Father."

"Can you reach them?"

I let go of his hand and stretched up on my tiptoes as high as I could. Then I fell back on my heels and shook my head.

"Do you know what causes them to shine?"

I frowned, perplexed.

"Do you know what I think?" he asked.

I bit my lip.

"They were born in an instant. One moment there was darkness, and then"—he snapped his fingers—"there was light."

I stared at the sky, but I couldn't imagine it without the stars.

"They shine because they must," he whispered. "Because they can't contain the light."

"There." Selma carried a white satin pillow bearing the starlight slippers. The salt-and-pepper-haired Head Laundress, with her rough hands and canvas apron, made quite a contrast with the dainty pillow. "Clean as a new day and white as white can be!"

The slippers gleamed, a lace confection floating on leather heels. The creamy opals glistened. The sparkle of rose, gold, and azure captured in the painting didn't do justice to the real things. Light coruscated across the surface of the gems, setting the captive specks dancing like miniature fireflies.

I picked up the enamel button to sew it back onto the watercolor floral dress. I'd waited until late the previous evening to talk to Bonbon, but when I checked my crate, it was empty. No mice. Then this afternoon, I'd found the enamel button beside the button box on Marci's desk. Lined up next to it were a big bronze button and four little pearl buttons. Marci thought I'd been playing with them.

"You're an artist, Selma," Marci said with an overly bright smile.

"It's delicate work," Selma agreed. "Had to wear gloves and clean with a paintbrush. Opals are fragile bits of stuff. Why anyone would ever put 'em on their feet is beyond me!"

"Her Highness will be so pleased," Marci said, staring at the shoes.

Selma set the pillow on the desk. "What's the matter?" she asked. "*You* don't sound pleased."

"Nothing. Nothing at all. I'm just . . . amazed at your talent," Marci said.

Selma frowned; she'd known Marci too long to be easily deceived.

"You should show them to Her Highness," Marci urged. "She'll want to try them on."

"I'm not one to fuss over my work like some Duster who's just discovered polish!" Selma said. "It's a-getting late. You can take them to her when she dresses for dinner."

With a nod, Selma took herself back to the undercellar. Marci opened and closed her hands as if deciding whether or not the slippers were safe to touch.

"They didn't do Selma any harm," I said.

"The dragons would chip a tooth on Selma," she retorted.

"They didn't bother the Princess," I said. "Maybe your grandmother didn't mean the slippers at all. Maybe the dragons were drawn to the magic and it was in something else?"

Marci considered that for a fraction of an instant, her frown deepening. "Look at those opals, all cleaned up," she whispered. "They look almost . . . *alive.*"

I squinted at the opals, which sparkled marvelously. But if there was anything odd about them, I couldn't see it. I glanced up at Marci, who glared at the gems as if they were poisonous.

Then she caught me watching her.

"Don't you have work to do?" she asked.

I poked my needle through the metal loop at the back of the button. Then I pushed the needle into the dress's fabric. Studiously. As if sewing on buttons required great precision. Which it didn't.

With a grimace, Marci scooped up the pillow, took a step, and stopped.

"Darling," she said, "go get a dress, and tell it you need to be Lady Kaye."

Startled, I stabbed the needle into my finger.

"Ouch!" A drop of blood welled up on my fingertip. I set the dress down so that I wouldn't accidently stain it. Then I dug out my handkerchief and dabbed at my finger.

"Well?" Marci said, planting her free hand on her hip. "Get moving."

"I can't," I told her. "I already was the Baroness ... once."

"Then tell the dresses you need to be Lady Marie."

I bit my lip. I tucked my soiled handkerchief in my pocket.

"Oh for goodness' sake, Darling," Marci said. "Be Pepperwhistle."

I shook my head. I'd been her, too.

Marci scowled. She turned to go but then whipped back around. "Go tell those dresses that you need to be somebody the Princess trusts," Marci ordered.

"She trusts me," I protested.

"Go. Do it now," Marci said, pointing at the closet door.

"Yes, ma'am," I said, biting back a complaint. If Marci wanted me to waltz around the castle as someone else, then I would. But it seemed silly. Why didn't she just take the shoes to the Princess herself?

I went into the closet, where Lyric was singing in the spring sunshine. The stained-glass canary glowed, casting slivers of yellow and gold across the carpet. The dresses fluttered in anticipation.

"Marci sent me," I warned them. "She wants me to be someone the Princess trusts."

At the mention of Princess Mariposa, a flurry went through the dresses as if they were unsure about this request. I waited as the dresses decided.

A sharp knock sounded.

"Now, please," Marci called through the door.

"I won't do anything I shouldn't," I told them. "I promise."

Ten, an opalescent taffeta ball gown, roiled on its hanger like a carrot simmering in a stew.

"Thank you." I picked it up and stepped into it.

A louder knock rattled the door.

The crisp taffeta swooped up over my shoulders and clasped me in its folds, shrinking to fit. The skirt shimmered in waves of white, pink, and lavender as the light caught it.

"Just like the slippers," I said, admiring it.

"Darling!" Marci thundered on the other side of the door.

"Coming!" I looked up. Francesca smiled in the mirror, sizing me up. "Whoa," I told Ten. "Are you sure about this?"

The door swung open. Marci stopped in midstride, her fist glued to the doorknob. The pillow in her free hand shook. The slippers bobbled on their satin perch.

"I told them I needed someone the Princess could trust," I said.

Marci glowered at me.

"Francesca is loyal to Her Highness," I said. "It sort of makes sense."

"I suppose it could be worse," Marci growled, and shoved the pillow at me.

I carried the pillow with my chin in the air and a bounce in my step. Being Francesca came easily, like singing a familiar refrain. I didn't have to ask myself what she would do or say. I already knew.

Ten bounced along with me, the occasional ripple in

its skirt. I had the impression that it had been yearning to get out of the closet for a long time.

Marci strolled beside me, a mask of serenity plastered on her face. But the white knuckles of her hands clasped together before her spoiled the effect.

"Did you wear all of them?" I asked, referring to the dresses. Marci had had a turn with the closet when she was a child and her grandmother was the Wardrobe Mistress, but she never talked about it.

"No," she replied in a frosty tone.

"Why not?"

"Because I got caught," she retorted. "Which I've advised you not to do."

"By who?" I asked, smiling at a passing Footman. (Francesca never missed an opportunity to smile at adults.)

"My grandmother," she replied. "Otherwise, I doubt I'd still be here." She shot me a look that said I too could disappear if I asked any more questions.

But there was one I couldn't resist asking. "How many did you wear?"

We flew by corridors and stairs as Marci remained silent.

I bided my time; I knew better than to insist on an answer.

Finally, she said, "Thirty-six."

"Could you still wear the others now? Since you never wore them all?"

Marci swallowed as if trying not to cry. "No," she whispered. "Once you grow up, it's too late to go back."

I had the sudden image of Marci as an adult, struggling into one of the dresses—only to be disappointed.

"Oh," I said, having nothing else to say.

We walked down the back stair to the main hall, and there—to my dismay—was Mrs. Pepperwhistle, instructing a Messenger Boy.

"Take this note to the Head Footman," she told him. "Lady Teresa arrives this evening. Her Highness expects everything to be ready."

Marci nudged me, hope blooming in her eyes.

I shook my head. It wouldn't do any good to wait until later. I'd been Lady Teresa.

Marci groaned, exasperated.

"See to it that he reads it at once," Mrs. Pepperwhistle concluded.

The Messenger Boy nodded eagerly. The Head Housekeeper had no business ordering him about, since he answered to Esteban, the Head Footman. But the Messenger Boy didn't argue, because Esteban would punish any Boy who ran afoul of the Head Housekeeper.

It wasn't fair. But it was the order of things among the servants.

The Messenger Boy, note in hand, vanished as quickly as he could.

"You've had them cleaned!" Mrs. Pepperwhistle exclaimed, seeing the slippers.

"Indeed," Marci replied. "We're just on our way to present them to Her Highness."

"It's very kind of you to allow Francesca this privilege," the Head Housekeeper purred.

"Only fair," Marci replied tersely. "She did find them."

"I can't wait to see the Princess's face," I said, hoping Mrs. Pepperwhistle would take the hint and let us go.

"Yes, well, remember our little discussion," she replied. "Princess Mariposa is sentimental, but Queens do not keep Girls. They employ Ladies-in-Waiting."

"Y-yes, ma'am," I sputtered.

What did she mean, *Queens do not keep Girls*? My heart pounded. My palms grew moist. The pillow wavered in my hands.

"Mustn't keep Her Highness waiting, Francesca," Marci said.

"Smile!" Mrs. Pepperwhistle commanded, and let us go.

Marci led me across the main hall to the west corridor.

"What did she mean? Queens don't keep Girls?" I squeaked.

"They don't. Usually. They appoint adults as Ladies-in-Waiting to handle some of their personal chores and turn the rest over to the Ladies' Maids," Marci replied. "But the

Princess is fond of the lot of you and isn't eager to do that."

"Does that mean"—I sniffled—"that we won't have jobs much longer?"

Marci softened slightly. "Darling, it means *I'm* keeping you, no matter what."

I glanced up at the stubborn set of her chin.

"I don't fancy doing all the mending by myself," she added. "Now, stop asking questions."

She paused before the door to the Princess's private office, waved the Footman aside, patted the crown of braids on her head, tidied the knot of her scarf, and took a deep breath.

"No matter what happens," she whispered, "you're here to convince Mariposa that nothing out of the ordinary is going on. Got that? Follow my lead."

"Yes, ma'am."

"And, Darling, if anything *bad*—" Marci's chin quivered. "If those slippers do anything at all other than look pretty, you yank them right off her feet!"

Her reasons for wanting me there crystallized into focus: *Marci was scared of the slippers.*

But you wouldn't know it to watch her. Marci rolled into the royal office like the Pastry Chef flattening dough. Nothing dared stand in her way.

The Princess sat at her desk, writing letters. Alone.

"Marci!" she said, surprised. "Oh, you have the starlight slippers! You brought them to me."

She dropped her quill and stood up, holding out her hands.

I walked forward and placed the pillow on them.

"You needn't have come all the way down here," she said, admiring the slippers. "But I'm pleased you have."

"I knew Your Highness would be anxious to see them," Marci replied.

"They're beautiful. They're perfect," Princess Mariposa sighed. "Oh, I must try them on!"

"As you wish," Marci said smoothly, as if she weren't dreading it.

"Let me assist you," I said. Because Francesca would jump at the chance.

Princess Mariposa walked over to a small sofa by the window and sat, placing the pillow at her side. I knelt down and helped her out of her shoes. Then she handed me a slipper.

I felt Marci stiffen beside me.

The shoe felt weightless, like a whisper of cloud in my hand. I set it down for Princess Mariposa to slide her foot into. I held my breath. Nothing happened. Then the Princess handed me the other shoe, and I helped her put it on.

Princess Mariposa stood, held up her skirt, and whirled across the room.

"Like dancing on air!" she cried.

Marci twisted her fingers together as the Princess bent and swayed with her imaginary partner. The starlight opals flashed as she moved. Princess Mariposa pirouetted, then ground to a halt. The color drained from the Princess's face. "I'm dizzy," she gasped, putting her hands to her head. "The room won't stop spinning."

Marci caught her arm and led her back to the sofa.

"Your Highness has been working too hard," Marci said, clucking. "All these wedding plans. And those shoes! Obviously, they're not well balanced. *You shouldn't wear them.*"

White-faced, Princess Mariposa stared at her. *"Not wear them!"*

"Maybe you shouldn't," I said, echoing Marci. "You spun so fast; I think the soles are slippery. You might fall."

"Take them off—for now," Princess Mariposa said, holding her foot aloft. She looked strained and tired. "But I will wear these slippers to my wedding—if it's the last thing I do!"

I pulled the shoe off her foot. It didn't feel any different than it had earlier.

But I could have sworn the opals glimmered a darker shade than before.

14

Marci put the pillow with the slippers on her desk, muttering about stubborn people. Which was funny, considering she herself was the most stubborn person I knew. I debated whether I should tell her about the change I'd seen in the opals. But that would only upset Marci more. Besides, I hadn't felt any magic in the slippers. Not a bit. —

That evening, the arrival of Princess Mariposa's cousin Lady Teresa turned the entire castle upside down. The Princess insisted that Lady Teresa's days be an unending whirl of feasts and entertainments. I felt sorry for Teresa; she was so shy she'd hidden from the court during her previous visit. And equally sorry for the servants, who were kept running, cleaning, cooking, washing, and fetching.

Marci was frazzled organizing the Princess's changes of clothes—three or four a day. Not only did Her Highness require a certain kind of dress for every event, but shoes, jewelry, shawls, and even gloves and parasols. Each selection had to be perfect. Not just any pair of gloves would suit the fawn-colored walking dress; Princess Mariposa must have the turquoise cotton gloves. Which she hadn't worn in two years. (It was a good thing Marci and I had just turned the closets inside out searching for the starlight slippers. Otherwise we might not have been able to produce the gloves on demand.)

Once Princess Mariposa had worn something around Lady Teresa, it could not be repeated. Whether anyone had noticed it—like the pearl bracelet she wore half-hidden by the lace trim on the sleeve of her rose-colored afternoon gown—or not.

For the first time, I understood why the Princess had six closets.

And in the middle of all this, the wedding preparations continued.

Gillian and I dropped onto the bench in the kitchen. My dinner plate steamed on the table before me. I was so tired I didn't think I'd be able to pick up my fork, let alone get it into my mouth.

"I ache so much my curls are sore," Gillian moaned.

Roger sat down across from us. The Stable Boys had all been so busy; he'd forgotten he was mad at us.

"You girls were *mooning* over the royal wedding," he said. "You're singing a different tune now."

"We are not." I snatched my fork off the table.

"What a goose you are, Roger," Gillian said, unfolding her napkin. "I'm *glad* to suffer in the service of my Princess."

"Yeah," I said.

I neglected to mention that Gillian's extra work had been dumped on her; I'd volunteered for mine. Late afternoons, when I'd ordinarily be finishing up, I had to work on the Girls' dresses. I'd sewn so many pieces of blue silk together that I'd begun to dread the sight of it. But I knew better than to complain to Marci.

And I'd jump off the castle roof before I'd admit it to Roger.

"What have you been up to?" Gillian asked. "Polishing your ponies?"

Roger slapped his leather cap on the table. "I came here to eat," he said, and dug in.

Gillian hid her smile behind her napkin, dabbing her lips ever so delicately. "So, Darling, did you hear the latest?" she asked.

Between the Baroness and Lindy, she heard most things before I did.

"No, what?"

Gillian cut her chicken into tiny, bite-sized pieces. "You know how excited the Princess was about those slippers?"

"Uh-huh."

"Ann told Kate that her mother said *every* lady in the court ran to the Royal Cobbler begging for lace shoes."

"Better off with a decent pair of boots," Roger said.

"Well, the Prince sent the Royal Cobbler a note saying, 'Please don't make lace shoes,'" Gillian said, ignoring Roger.

"Cost him a lot of business, that would," he said, gesturing with his fork. "The Royal Cobbler's got wages to pay and a family to care for, same as everybody else."

"We know," I told him. "So what happened?" I asked Gillian.

"So the Prince sent the Royal Cobbler a purse of gold—much more than the shoes would have cost—just so Princess Mariposa will be the only lady in the kingdom with lace slippers. Isn't that romantic?"

"Really?" I sighed. "He's so nice."

"And handsome," Gillian breathed.

Roger snorted in disgust. "All you girls are in love with that guy," he said.

I gasped, appalled by the very idea. Prince Sterling was the *Princess's* own true love.

"No, we're not!" I said, banging on the table. "It's that he's—he's a—"

"A prince," Gillian said, as if that explained everything.

Before Roger could retort, Dulcie slid onto the bench next to him.

"Hi, Roger," she said, blinking up at him. As usual, her braids were mussed, and she had a suspiciously jam-colored smear on her apron. "Whatcha doin' tonight?"

"I'm *poofing*," he said, and shoveled in the last of his supper.

"Can I disappear with you?" Dulcie asked.

"No," Roger said. "I have to get back to the stables. The horses I care for are *huge*. Big, scary, stamping monsters."

"But I like horses. I fed them carrots on the farm," Dulcie said. "Horses like me too."

"You grew up on a farm?" Roger asked, collecting his cap.

Dulcie sat up straighter to demonstrate how grown up a nine-year-old she was.

"Yep," she said. "I fed the chickens and gathered the eggs and weeded the garden and snapped the beans and shelled the peas and—"

"I'm working, not playing," Roger said.

Dulcie turned the full force of her pleading, little-neglected-orphan eyes on him.

"Okay," Roger said. "Meet me after supper. But no talking."

Dulcie sealed her lips together.

"See you guys later," he said, and left.

"It's Girls, Roger." Gillian stuck out her tongue after he left. "Not *guys*."

I giggled at her expression and forked up another bite of mashed turnips.

"Prince Sterling never gets confused," I said. "That's one reason why we like him."

"And there are *so* many others," she agreed.

"I have to go," Dulcie said, wiping her chin off on her fist. Which I was pretty certain she'd later brush off on her clothes.

"I need the key," Gillian said as soon as Dulcie was gone.

"What?" My fork stopped in midair. I'd been planning to have a look through Lady Amber's armoire that evening.

"To go to the library," Gillian said. "The Baroness wrote Master Varick a note. Remember?"

"Oh," I said, eating my turnips, stalling.

I could feel the key through my clothes, a reassuring weight on my thigh. In my mind, Lady Amber + armoire + missing key = Inheritance. A deed. A jewel. One of Magnificent Wray's secrets written on a sealed scroll.

"I finally have the chance," Gillian said, not noticing my discomfort. "I've been waiting for days. I'm *so* excited." Her curls bounced with her enthusiasm.

It was her turn. I fingered the key. Fair was fair. I took it out of my pocket. The starburst on the bow twinkled at me. My pulse raced. I glanced up, ready to protest.

Gillian slid her hand under the table, palm up. Her eyes danced.

I surrendered the key to her.

"I'll try to test as many as I can tonight," she said.

"Sure," I said.

"Just think," she breathed. "In a few days, we'll have our hands on it. Whatever it is."

"Yeah," I said, torn by jealousy.

I wanted to be the one to find the right lock. Me, Darling Skunk, False Friend, and Inheritor of All Things Wray. For a moment, I knew how Magnificent had felt in his search for magic. It had to be there, and *he* had to be the one to find it.

15

The loss of the key jabbed me like a pin forgotten in a hem. Marci didn't help matters. She stalked into the wardrobe hall, armed with a box of mousetraps and a block of cheese. She made me bait and set the traps and then follow her from closet to closet while she strategically placed them where she thought a mouse was most likely to squeeze in.

As the traps guarded the closet floors like wooden soldiers with sheathed swords, I spent the remainder of the afternoon on pins and needles. I didn't think Iago or his family would run around the wardrobe hall during broad daylight. But I had to warn them.

The sooner the better.

I gobbled my supper down, and then I bolted upstairs

to the Girls' dormitory. My crate marked ARTICHOKES was empty.

I sat on the rug next to my bed and thought. Should I wait for Iago to return? Leave a note? Go look for him?

Iago watched the dragons on the roof for me, but the only way up there was through the door in the north tower, to which I didn't have a key. The only person who did was Marsdon, the Head Steward, who had definite opinions about children doing dangerous things like climbing out on roofs. And if Iago wasn't there, he could be anywhere in the whole enormous, sprawling castle.

In the end, I promised myself I'd wait up and talk to him after everyone was asleep.

Which left me, Darling Wray Fortune, All-Important Under-assistant to the Wardrobe Mistress and Storyteller Extraordinaire, with absolutely nothing to do. It was too dark to sew on the Girls' dresses, and my best story audience, Gillian, was unavailable.

At times like these you appreciated your true friends.

I headed for the wardrobe hall, whistling, certain there was a dress or two that required my company. As I passed Marci's desk, the starlight opals glimmered in the dim evening as though someone had poured the Milky Way into a cup. I felt that I could dip in my fingertip and bring it out wet with stars.

I picked up one of the slippers, cradling it in my hand.

The opals didn't look as dark as before. It must have been my imagination. I turned the slipper over. A starburst was etched in the sole. I cocked my head to one side, considering.

The slippers were older than the closet, than the dresses. Well, older than *most* of the dresses. It was possible that One Hundred had been sewn before the slippers had been cobbled. But maybe not. Maybe One Hundred had been made for *them* instead of the other way around.

I scooped the other slipper up and headed into the closet. Lyric chirruped at me. The dresses jangled their hangers. The starlight opals glowed.

"Good evening, ladies," I said.

One Hundred's crystals sparkled as it flared its train.

"Have you missed them?" I asked, holding up the slippers. "They're really pretty."

I set them down on the rose-patterned carpet, where the rising moon kissed them with shimmering light. My toes twitched. I sat down and unlaced my boots.

"I wish you could talk," I told the dresses. "Then you could tell me things."

A dress near the door—one that Gillian always made a fuss over—waved a ribbon at me.

"She's not here," I said. "Tonight it's just me and you, ladies. Like it used to be."

The dresses grew quiet. I pulled off my boots and

tossed them aside. I popped one of the slippers onto my foot—all the better to admire the starlight opals. And then, because no one could see me and no one would know, I put on the other. I stood up and faced the mirror so that I could see me, Darling Damsel, Princess of the Night Sky, wearing Queen Candace's slippers.

They weren't magic, but they *were* beautiful. And I felt very pretty wearing them.

"What would it be like to dance at a ball?" I wondered aloud.

A vermilion ball gown fluttered a ruffle at me.

"Thank you, my dear," I said. "But these slippers require an extra-special dress."

I reached for One Hundred. It shrank from my touch, pulling against my hand and clinging to its hanger. Startled, I let go. I'd never had a dress refuse before. In fact, I didn't know they could.

"You don't want me to try you on?" I asked, stunned. "You don't want to go out? See Her Highness? Visit the Prince? Have some fun?"

One Hundred receded even further.

"All right," I said, holding up my hands. "I just wanted to see them on. I wasn't going to let anything happen to them."

I stepped out of the slippers.

"Anyway," I continued, "as I was saying, if you could

talk, you could help me." I picked up a slipper to show the dresses the sole. "I have a key with one of these on it. It belonged to Magnificent Wray. Do you know what it opens?"

Lyric rustled his feathers. The dresses folded their sleeves and listed sideways on their hangers as if they were thinking.

One Hundred bobbed on its hanger. It wanted to help me. But evidently *not* by being worn. Maybe it had something else in mind.

Maybe it missed the slippers. Maybe my wearing them had made it jealous. A burning desire to see the slippers with the dress overtook me.

I lifted the lace-covered hem of One Hundred, slid the slippers under it, and let the lace drift down over the shoes, leaving the starlight opals exposed. I rocked back on my heels. The shoes were the perfect complement to the dress.

One Hundred lifted its sleeves as the entire dress *shivered* with magic. Flashes of magic ran across the bodice and sparkled in its lace. A ripple spread through down the skirt, glazing crystals and pearls with a milky glow in the dark closet.

"Wait," I told One Hundred. "What are you doing?"

Magic frothed in the garment's hem and spilled into the starlight slippers like a gallon of comets soaring down from the night sky. The gems blazed, and all the little specks and glimmers of color in their surfaces twinkled like miniature galaxies. Each one pulsed with magic.

I snatched the slippers up, but it was too late. The magic in them throbbed in my hand, excited, eager, and *aching* to be released. I dropped the slippers to the carpet before the magic could do any more.

Lyric squawked in his cage.

"What have you done?" I asked One Hundred. "They're full of magic now!"

One Hundred swayed on its hanger, turning a lace-covered shoulder to me.

I poked the shoes with a finger. Magic sizzled under my touch.

"I can hardly hold them," I grumbled. "How am I going to carry them? I have to put them back."

And then it hit me: an image of Princess Mariposa sliding her feet into the magic-drenched starlight slippers.

"The Princess is wearing those shoes to her wedding!" I cried. "What will happen when she does?"

One Hundred drew its train around itself like a cat curling up in its tail. If it could have talked, it would have purred. It was that pleased with itself. And the starlight opals crackled with magic as they echoed the dress's delight.

16

When the dragons came, Father rose to the challenge. No longer did he seek magic for his own devices, but in the service of his sovereign. As the beasts ran rampant over the mountain—burning, stealing, killing—all the people of Eliora cowered in terror. Yet Father was fearless. He would halt these monstrous deeds. He would forge a great weapon.

Then the dragons took Mother. Father changed. His desire for magic's power changed, and all our destinies changed with him.

I wrestled the starlight slippers into my apron and put them back onto the satin pillow in the wardrobe hall. The opals sparkled in the darkening evening. Worry gnawed a hole in the pit of my stomach. What was I going to tell Marci? *Oops, I might have unintentionally soaked these shoes in magic. But not to worry, Marci. I'm sure that nothing very terrible will happen when Princess Mariposa puts them on.*

Who was I kidding? I was doomed.

I sought comfort in the kitchens.

Jane sat knitting socks, eyes blurry, her mouth pursed in concentration. At the table next to her, the Head Cook scribbled in a recipe book while the Pastry Chef waved his rolling pin about, lecturing.

"You have to roll the marzipan thin, very thin, but not too thin," the Pastry Chef said, demonstrating by flattening a ball of the stuff.

A row of delicate swans lined the table. Each one had sparkling black sugar eyes, arched necks, and dazzling white feathers. And they were all distinct and individual, no two alike.

"You have a wonderful attention to detail," Jane remarked, counting the stitches on her knitting needle.

Jane couldn't see past the end of her nose. But she had mastered the art of conversing about things without actually knowing anything about them.

"Can you eat them?" I sat down and pointed to the swans.

"Eat them!" the Pastry Chef exclaimed. "These are works of art! Not food."

"But aren't you making them for the wedding cake?" I said.

"Of course," the Pastry Chef said, taking a shaped tin cutter and pressing it into the marzipan. "But these beauties will swim along the rose-strewn layers of the royal cake—a glorious fantasy of sugar and marzipan!"

"So, after the Prince and Princess cut their cake, they're just going to admire it?" I said, reaching out to pick up one of the swans.

"No touching!" The Pastry Chef slapped my hand away. "They *will* admire it. *Everyone* will. The applause will be stupendous."

The Head Cook rolled her eyes.

"And, Charlotte," he added, glowering at the Head Cook, "I will bake separate—supremely delicious—cakes for eating."

"I'm sure you will," she said, blotting her writing. "And the feast I'll create for *this* wedding must be unlike any cooked for any *other* wedding!"

I'd been impressed with the feast for the failed wedding; I couldn't wait to dig into this one.

"It does present a challenge," Jane agreed. "But no one cooks like you do."

The Pastry Chef cleared his throat ominously.

"Or creates dessert like you," she added.

The knowledge that everyone was outdoing themselves so that Princess Mariposa's wedding would be her dream come true stabbed me in the heart. While they slaved away, I was busy ruining it all. I squirmed on the bench.

"If you're going to fidget, you should go outdoors," the Pastry Chef snapped when I jostled his elbow.

Gillian came swinging in from her evening's adventure with a fat book tucked under her arm. She slapped it on the table, setting the swans aflutter.

"Children should be kept in cages," the Pastry Chef muttered, rescuing a swan from falling.

"What have you got there?" the Head Cook asked Gillian.

"*The Perils of the Indigo Isles,*" Gillian said. "It's a memblar."

"Memoir," the Pastry Chef corrected.

"Yeah," Gillian said. "It's written by a ship's cook, all about pirates and stormy seas and—"

"Sounds interesting," Jane said.

I folded my arms across my chest. It sounded like Gillian had spent the evening doing everything but trying the key.

"Just the sort of thing that fills young minds with nonsense," the Pastry Chef said, clipping the marzipan to resemble feathers.

"Where did you get that?" the Head Cook asked.

"The royal library," Gillian said. "I had permission," she added quickly as the Head Cook's eyebrows shot up her forehead.

"I hear there are a great many books there," the Head Cook said.

Gillian scooted in next to me and stood the book on its spine.

"Thousands," the Pastry Chef said. "Next time, look for something improving."

"History," the Head Cook suggested.

"Or something practical," Jane said. "Like cooking or gardening."

"Gardening!" the Pastry Chef exclaimed. "Digging about in dirt! Where is the artistry in that?"

"I like flowers," Jane said, clicking her knitting needles.

"You'll like this page." Gillian nudged me.

I glanced at the book she'd opened a crack. The key was tucked in the center, along with a scrawled note: *Top row, nothing.* Relief washed through me. She hadn't found it without me. And only five more rows to go.

"Sounds like a good book," I said, eyeing how thick it was. "You'll have to read fast so you can get another."

"As fast as I can," Gillian said, beaming.

I smiled back, but all I could think about was *my* turn with the key.

Iago and his family were nibbling on a feast of bread crusts and cheese when I interrupted them.

"Good evening," I said. "You have to stay away from the wardrobe hall and the closets."

Iago twitched his whiskers. Bonbon batted her lashes. And others quivered in fear. Sleeping Girls rustled and snored around us.

"Marci put mousetraps everywhere," I said. "And I mean *everywhere*. They're loaded with cheese."

The mouse I'd named Éclair chattered excitedly to Anise and Flan.

"You can't eat it, though," I said. "If you touch it—" I gulped, not knowing how to tell my little mouse friends what happened when the trap snapped.

But I didn't have to. Iago pointed his bread crust at his children and let loose. His tiny brow furrowed. His voice rose in pitch. And the four mouselings shrank under his scolding.

When he'd finished, I bid them good night and went back to bed.

The next morning, despite my warning, the enamel button from the watercolor dress again sat on Marci's desk. Along with five other buttons.

Princess Mariposa hummed as Marci helped her into her new pink-and-white-striped dress. Her cheeks glowed. Her eyes shone.

"You are a picture in pink," Lady Kaye observed.

"Everything is falling into place," Princess Mariposa said. "The Royal Dress Designer sent word that the dress is nearly ready for fitting. The Head Cook reports that exciting new culinary ideas are simmering in her brain." She paused to laugh at her own pun. "The musicians are practicing a new waltz. The roses are blooming in the greenhouses. Teresa is here! And best of all, I have the most perfect slippers ever made."

"Indeed," Lady Kaye replied.

"This will be the—the most *enchanted* wedding of all time," the Princess exclaimed.

"I'm sure it will," Marci agreed, buttoning a cuff.

I stood, sodden with misery, a lace shawl draped over my arm and a fake smile slapped on my face. I dipped my spare hand in my pocket. The key was my only comfort. Maybe I could discover my inheritance *before* the wedding and somehow save the day.

If that was going to happen, that inheritance had to be something more powerful than a deed to a moldy old mansion or a string of rubies.

"Why are you glum?" Lady Kaye asked, poking me with her cane. "Jealous?"

"No, ma'am," I said. "I'm thrilled that the Princess is happy."

"You don't look it," Lady Kaye said.

"Darling's a bit overworked these days," Marci said, coming to my rescue.

"Ooh, Darling, are you?" Princess Mariposa asked, her brow wrinkled in concern.

"No, Your Highness, I'm fine," I said.

"She's been doing her chores *and* sewing for Rose," Marci said, straightening the Princess's collar. "Working after hours to get everything ready for the Girls."

"She has!" The Princess's cheeks grew a deeper shade of pink.

"I volunteered," I said quickly, not wanting to get Rose into trouble.

"Did you?" The Princess's sea-blue eyes turned sapphire with tears. "Darling, I don't deserve an Under-assistant like you."

"Give the child the day off, for heaven's sake," Lady Kaye said. "Before you get water spots all over that bodice."

Princess Mariposa took the handkerchief that Marci offered, and dried her eyes.

"Do," she said. "Take the day off and get some rest."

"Thank you, Your Highness," I said. More miserable than ever.

What would Princess Mariposa say when her wedding day dawned and the starlight slippers ruined it?

I chewed on my thumb as I stared out the closet window at the bright spring morning. A day off was a pickle. Where to go? What to do? I was liable to be shooed out of the kitchens—and everywhere else. Both the Upper- and Under-servants were busy. And not one of them would be glad to watch me sit idly by while they worked.

There was nothing to do in the Girls' dormitory.

I wasn't allowed in the library.

Jane wasn't a Picker anymore, so I doubted I was welcome in the greenhouses or the gardens.

And while Roger had forgotten he was mad at me, I hadn't quite recovered from the sting of being unfavorably compared to one of Lady Marguerite's horses.

Lyric whistled at me. Startled, I turned around to find the entire closet trembling with anticipation.

"What do you think I should do today?" I asked the dresses, stealing a glance at One Hundred.

It hung from its hanger like an icicle of indifference. Clearly, having ruined the starlight slippers with magic, it had no further interest in my adventures. I cast my attention on the other dresses. Ninety, a sunshine-yellow dress with a garden of ribbon flowers scattered across the skirt, fluttered in an imaginary breeze.

"You want to go out?" I said.

The weight of the starburst key in my apron pocket tugged at me. I could sprint over to the Duchess's rooms and try the key out on Lady Amber's armoire, but I was pretty sure that Aster was doing all those things Lady's Maids did when their mistresses were busy. And Aster was not someone I cared to tangle with. Not even in a dress.

Ninety fluttered faster.

"But where would we go?" I said. "I can't use the key until this evening, and I've got the whole"—I swept my hand dramatically to emphasize my point—"*day* to fill."

Ninety jerked so agitatedly that it knocked itself off its hanger. As I bent down to scoop it up, a flash of gold outside the window caught my eye. Holding Ninety, I went over and peered out. The Footmen were putting up the canopy Princess Mariposa liked to use for entertaining outside. I'd attended a luncheon out there with her last spring—well, I had as Lady Teresa.

"I have a marvelous, fantastic, stupendous idea," I told Ninety, slipping it on. "Let's go spend the day with the Princess."

Ninety swooped me up in its folds with a giddy abandon. Obviously, the dress liked this plan. And it occurred to me that while Marci couldn't convince the Princess not to wear the slippers, and I couldn't, somebody more important might be able to.

"I need to talk to Her Highness," I told the dress before I looked in the mirror. "I need to be someone she'll listen to."

Ninety waved a ribbon rose.

I glanced over my shoulder at the mirror.

Madame Zerlina blinked back at me.

17

I hovered behind a bronze peacock at the edge of the garden, where Princess Mariposa chatted with her guests. The *chink* of china sounded from the open-sided tent as the Footmen set the cloth-covered table. I straightened my shoulders. Ninety rippled gleefully in the breeze; the petals of its silk flowers trembled with excitement.

But my feet remained planted where they were. Madame Zerlina was tall, taller than the Princess and much taller than I was. When I put on Ninety, I hadn't picked a dress with shoes. So although I looked like Madame Zerlina in a taupe silk dress with chocolate beading on the skirt and a wide chocolate sash tied in a dramatic bow at the hip, I felt as if I were Bonbon's size. Whatever I did, I couldn't let anyone get too close to me.

"Madame Zerlina!" A buxom lady with a reddish complexion accosted me. "How good of you to come! Her Highness said you were so occupied with fittings today that she doubted you would."

Which immediately reminded me of the other problem with being Madame Zerlina Trinket: every lady in the court knew her, and she knew all of them.

But I did not.

"What a beautiful day!" I spoke with gusto, impersonating the Royal Dress Designer. "How lovely you look!"

"Oh, do you think so?" The lady quivered with emotion, swishing her mint-colored lace dress. "I got this last year in Boquebec. *Not* as good as anything you'd create, but still—" She broke off to giggle nervously. "Rather fetching, I thought."

"Indeed," I agreed, edging away.

A lady in a violent green-and-purple-striped dress grabbed me.

"Oh, Madame Zerlina, you must tell me what shoes I should wear to the royal wedding," she said with a pout. "Everyone says buff would be best. But you know I can't *abide* pale-colored shoes. They give me fits."

Without any idea what this lady was going to wear, I looked right in her eyes and announced, "This is a spring wedding! So you *must* wear robin's-egg-blue shoes!"

"Oooh," she breathed. "What genius! Oh, but don't tell anyone else! Please, Madame Zerlina, I beg you."

"My lips are sealed," I assured her, hoping that whatever color her dress was wouldn't clash too badly with robin's-egg blue.

I sidled through the press of guests toward Her Highness. Eager ladies waved at me and shook fans my way, vying for my attention. I pretended not to see them, but a determined woman caught my elbow and began quizzing me about her wedding attire.

"Low heels or high heels?"

"Low," I guessed, wiggling loose.

"What about a camellia in my hair?" another joined in as a group of fashion-hungry women encircled me.

"Flowers wilt so easily," I said, thinking that her elaborate arrangement of curls didn't need any adornment.

"Green goes with my eyes, don't you think?" a blue-eyed lady demanded.

"Well . . ." I glanced around, anxious to keep moving, to talk to the Princess before the real Madame Zerlina made an appearance.

"You aren't wearing stripes!" an elderly woman in a black-and-white-striped gown complained. "I thought they were *all* the rage."

I felt a stab of sympathy for Madame Zerlina. I looked about for a way to escape.

"Should I wear opals or diamonds?" an orange-haired lady asked.

Before I could respond, a tall lady squealed, "Opals are bad luck!"

That gave me an idea.

I took a step backward, thinking it might be easier to retreat and work my way around to the Princess than to wiggle through the crowd.

"I'm told a train would make my waist slimmer," yet another told me as the group pressed closer.

"Is there still time to change my gown? I thought perhaps I should add a few ruffles," a stout woman asked.

One woman—in a skirt so full that she knocked another lady out of the way—demanded, "Will four petticoats be sufficient? Or should I wear five?"

I gaped at her, at a loss for words.

"Ladies," Prince Sterling said, stepping between them to rescue me. "Madame Zerlina is available for consultation at her salon. *Here,* she is the Princess's guest."

"Well!" the wide-skirted woman snorted. "I see how it is. Too important."

"Keeping her best ideas for the Princess," another exclaimed knowingly.

"Stingy," a third muttered darkly.

"*Ladies!*" I snapped, losing my patience.

Prince Sterling stifled a grin.

Several ladies blinked at me in surprise. One or two blushed.

"Of course," the lady worrying over ruffles said. "Please accept my apologies. I shall direct my secretary to make an appointment."

"Let's not keep the Princess waiting," Prince Sterling said, offering me his arm.

I slipped my hand around his coat sleeve, holding on as lightly as possible. As he threaded me through the crowd, I chattered about the weather, hoping to distract him from my Darling-sized hand. And being kind—and handsome—and having the warmest brown eyes and the nicest smile, Prince Sterling offered his opinions about how blue the sky was and how fine the day. I slipped free from his arm as soon as we reached the Princess.

Her Highness glowed in her pink-and-white gown, from her cheeks to the deep rose of her lips to the sparkle in her sapphire eyes. I had no idea how I was going to talk her out of wearing those shoes, but I had to try.

"Madame Zerlina!" she said. "I'm so pleased you've come. You must meet my dear cousin Teresa."

Lady Teresa blushed a deep crimson, fluttering her dark eyelashes and setting her dark curls dancing. She looked as though she wished she were somewhere else.

She wore a white silk dress embroidered with violets and trimmed with green ribbons, which she toyed with nervously.

"A pleasure," I said, curtsying.

"I was just telling Teresa all about the wonderful wedding gown you are making," Princess Mariposa continued, "to match the starlight slippers."

"Indeed," I said.

"She talks of little else," Prince Sterling said.

Princess Mariposa laughed.

"The starlight slippers are so very lovely," I said. "But I am concerned."

"About what?" Princess Mariposa asked.

"Omens," I said ominously, lowering my voice.

"Omens?" Princess Mariposa echoed, startled. "What sort of omens?"

"Oh, never mind me," I said. "It's just . . ."

"Yes?" the Princess asked. "Just what?"

"My dear," I said, drawing her aside, "suspicion hounds me. My heart is troubled over these"—I dropped my voice to a whisper—"*opals*. I don't like to say so, but they're terribly unlucky. Perhaps you should not wear them to your wedding."

"But—" she began.

A tale of doom and disaster—embroidered out of

Master Varick's dire hints about the ghosts of Umber—bloomed on my tongue.

But before I could tell it, Princess Mariposa shook her head. "Opals are mere stones, nothing more," she said with an understanding smile. "You mustn't trouble yourself, Madame. I shall be perfectly safe! My grandmother, Queen Candace, wore them. Nothing bad ever happened to her."

"If you're sure . . . ," I said, casting around for another reason she shouldn't wear the slippers. "But then you can't wear the shoes *I'd* imagined for you."

"Oh?" the Princess replied.

"Lace slippers trimmed with pearls and butterflies. *So* enchanting! *So . . .* you!" I stopped. Even if I could interest Princess Mariposa in another pair of slippers, how would I get Madame Zerlina to whip up *my* idea?

"You are such a dear, Madame." The Princess patted my arm. "You probably slaved for days designing dozens of marvelous shoes just for me, but my heart is set on the starlight slippers!"

A gong rang, and the Princess, turning back to the crowd, invited everyone to join her for lunch. My shoulders sagged; I'd had my chance—and I'd mucked it up. I followed a few steps behind, slowing as I walked, thinking *now* would be a good time to slip away. But a short gentleman in a lavender cutaway coat snagged my arm and buoyed me into the tent. Once there, I had no choice but to find the place card with Madame Zerlina Trinket's name on it and sit down. To my chagrin, the lavender-coated gentleman sat next to me.

The menu by my place setting read:

Mariposa's Spring Feast
Cucumber Soup
Spinach Cheese Soufflé
Cod Fillet in Escarole
Lobster Salad with Avocado Cream
Minted New Peas
Roasted Asparagus
Lime Tart

Last summer I'd eaten the Ruby Luncheon. Evidently, Her Highness liked her meals color-coordinated. And loaded with vegetables.

"It all sounds divine," the lady next to me said, fluttering her menu in my direction. "Don't you think so?"

"It sounds delicious," I said, thinking I would eat only a course or two and then excuse myself.

A Footman set a bowl of pale green soup before me.

"Such a fashionable color for soup," the lady said.

I picked up my spoon.

Ninety jiggled around my knees. I'd asked to be

someone the Princess would listen to. And obviously, she respected Madame Zerlina's opinion. But the Princess had a mind of her own. I couldn't save her from the slippers by scaring her—or tempting her with something fancier. Still, there had to be *some* way to keep her out of those shoes!

But what?

"You must really like it," the lady said, interrupting my thoughts.

I glanced down at my empty bowl. I hadn't tasted a bite.

18

 I ended up remaining for the entire affair. Between the eager lady on my right and the lavender-coated gentleman on my left, I'd been shoveled full of food and forced to converse. All the while I kept glancing over my shoulder, praying that Madame Zerlina wouldn't appear and expose me as a phony.

It was only after the last plate had been cleared away that I was able to steal off. I was stuffed. So after I returned Ninety to the closet, I waddled to the Girls' dormitory to rest before my evening's adventure.

A gloss of sunshine coated the room. The beds were made. The vases freshened with new daisies from the greenhouses. The floors swept. The rugs beaten. And I had it all to myself. I went to stretch out on my eiderdown, when I found a row of buttons on my pillow. A big blue button, four small diamond buttons, and the enameled button from the watercolor floral.

Bonbon!

I scooped the buttons up and stashed them in my pocket. I'd have to get them put back before Marci noticed they were missing. One diamond button was worth more than her year's salary. She'd baste me into a shroud if she thought I'd taken them!

I plopped down on my rug and yanked my crate out from under my bed. I'd give that mouse miss a piece of my mind!

The crate was empty.

Where *did* those mice disappear to?

I pushed the crate back under the bed and lay on top of my covers. The next thing I knew, the white dormitory walls were drowning in a rose-gold sunset. I sat up and stretched. I'd missed supper, but I wasn't hungry. I combed my hair, retied my ribbon, and made sure the key was in my pocket.

Then, whistling, I set off on my next jaunt. On my way, I passed Marci's desk, put the buttons back where they belonged, and eyed the glimmering opals on the starlight slippers.

"I'm watching you," I told them, just in case they were listening. The starlight opals sparkled with a bluer gleam.

If they hadn't heard me, the magic had. Satisfied, I opened the closet door.

The dresses stirred in the evening breeze from the open window. Lyric sang on his perch.

"I need to go to Lady Kaye's room," I told them. "Who wants to come?"

Forty flared its sapphire taffeta skirt my way. I helped it off the hanger and stepped into its crisp folds. The taffeta made a crinkly sound as it rustled around me. In the mirror, Aster, Lady Kaye's maid, glowered at me. I grinned back.

"This is great," I told Forty.

I started for the door and then stopped.

"Pardon me," I said.

I hiked up Forty's skirt, dug the key out of my apron pocket, and tucked it in the sash around the dress's waist.

"All set," I said. "See you later, Lyric."

The canary trilled at me, but I was already turning the doorknob. Dulcie stood on the other side of the door, grinning from ear to ear.

"Good evening, Darling," she said.

"*Dulcie,*" I said before I remembered that I wasn't supposed to be Darling. "Er, little girl, shouldn't you be somewhere else?"

Dulcie laughed so hard she slapped her thigh.

"You should see your face!" she cried, laughing harder. "You look like you swallowed a lice-infested prune!"

"Now see here, young lady," I said, wagging a finger in her face. "Don't make me speak to Mrs. Pepperwhistle about you."

"You won't," she said, wiping away tears. "You like me too much, Darling."

Exasperated and desperate to get rid of her, I tried again.

"I don't know who this Darling person is, but—"

"I've been following you," she said. "I know all about those dresses."

At that, I grabbed her by her skinny little arm and hauled her into the closet.

"Dulcie, this isn't funny," I said. "You could get us both in serious trouble."

"You never get caught," she said. "And if you take me with you—" She pantomimed locking her lips and tossing away the key.

"So that's how it is," I said.

She nodded, lips clamped shut.

"Do you know that they send blackmailers to prison?" I asked.

"Sure, but what do they do to Girls who take dresses that don't belong to them?" she shot back, unsealing her mouth.

What could I do?

I warned her not to say *anything to anyone* we saw, threatened her with dire consequences if she got me in trouble, and took her with me.

At this time of evening, the castle sat bathed in sunset colors, breathless and waiting for dinner to end and the halls to spill over with people. I hustled Dulcie along to the west wing as fast as her feet could fly. Aster was probably in the Upper-servants' lounge, since the Baroness would be dining with the Princess. But I didn't know if the private servants lingered over tea and conversation, as the Under-servants did in the kitchens. Gillian was almost finished with her book, and she'd want the key again as soon as she was.

I didn't intend to wait one more day to get my hands on the armoire.

The peach-colored corridor by the Baroness's room glowed in dark salmon shadows. Dulcie ran her finger along the frieze of mice as she skipped beside me. When she hit the missing patches, she yelped.

"There's holes here," she said.

"The plasterers probably haven't gotten around to fixing them yet," I told her with an oh-so-casual shrug. "Wedding stuff."

She looked dissatisfied with that explanation, but I pulled her along to the Baroness's door.

Which is when I reached my first big complication.

How could I, Darling Wray Fortune, Heiress, find my long-lost and all-important inheritance with a nine-year-old busybody poking her nose into *my* armoire?

I had to improvise on the spot.

"Dulcie," I said in the sort of whisper you save for really big secrets, "I need your help."

"What do you need?" she asked, all wide-eyed and sweet.

Pushing down the weaselly-rat feeling that nibbled at my conscience, I said, "I need you to stay here in the hall." She blinked. I plunged on, "Right here by this door. And be my lookout. Can you do that? It might be dangerous. If anyone comes, you need to knock twice on the door—and then have a hysterical fainting fit. Okay?"

"Should I fall down on the floor after I'm done screaming?" she asked.

"Sure, but only if someone comes," I said.

She planted herself by the door, in the same rigid posture adopted by the Princess's own Guards.

"I'll be quick," I said, patting her on the head, and slipped inside the Baroness's rooms.

The armoire waited in the purple-edged shadows of the darkening pink bedroom. The painted swan on the top glistened a pale shade of lavender. I knelt down and slipped the key in the top lock. Nothing. *This* had to be it!

172

I knew it. It had belonged to Lady Amber; where better to have hidden an inheritance?

I took a deep breath and tried the next drawer. One by one, I jiggled the key in each lock until I reached the last one.

Forty trembled around me. I braced myself. This was it! This was *the* keyhole!

I slipped the key into the lock and turned.

The key stuck fast. Gritting my teeth, I jangled the key as hard as I could. The key refused to budge, but the drawer flew open. Shocked, I yanked the key free and stared in the drawer.

Yellowing handkerchiefs sat atop a pile of objects in the drawer. I drew them out. Faded hair ribbons. An ebony brush with a broken handle. A wad of musty letters tied together with gold cord. And a small, flat leather case.

A jewel case?

I picked it up and it flopped open. Inside was a miniature portrait of an old man with thick white hair, a white beard, and startlingly aquamarine eyes. He was handsome, with chiseled features and an air of nobility about him. He radiated authority; if he'd been an Upperservant, he'd have ruled the castle. But at the same time, I couldn't imagine *this* person serving anyone. He looked more kingly than King Richard did in *his* portrait hanging in the throne room.

MAGNIFICENT WRAY, a tiny brass plate read.

"Where'd you hide it?" I asked him. But of course the portrait didn't answer.

Boiling with frustration, I set it down and went back over the drawers, tweaking each handle. *None* of them were locked. And all of them were filled with assorted bits of junk and several pieces of jewelry: dangly pearl earrings, a pearl-and-ruby brooch, and an onyx ring, among others. But nothing that screamed *inheritance*.

I stuck it all back in the armoire—except for the portrait. The more I stared into that face, the more it commanded my attention. This was my ancestor, the great architect, the man who had designed the castle. The one who'd poured into it all the magic he'd created from the siphoned virtues of the Wrays. I caressed the leather backing and felt a faint stirring of magic.

I wanted to tuck the portrait into my pocket. I knew I shouldn't, but he was my ancestor, not Lady Kaye's. And she'd give it to me if she knew she had it.

But she didn't. And she hadn't said I could have it either.

Then I remembered what she'd said in the green room: *People used to write secrets on the backs of paintings.* Secrets like the location of family heirlooms.

I flipped the case over. Nothing. And then I noticed a piece of paper peeking out of the bottom edge. I pulled the paper out. Magnificent Wray had written on it. *Darling*, it said, just as if he were speaking to me.

A nearby wall rumbled. Startled, I stashed the paper in my apron pocket under Forty's skirt. A piece of the wall slid away. Roger fell out onto the carpet, dropping a burlap sack and scattering a coiled rope, chalk, folded papers, and several unlit candles.

"Uh!" he said, scrabbling for the wall's edge.

I tossed the case back into the drawer and shut it. Then I stood up and shook out Forty's skirts. "What are you doing here?" I asked.

"Um, um . . . ," he babbled, his freckles white with fear.

"It's *me*—Darling," I told him. "Not Aster." I resisted the urge to giggle.

"Why'd you scare me like that?" he demanded. "Jumping at me from behind walls? In a disguise, no less?"

"What do you mean, jumping at you? I was here first. I have important key business to attend to," I said, planting my fist on my hip. "What are *you* doing here?"

"Looking for the library," he said, scooping up his stuff and shoving it into his sack.

"Without your maps?"

"I've retraced some of my steps," Roger continued. "I figured I'd work on the upstairs first. The cellars can wait."

"Huh," I said, not wanting to seem too pleased. "Well, this is Lady Kaye's bedroom, so you're way off."

He scowled.

"Thanks for trying," I said. "Really. But Gillian got Lady Kaye to write her a note saying she could read the books. She's been snooping around in there already."

"You might have told me that," he said.

"Sorry," I replied. "We've all been so busy."

He took off his cap and dusted it on his pants. "I found something *really* special. Come see," he said, and held out his hand.

It was such an un-Roger-like thing to do that I took it.

And he pulled me through the wall.

19

My brother, Noble, yawned, bored. He'd never had the interest in Father's pursuits that I had. I leaned so far forward, clutching my fur muff in my gloved hands despite the heat from the nearby furnace, that the goldsmith scolded me.

"Stand back, Lady DeVere," he said, beads of perspiration on his brow. "It's a deadly beauty."

"So is she," Noble said, laughing at his own joke.

I smoothed the fur on my muff, ignoring him.

"Will it hold them?" I asked Father.

"Mere metal?" he said, raising his bushy white eyebrows. "Bosh. No. It's not the gold; it's what I'll pour into the collar that counts."

"You can't pour anything into solid gold, sir," the goldsmith said, wrenching off his gloves as if ridding himself of the whole business.

"You can't," Father said, his aquamarine eyes gleaming. "I can."

I shivered, knowing what he meant. I could feel the magic dancing in his fingertips. Humming in the air. I was filled with dread.

Before he'd first squeezed magic out of nowhere, I'd been happier. More certain of myself. But since then it was as if someone had combed through my soul, and tiny fibers of it had been teased out. I felt thinner, somehow. Less.

Noble laughed at him. "The Great Magnificent One," he said. "Always good for a little excitement." He sounded jolly, but his eyes were cold.

Roger collected the lamp he'd stashed and led me up stair after dusty stair until my head swam.

"We have to be almost to the roof," I said, stopping to catch my breath.

"We are," Roger said. "We're so high up that the dragons can hear us breathe."

"Really?" My heart thudded against my chest.

Roger laughed at my discomfort. "Nah, they're asleep, remember?"

"Sure," I said, knowing that they weren't asleep. Not

really. Underneath their hardened stone exterior, they were awake and aware. And watching. "What were you going to show me?"

"This way," he said. "Cleaning out the stable attic, I found stuff, *great* stuff. Nothing that would interest *you*, but it gave me an idea."

I bit my lip, resisting the urge to point out that he wouldn't have been cleaning the stable attic if it weren't for me.

Around the next corner, under the massive wooden beams holding up the roof, was an alcove crisscrossed with chains. Heavy padlocks attached the chains to enormous bolts set in the stone walls. Behind the chains sat an iron-bound wooden door. A brass lock glimmered under the heavy brass doorknob.

"What is that?" I asked.

"Look real close," Roger told me, holding his lamp out.

I ducked my head under the chains and squinted.

A starburst circled the brass keyhole.

"That could be it," Roger said.

I dug the key out of my pocket and leaned as far forward as the chains would allow. But I was still inches short of the lock.

"Oof," I said, falling back. "I can't reach it!"

"Whoever chained this up saw to it that nobody would

reach that door." Roger's grin split his freckles. His brown eyes glowed. "Which makes me wonder what's behind it."

I studied the door as if the wood, iron, and brass contained some hint as to its purpose.

"Know what I think?" Roger asked.

"What?"

"It's a workshop." He bumped my shoulder. "That Magnificent guy's *secret* workshop."

"Who puts a secret workshop in the attic?" I said. "I'd put one in the cellar."

"The cellars are full of folks doin' some kind of work," he replied. "How would you keep that secret? Up here is perfect. Where else can you go in this castle that nobody else goes?"

I chewed my lower lip, thinking. Roger was right; this was the perfect hiding spot. If the starlight slippers had originally held magic, like Magnificent Wray's letter suggested, then he'd discovered it before the castle was built. So this wasn't the place where he'd done *that*. But once the dragons were collared and the castle completed, he'd have wanted some place to explore his discoveries where he wouldn't be disturbed.

This had to be it.

And if Lady Amber had told all she knew in her little book, he'd kept his room secret even from her.

"Magnificent Wray burned most of his papers the night before he died," I said. "But what if he only destroyed what was in his house? What if there's more in *there*?"

Roger tugged on the chains.

"These are solid; you'd have to pick those padlocks to get at that door."

"Can you?" I exclaimed. A burning desire to try that lock bubbled in my veins.

"Nope," Roger said. "But maybe I can talk to the blacksmiths."

"Oh," I breathed, "when?"

"Darling." Roger rolled his eyes. "Asking about breaking into padlocks is the sort of thing that gets guys into trouble. I have to wait for the right chance."

"Oh. Sure." My excitement dimmed. Who knew when that would be? "I don't want you getting into trouble."

I took another look at the door, imagining all the thrilling possibilities behind it. Secret workrooms. Hidden notebooks. Vials of . . . magic waiting to be poured out? A shiver traveled down my spine.

"Thanks for finding this," I said. "It's really great."

A blush stole over Roger's face. He scuffed his boot against the floor.

"I figured that if you got an inheritance coming, you should get it," he said with a shrug.

I felt bubbly inside. He *did* like me.

I punched him in the shoulder. "You're a good friend, Rog," I told him. "A bit freckly . . ."

He swatted me with his cap, but I could tell he didn't mean it.

On the way back down, he showed me the scribbled pages of his reconstructed map.

"This here," he told me, "is a back door into the Guard room. You never know when that will come in handy."

"Yeah," I agreed. "If Cherice ever gets out of the asylum, I might need it."

"I heard that crazy lady is locked up tighter than the King's crown."

He grinned, but the reference to the King's regalia made me cringe. They'd be getting it back out for the royal coronation—and the talisman that unlocked the dragons' collars was among those pieces. I rested my palm against the wall of the stairwell, running my hand over the smooth stones as we climbed down.

Magic gurgled just below the rock surface. I felt the humming and singing of the myriad creatures caught in its web. And the low threatening growl of the dragons.

I snatched my hand back.

Did One Hundred realize what a really bad idea it had when it loaded those slippers up with magic? And at a time when the talisman would be out in plain sight? Suddenly, I couldn't wait for the wedding to be over and done with. And for the King's cuffs to be back where they belonged—shut up in a chest deep in the royal treasury.

"And I'm done with the new map of this part of the castle," Roger continued, unaware of the magic. "I just have to double-check a couple of passages. But there's a whole bunch of places you can get to where you shouldn't be going."

"Do any of them lead to the royal treasury?" My throat tightened. All the air squeezed out of my chest.

"Are you nuts?" he said. "If one did, I'd get me some wood and board it up myself. A guy could get slammed into jail if he was caught going in there."

"I didn't mean you should go there," I croaked. "I just wondered."

"You sure look spooked," he said, folding his papers. "Are you still worried about ghosts?"

I shook my head. Once we'd caught Cherice and realized *she* was our phantom, I'd stopped thinking about ghosts. They were the absolute least of my worries.

"Well, here's a good place to sneak out," he said, reaching for a latch he'd numbered *W2-3-2* in chalk. "You can scoot back to the wardrobe hall and—"

"Oh no!" I cried, having realized my second big complication for the evening.

"What?" Roger said, whipping around as if a battalion of phantoms were on our heels.

"Dulcie!" I said. "I left her outside the Baroness's room!"

"She knows about the closet now?" He grabbed my arm.

Forty squeezed my waist, reminding me it was still there, that I still looked like Aster. That made me flutter uncomfortably inside. Roger had been talking to me the whole time like I was just me, not like I was me being someone else.

"It's a long story," I said. "She caught me coming out of the dress closet. She's been following me. You know how she is."

"Just go back and get her," Roger said. "And send her to bed. It's getting late."

"How late?" I asked, a sinking feeling in my gut.

"Late enough," he replied. "It might be better to go around to the outside of the Baroness's door, instead of going back through her rooms. In case you run into her—"

"Or Aster," I added, thinking that would be worse.

I, Darling Wray Fortune, Sightseeing Shirker, scurried back through the dark castle. Evening had turned to night while I'd been with Roger. Visions of Dulcie acting on my poorly thought-out instructions and thrashing about faking a fit in front of a returning Aster—or, even worse, Lady Kaye—boiled in my brain.

That would be the big complication to end *all* complications!

Maybe she got bored, I told myself as I whipped around a corner, *and left. Or tired,* I thought as I bounded down a stair, *and she went to bed. Or maybe she's sitting there all quiet and unnoticed, like a good little girl.*

That seemed the least likely of the three.

I plunged through an arch and heard a familiar sound.

"You're up to your old tricks," Francesca's voice echoed off the paneled walls. "Pretending to be me!"

I froze with one foot in the air. A door stood open a few steps in front of me. The sound of Francesca's voice came from there.

"*Nobody* wants to be you, Franny," said a voice I recognized as Faustine's. "I haven't done anything."

I eased my foot to the floor—the polished marble tiles that decorated the finer corridors. The kind of tile that magnified every noise. I held my breath and glanced around for an escape.

"Oh yes you have!" Francesca retorted. "You dressed up in *my* clothes and took the starlight slippers to Her Highness. *I* should have been the one to hand them to the Princess. You cheated me out of it."

Oops. It hadn't occurred to me that either sister would find out.

But it should have. Really. How likely was it that Mrs.

Pepperwhistle would resist asking her daughter for all the details of her conversation with the Princess? Not very.

"Did not," Faustine said.

"Did. So."

"No, I didn't," Faustine insisted. "Why would I?"

I chewed my thumb. This was it. This time Francesca wouldn't let go. She'd chase the tail of *this* rabbit until she caught it. And I'd be the one in the bunny suit when she did.

"You're jealous because I'm still a Princess's Girl and you're not!" Francesca yelled.

There was a long silence before Faustine replied.

"Bah! I never wanted to be a Princess's Girl to start with," she said. "And I'd still be one if Lindy hadn't gone off to chase Captain Bryce and left me to finish her work!"

I exhaled slowly. Faustine's remark had the ring of truth about it. Lindy *did* flounce off every opportunity she had to spend time with the Captain. But I'd never thought about it like that before: that Lindy could have been to blame. I'd always assumed Faustine was a lousy Under-presser.

Forty jiggled impatiently.

"Mother says you didn't apply yourself," Francesca replied. "Mother says you lack determination. Mother says—"

"You still think *you're* Mom's favorite?" Faustine asked.

"Wake up. One mistake and"—Faustine snapped her fingers—"it's over. And anyway, Faye's her favorite, in case you hadn't noticed."

"That's ridiculous!" Francesca shrieked. "Mother says—"

I decided that I didn't want to hear any more. I was Aster, not me. Neither girl would pay attention to *her*. I straightened up and marched myself right past that open door with quick, purposeful steps, as if the Baroness needed me right that minute. I didn't look inside the door as I passed. And I didn't stop until I'd walked all the way down the corridor and around the corner.

Then, not having another minute to lose, I barreled down the dark corridor to the Baroness's door.

And straight into Aster.

20

My heart stopped. A kaleidoscope of miserable futures flashed before me, Darling Wray Fortune, Disgraced Outcast. Beggar. Exile. I staggered back. Forty bunched around my knees as if it too were frightened.

"Well, I never!" Aster exclaimed, stepping back and dusting off her stiffly pleated skirt. "Watch where you're going."

I felt like I should say something, excuse myself. But my tongue stuck to the roof of my dried-out mouth. My heart hung in my chest like a cold, hard rock. Any second now, I would simply fall over dead, and *that* would be it.

"You ought to straighten that collar and comb that hair," she said, scrutinizing me. She clicked her tongue. "Disgraceful. Haven't you any pride?"

She didn't recognize me—her—er, *me* being her! My heart roared back to life, racing away at a million beats a minute.

"Well?" Aster said. "What do you have to say for yourself?"

She was looking straight at herself and she didn't even know it. Did she have the same problem with mirrors? How could she *not* notice that she was *talking to herself*?

"You should take a lesson from we better servants," Aster continued, patting her fraying dishwater-colored bun. "Pride of position, attention to appearance, zealousness for one's work—all these things determine *who* serves *whom*."

For a heartbeat, I wondered if the Baroness would agree with Aster's opinion of herself. But it didn't matter. I had to get to Dulcie before anything else happened.

"Um, well, um," I said, "pardon me."

I started to squeeze past her so I could grab Dulcie and scram, but Aster blocked my path.

"What on earth is *she* doing there?" Aster cried, pointing at Dulcie, who lay curled up against the Baroness's door, sound asleep.

For an instant, I was tempted to turn and run the other way. But I'd gotten Dulcie into this mess by leaving her in the hallway. I owed it to her to rescue her.

I sighed an exaggerated sigh. "Children!" I said. "You

tell them 'don't bother the Baroness.' But do they listen? No."

"What does she want with the Baroness?" Aster asked.

"Oh, you know," I said, as if Aster knew *everything*. "Day and night: 'Is the Baroness still ill?'" My voice rang down the corridor.

Dulcie stirred and pushed her disheveled red braids out of her eyes.

"But she's *so* tenderhearted she had to see for herself that Lady Kaye was well," I continued.

Dulcie saw us—two identical Asters. Her eyes widened to the size of goose eggs. She swallowed as if she was trying to determine which Aster was the real one and which was me.

Aster took a step toward Dulcie.

"Don't scold her," I said, grabbing Aster's arm. "Tragic tale, you know," I continued as if I were confiding something. "Such a dear little *orphan*," I said meaningfully, willing Dulcie to take the hint. "The Baroness is such a kind, generous woman that I am sure she would understand."

At that moment, Dulcie jumped to her feet. "I'm sorry I fell asleep at your door," Dulcie said. "I promise it won't happen again."

"I'm sure you're very sorry," I said, walking over to her and taking her hand. "Now, Aster can tell you *herself* that the Baroness is quite well." I smiled at Aster. "Can't you?"

Aster's face screwed up with disapproval—of me, the Inferior Private Servant, and of Dulcie, who took advantage of the situation to burst into tears.

"Oh, oh!" she cried. "I knew it! She's *dying*!"

"Really," Aster said. She glared at me as if *this* were my fault. "Stop this at once, little girl. The Baroness is in perfect health. She's downstairs, spending the evening with Her Majesty as we speak."

"Oh, you poor little thing!" I exclaimed. "Now, don't cry. We'll get you right off to bed before you catch a *fever*."

At that, Dulcie's eyes sparkled with mischief. Before I could stop her, she threw her hand over her forehead dramatically.

"I feel faint. Ah-ah-ah-*choo*!" She sneezed furiously.

Aster jumped backward. "Goodness!" she wailed, yanking out a handkerchief to cover her mouth. "The child is contagious!"

"Nonsense," I said firmly, giving Dulcie's hand a squeeze. "Just a little sniffle."

But Aster wasn't taking any chances; she grabbed the doorknob and vanished inside the Baroness's rooms.

I hustled Dulcie down the corridor as she broke into giggles.

"Save it!" I commanded. "We're not safe yet."

I walked on, determined to reach the wardrobe hall before we ran into anyone else.

"Darling," she said when we reached the closet door, "this was fun. What else can these dresses do?"

Forty bounced in reply.

"Nothing," I said, giving it a warning slap. "They're just dresses. They don't do anything interesting."

"I don't know," Dulcie said. "They seem sorta dangerous. In a fun way."

"That," I told Dulcie, "was *not* fun."

I wasted no time, bustling Forty back into the closet and Dulcie off to bed, despite her pleas to try on the dresses for herself. *Some other time,* I told her. And what I meant by that was *never.*

When we arrived at the dormitory, most of the Girls were already in bed. Including Gillian. I stashed the piece of paper in my pillowcase and went to bed. I'd have to wait until morning for a chance to tell her what I'd found out.

Early the next day, I tied my apron, simmering with the need to tell Gillian about Roger's newfound door. She dressed in her usual meticulous fashion, tying her bootstrings into perfect double-knotted bows.

I snatched up two apple fritters off the breakfast tray and tossed one to Gillian. "Catch!" I told her.

"What's the rush?" Gillian asked, balancing the fritter and the borrowed library book.

"Tons of work," I said. "The wedding's almost here."

"Tons," Dulcie echoed, brushing crumbs off her apron. She looked bright-eyed and ready for trouble.

"Have a great day, Dulcie," I said over my shoulder, and rushed Gillian out the door.

"Clean up those crumbs!" Francesca thundered behind us as the door swung shut.

"Listen up," I told Gillian, and I whispered the whole tale to her as she chewed thoughtfully.

"Why didn't they just lock that door and throw away the key?" she asked. "I would if I wanted to keep someone out." She waved her fritter at the walls. "It seems rather silly," she continued. "Chaining up a door! That won't keep anyone out. If you were the Princess, you could order the Guards to cut the chains."

Her words irritated me. Why couldn't she be excited with me instead of doing all this thinking?

"It's much more likely that they *chained* the door on the outside to keep something behind it from getting out and *into* the castle," Gillian finished.

The dragons flashed across my mind. That was stupid. They were already outside the castle. And if they were free, they wouldn't care about coming inside. They'd burn the place down! So *what* would you keep out?

Ghosts? Sorcerers? Monsters? I couldn't imagine any of those throwing up their hands and saying, *You got me! I can't break down this door or vanquish those chains!*

But something enchanted—

"When can I see the door?" Gillian said, interrupting my thoughts.

"Talk to Roger," I said. "He'd probably take you tonight."

"Tonight is my turn with the key," she said.

I eyed the thick book in the crook of her arm. "You read that already?"

"I finished it just so I could go back," Gillian replied. "All those locks are *waiting*," she said in a singsong tone. Her eyes gleamed. She was positive she'd find my inheritance in that desk.

But I wasn't so sure. Not since I'd seen the chained door. If the key didn't fit that lock, then it might open something that lay behind it. Which made sense, since Cherice had never found what she was looking for.

When we arrived at the wardrobe hall, Lindy was waiting for us. She eyed the last bite of pastry in Gillian's hand.

"You're going to wash those hands, my lady, a-fore you touch those linens," Lindy said. "Step lively. Pack o' work!" She snapped her fingers under Gillian's nose.

"There's always work," Gillian said with a naughty grin, and polished off her fritter. "Ta-ta, Darling." She waggled her fingers at me as she waltzed into the pressing room.

"Well, what are you doing?" Lindy asked me. "Waiting for an invitation?"

"Nope," I said, sitting on my stool. "Just waiting for Marci, Queen of Closets."

Lindy grinned. "Queen o' Closets," she said, leaving. "That's a good one."

As the pressing room door shut behind her, I picked up my sewing basket and pulled out my pincushion. Then I reached for the stocking I had been darning the day before.

Someone had moved the pillow with the starlight slippers over to my side of Marci's desk. I poked a finger into the satin and pushed the pillow back where it belonged. The starlight opals crackled with light as the pillow moved. I glared at them.

"You weren't full of magic before," I told them. "If you had it to start with, it must have leaked out of you over the years."

A blue spark flared in the center opal as if it agreed with me.

"So," I said, eyeing the center opal, "what do you need it for now? You should let go of it before anything bad happens."

A blaze of rose and gold lights swallowed the blue spark. The opals glowered from their lace perches. They didn't act as if they meant to let loose their magic anytime soon.

"Spoilsports," I muttered.

Two white ears popped up out of one of the slippers, followed by a pair of blue eyes and a twitching nose.

Bonbon.

"Get out of there," I said.

Bonbon climbed out and scampered across the desk to the button box.

"You go right back to the dormitory, where you belong," I said. "Didn't you listen when I told you how dangerous it was in here?"

Bonbon dug in the box, flinging buttons out onto the desk.

"Stop that!" I reached out to grab her.

But Bonbon eluded my grasp and had six buttons lined up next to my sewing basket before I knew it.

Not this again. Really. She had to stop playing with the buttons. I grabbed for them, but Bonbon hopped in my way, chattering excitedly.

"I don't understand a word you're saying," I said. "And Marci will be here any minute. You've got to get—"

Bonbon scooped up a button and threw it. It bounced off my arm and rolled off the desk.

"Nice," I said. "Go pick that up!"

Bonbon shook her head and went back to the other five buttons. She picked each one up and set it down deliberately. One big button and four little—

"That's your family," I said, suddenly understanding.

"Your dad," I said, pointing to the big button and then the smaller buttons, "and you, Éclair, Flan, and Anise!"

Bonbon clapped her paws together. Her tiny blue eyes swam with tears.

I looked at the button on the carpet beneath me.

"That's your mother," I whispered, remembering the five holes in the frieze. "That's why you four don't stay in the box; you're trying to get her back."

Bonbon sniffled, curling her tail and wiggling her ears.

"She's still in the wall, isn't she?" I said. "And you want me to rescue her?"

Relief broke out on Bonbon's furry face.

"Okay," I said. "I will. But," I said, holding up a hand to stop a celebrating Bonbon from dancing her way off the edge of the desk, "I'll have to do it later today."

Bonbon stopped in mid-waltz and assumed a dejected air.

"Right now I have to work," I told her. "But *later* I will. I promise."

Bonbon squeaked excitedly. Then she pirouetted across the desktop, vanishing over the edge with a farewell flick of her tail.

21

After lunch, I found several Guards lugging pasteboard boxes into the wardrobe hall. Princess Mariposa, Madame Zerlina Trinket, and Marci were gathered together at Marci's desk, examining a lace butterfly in the Princess's hand.

"See," Madame Zerlina instructed, "underneath, there are very thin wires sewn into the wings. That way each butterfly can be shaped and positioned on your dress so that we will give the illusion that they have just landed." She clapped her gloved hands together. "Perfection!"

"How clever," Marci said.

"Marvelous," Princess Mariposa told Madame Zerlina. And then she turned to the Guards, who'd set the boxes on the carpet. "That will be all for now."

The men bowed and left.

"Is the wedding dress done?" I asked, surveying the boxes.

"Done?" Madame Zerlina Trinket exclaimed. "My dear child, one does not rush great art!"

She flung her arms wide as if *she* were the work of art in question. She wore rose-colored leather gloves and an avocado-green dress with a narrow skirt tucked up in the back with jeweled clips. An ostrich feather curled over one eyebrow.

"No, one can't," Princess Mariposa replied for me. "But one can nudge it along a bit."

Madame Zerlina laughed in a full-throated manner. "Feast your eyes, ladies, on a *masterpiece* of fashion," she said.

She ripped open one of the boxes and brought out a white satin skirt with jewels scattered across the front and a ripple of lace around the hem. The waist of the skirt was ragged and unfinished.

"Oh my," Princess Mariposa breathed. "It's stunning."

"I am so glad you are pleased, Your Highness," Madame Zerlina replied.

"Is the rest in pieces?" I asked. There were a lot of boxes.

"Each portion of the gown is complete: skirt, bodice, sleeves, train, underskirt, petticoat," Madame Zerlina explained. "But they must all fit perfectly. So we will adjust and then assemble." She flashed a wide smile. "Then we add the crowning touch—our butterflies!"

"That's a lot of sewing," I said.

"So it is." Madame Zerlina laughed. "I will unpack and make ready. I am at your disposal, Your Highness, all day."

"I'll go change," Princess Mariposa said, handing the lace butterfly over to Madame Zerlina as if reluctant to relinquish it.

Then the Princess and Marci went into the dressing room.

"You," Madame Zerlina said to me after they left, "may assist." She pointed to a box. "Unpack that one first." Madame Zerlina settled on Marci's chair as if she meant to stay.

So, despite her announcement that *she* would unpack, I did. Not that it wasn't fun. Each piece of the gown was beautiful, even the petticoat, which was a delicate, shimmering mist of tulle and lace. One box held lace butterflies, which Madame Zerlina instructed me to leave alone. And lastly, I opened a box that held a simple mauve gown with a cream lace jabot and a mauve leather belt. It looked too short and too wide to fit the Princess, but I set it out just the same.

By the time I was finished, Marci returned to announce that the Princess was ready.

Madame Zerlina swept off her chair and fetched the petticoat.

"We shall start with this," she said, and whirled away.

I went back to darning stockings while all the excitement happened in the next room. Occasionally, Madame Zerlina would return for another piece. And when she carried it into the dressing room, the Princess would admire it profusely.

I craned my neck to catch a glimpse, but each time the door swung shut before I could.

When Madame Zerlina retrieved the last piece, the train, she gestured to the slippers.

"We'll want those in a few minutes," she said. "Perhaps when you have completed your current task, you can bring them in for me."

"Sure," I said uneasily. "I'd be glad to." It hadn't occurred to me that the Princess would wear them before the wedding.

"Thank you," Madame Zerlina said, and left.

I stared at the shimmering starlight opals. I knew that if I touched them, I'd feel the surge of magic within them. What would happen when the Princess put them on? Would she change in some fashion? Grow? Shrink? Turn into somebody else? What?

And could I risk finding out?

I grabbed the slippers, cringing at the magical furor

beneath my hands. Then I dashed into the closet, shut the door, and set the shoes on the carpet. Lyric whistled sharply as if he didn't approve of my bringing the slippers in there. The dresses arched in my direction as I plopped on the floor and hurriedly untied my boots. I yanked them off, took a deep breath, and shoved my feet into the slippers.

I held my breath and waited.

A nearby dress fluttered at me. I ignored it as the rising tide of magic beneath my feet rippled up over my toes and lapped at my ankles. Unlike the pleasant sensation in the dresses, this felt like pins and needles stinging me. I gritted my teeth as the magic enveloped me, gushing upward until it sizzled in the roots of my hair.

Then I looked in the mirror. I had no idea what I'd see, but I had to know.

The only reflection I saw in the mirror was my own.

Me, Darling Wray Fortune, Under-assistant to the Wardrobe Mistress, looking odd in a silver-gray dress, a white apron, and a pair of lace shoes sparkling with opals.

With a sigh of relief, I kicked off the slippers and dived back into my boots. *There.* I'd worn the slippers, and nothing had happened to me. So it was probably safe to take them to the Princess. The opals might sparkle more than normal, but with all the excitement over the wedding gown, no one would notice.

I tied my boots, gathered up the slippers, and, still simmering with magic, trotted out to fetch the satin pillow. I set the slippers on the pillow and walked over to the dressing room door.

"No nonsense now," I told them, and opened the door.

Princess Mariposa radiated joy in her pinned-together wedding gown. It suited her exactly, from the lace over the bodice to the sprinkling of jewels to the butterfly alit at her waist.

Madame Zerlina knelt at the train, delicately creasing a lace butterfly's wing before placing it on the train. Marci handed her a long, straight pin to fasten it in place.

I set the pillow down on a nearby chair.

"What do you think, Darling?" Princess Mariposa asked, eyes sparkling.

"It's almost as gorgeous as you are!" I breathed.

The Princess laughed.

"And you need a butterfly for your hair," I added. "I can picture your curls piled on your head with a butterfly on one side." I pulled my dandelion-fluff hair up to demonstrate.

Madame Zerlina stopped what she was doing and stared at me.

"That is exactly right, Your Highness," Madame Zerlina said. "I can make a special butterfly just for your hair—jeweled, of course!"

"Hadn't you planned to wear a tiara and a veil?" Marci asked.

"I had," Princess Mariposa admitted, "but Darling's butterfly sounds much more romantic."

"There," Madame Zerlina said. "The fitting is all done. Now we can check the length. If you'd like to put on the slippers—"

Marci grimaced as I picked up the pillow and held it out. I gave her a reassuring nod. She took the slippers and walked over to the dais, where the Princess waited before the mirror. My grip on the pillow tightened as she bent down and helped the Princess into the shoes.

"Oh!" the Princess cried.

I nearly dropped the pillow.

"They are perfect!" Princess Mariposa held the skirt up to reveal the opals. "See!"

Marci sagged in relief.

"Your Highness, they are!" Madame Zerlina exclaimed, as if wearing the slippers had been *her* idea. "When His Highness sees you at the wedding, he will be *overcome* with your beauty."

The Princess laughed. "I hope not. I'm expecting him to dance at the ball afterward!"

I forgot about mending as Madame Zerlina wrapped the pinned-together gown and its petticoat in white cloth. Then she packed away her packet of pins and assorted sewing supplies, chatting with Marci as she worked.

"I prefer to take things back to my salon for the finishing touches," she said.

"I thought Rose did the sewing," I said.

"Oh, she does sometimes, for some of my designs for Her Highness," Madame Zerlina said. "But certain gowns I must see to personally. I have the *best* seamstresses in all the land!"

"But if Rose is the Head Seamstress for Princess Mariposa, isn't she the best?" I asked.

"She is *one* of the best," Marci said.

"Oh, indeed she is!" Madame Zerlina cried. "And I know Rose. I will leave the final sewing to her; I can trust her to wear gloves."

"Gloves? To sew in? Why?" I asked.

"To protect the satin from the oils in the hand!" Madame Zerlina answered, holding out her hand in its rose-colored leather glove. "See, I do not wear this for the fashion! I wear it to protect the fabric!"

"Oh."

"Not that my hands aren't spotlessly clean," she added sternly. "Because they are."

"Darling doesn't mean anything by her questions," Marci said. "She's just curious."

"Hmm," Madame Zerlina replied.

"And I admit to being a little curious about this mauve dress," Marci said. "I don't remember the Princess ordering one."

"She did not," Madame Zerlina said. "I have made this just for you!"

"For m-me!" Marci stuttered. "Oh, Madame Zerlina, I could never afford—"

"Tut-tut," Madame Zerlina said. "Afford! The idea! This, my dear, is a gift, a small gesture of appreciation. It's just your color; in *this* dress, you will glow like the last kiss of the sunset!"

"Oh," Marci breathed, fingering the rich fabric.

I couldn't imagine Marci *ever* glowing like the last kiss of the sunset.

"Thank you!" Marci exclaimed. "Thank you so much!"

Madame Zerlina patted her shoulder. "You should slip away and try it on."

"Now?" Marci said.

"But of course now! What better time?"

"Well." Marci giggled, tugging on the mauve scarf she wore knotted under her collar. "It *is* my shade."

I stared at her in disbelief. She was acting like a Kitchen Maid with a new beau!

"Go!" Madame Zerlina shooed her.

Marci melted, gathering up the dress and scooting out the door.

"My work here," Madame Zerlina said, "is done!"

And with that, she swept out of the wardrobe hall.

22

Father watched as the goldsmith released the metal from the molds. Beyond them, a furnace raged behind iron
bars. The goldsmith's workshop gleamed
with gold and sizzled with heat. The smith wore a heavy leather
apron and gloves, and he'd handled the molten metal with iron
tongs when he'd poured it the day before.

"It must still be polished," the goldsmith warned, holding the
large studded collar up for Father's approval.

"You followed my specifications exactly?" Father asked.

"Weigh and measure it yourself," the goldsmith replied.

Father caressed the collar. "Oh, I shall," he murmured,
studying his reflection.

I crouched at the intersection of two corridors in the
west wing, listening for footsteps. I had the tail end of

the afternoon to myself. Marci had not only tried on her new dress but planted herself before the closet mirror to admire her reflection. And when I'd mentioned an errand I needed to run, she'd waved me off without stopping to question me.

Of course, she was in the closet at the time, which made it impossible to use a dress without explaining myself. I couldn't very well tell her, *Oh, Marci, nothing to worry about. I'm just off to let another mouse loose in the castle.*

But I'd promised Bonbon, so there I was.

It was still early enough that most of the courtiers were too occupied with their various activities and amusements to think of dressing for dinner. But it was an hour when servants were apt to be about, fetching and carrying whatever Lady Such-and-Such might soon require. I'd cooked up an excuse for myself—a mysterious note that *must* be delivered; I'd even brought along a folded leaf of Marci's stationery as a prop—but I preferred not to use it. I planned to behave just like Iago and Bonbon—scurrying in and out without being seen.

I peeked around the corner; the corridor was empty. Holding my note out conspicuously as if I were engaged in urgent business, I trotted down the hall. Plaster mice cavorted along the frieze at my side. The break where the mice were missing was about halfway between the Baroness's door and the end of the hall.

I found it quickly and glanced up and down the corridor to be sure no one was coming. Then I reached a finger out and stopped.

Which mouse was Bonbon's mother? The missing stretch began and ended with two mice very similar in size and posture. I dithered for a moment. I could release them all, but the frieze lined the corridor on either side. There were dozens—or even hundreds—of plaster mice capering along its length. I needed to find the right mouse. And quickly.

I put the tip of my finger on the mouse to the right. A tiny bit of magic bubbled under my touch. I felt a curious sensation as if *I* were the mouse in the frieze. An anxious pattering around as if I were frantically searching. *That's* how the mice in the frieze saw their captivity. In the past when I'd touched the magic and felt the creatures trapped in its web, they'd been happy. But now they were desperately searching for a mousehole to crawl through to freedom.

My heart ached for the mice. I'd felt birds caught in the castle's magic, and they were jollier about their circumstances. Not exactly happy to be stuck, but . . . *hopeful*, that was the word. They felt hopeful that one day they'd soar again. But not the mice; they'd become worried, fearful, and dejected. I wanted so badly to release them all that I almost did.

Until I sensed the dragons' low growl behind the mice's

panic. Like the rumble of distant thunder, they warned of the storm to come. Naturally eager for shelter, the tiny mice hearts raced with the need to flee to safety.

"You'd be no safer out here than you are in there," I told the mice.

But they didn't believe me. Not for a second.

"I need Bonbon's mother," I said, forming a picture in my thoughts of Iago and his four children. "Which one of you is she?"

Like a magnet, the mouse on the left drew my finger, and there I felt the keen longing of a mother's concern. The magic word that unlocked the enchantment burned on the end of my tongue. Carefully, I latched on to the thought of the mouse under my hand. And with a heavy heart, I pushed the fretful clamoring of the others aside.

"Sarvinder," I whispered.

The magic rippled under my hand, and a solid mouse popped out. Startled, I caught her, squeezing her so tightly she squeaked.

"Sorry," I said, loosening my hold. "I didn't want to drop you."

She sat up on my palm, grooming her long, curly whiskers with her paws. She had large blue eyes and unusually long lashes. These she batted at me in surprise.

"I'm a friend of your husband, Iago," I told her.

Her long nose quivered suspiciously.

"Your family misses you," I said. "I'll take you to them."

When I went to slip her into my pocket for the journey, she squeaked angrily and darted out of my hand. She fell, head over tail, and landed with a *plop* on the floor.

"Just a minute," I said. "I can help you."

She flipped over on all fours, shook herself, and raced down the corridor.

"Wait!" I cried.

I took off after her, bounding along the hall and around the corner.

But she was gone. There was no sight of her in either direction.

I walked slowly down the hallway, looking for cracks or holes that she might have crawled through. But it was no use. She was gone, and I had no way to find her.

I went down to the kitchens, where the first rush of servants wanting supper had arrived. So I joined them. I fetched my plate and looked about for a place to sit. Ann and Kate waved me over to their table. I didn't especially want to eat with them, but it seemed rude to refuse. I sat down and unfolded my napkin.

Ann leaned over and motioned for me to come closer.

"Don't repeat this," she said in a low voice. "Francesca gets to go to the ball."

"First she gets that ring, and now this!" Kate said.

"She's just a kid," I said, not believing it.

"She's thirteen," Ann said, as if *that* were old.

"Ann's fifteen; I'm fourteen. If any Girls get to go, it should be us," Kate said.

"It gets worse," Ann confided. "Not only is she going, but so is Faustine!"

"Some of the Upper-servants get to watch, but none of *them* get to attend," Kate said.

"What are they wearing?" I asked, thinking of the sky-blue dresses I'd labored over.

"Pepperwhistle is having dresses specially made in the city," Ann said.

"They're wearing dresses from the Royal Dress Designer?" My voice rose in a crescendo of outrage. This was beyond unfair!

A table of Dusters glanced my way.

"Shh," Kate hissed.

"Imogene Tansy, Dressmaker at the Carnelian Dress Shop, is sewing for them!" Ann's aggrieved tone suggested that I should *know* the name Imogene Tansy.

I hadn't heard of her, but that didn't make me any happier. Francesca and Faustine got to dress up, attend the ball, and watch Princess Mariposa and Prince Sterling dance under the starlight. And I would most likely spend the evening in the kitchens, listening to everyone's stories of how they saved the wedding. Because all the kitchen staff thought the entire affair depended on them; never mind the rest of us.

I was just about to put these thoughts into words when Gillian arrived.

Gillian slid her plate beside mine and winked at me. She'd come for dinner—and the key. I dug it out of my pocket. And it occurred to me: I wouldn't spend the ball stuck in the kitchens! It'd be the ideal opportunity for Gillian and me to try a few unwatched locks.

I grinned at Gillian and slipped her the key.

"What's up?" Gillian asked.

"Well," Ann said, before I could answer, "you can't tell anybody, but—" And then she launched into the whole tale.

I crept into the Girls' dormitory after dinner. I wished I'd taken Bonbon or even Iago with me to the west wing. But I was so used to talking to my mice—and being accepted by them—that the outcome of the afternoon was entirely unexpected. And now I had to confess my failure.

I knelt down by my bed and pulled my crate stamped ARTICHOKES out from underneath it. I lifted the lid—and dropped it onto the rug!

Six mice sat huddled together on my lavender socks. Iago, Bonbon, Flan, Éclair, Anise, *and* their mother. It was such a warm, happy sight that I put the lid back on without interrupting.

23

Francesca threw open the windows and let the sweet-smelling breeze flow in.

"Let's get going," she chirped, smiling. "Lots to do. Wedding day is almost here!"

Ann and Kate flashed her sour looks, but the other Girls—who didn't know that she was attending the ball without them—smiled back. I ignored them. Sulking wouldn't change it.

I ran my brush through my hair. The bristles glided through my thick, silky locks.

I stared at myself in the mirror.

My once-dandelion-fluff hair cupped my face in smooth waves. I blinked. But the image in the mirror stayed the same. I put my hand on my head, feeling a few strands.

It was my hair. It was attached to my head. But it had

changed overnight. It had become an inch longer, easily tamed, and a gleaming shade of platinum! I turned my head back and forth, admiring the spring sunlight dancing in my tresses.

"What happened to your hair?" Gillian asked. "It's beautiful."

"I don't know," I said. "It just changed overnight."

"Like magic," Dulcie said, wiping jam off her chin with the back of her hand.

Magic. I gripped the bedpost, dizzy. The starlight slippers had done this!

"Look at Darling's hair," Gloria piped up.

Every Girl turned to stare at me. The bedpost rocked under my hand, shaking the whole bed. My pillow slithered onto the floor.

"What did you do to yourself?" Francesca demanded.

"Nothing," I said, lifting my chin.

Francesca frowned. I could tell she didn't believe me.

Ann marched over to the other side of my bed and gave me a once-over.

"She's tight with those kitchen folks," Ann said. "I'll bet they cooked up some tonic for her."

I crossed my arms over my chest, brazening it out. Letting them think that the Head Cook was behind this change was far better than having them suspect the truth.

"What's that?" Dulcie asked, pointing to the bed.

A folded-up paper lay exposed on my sheets.

Magnificent Wray's note! I'd forgotten about it. I dived to retrieve it, but Ann grabbed it and waved it triumphantly over her head.

"I guess Sugar Baby isn't the only one who hides goodies in her pillowcase," Ann said.

Several Girls chuckled.

"Hey!" Gloria said.

"What is it?" Kate asked. "A love letter?"

A couple of Girls snickered.

"Let's see," Ann said, and brought it down to her eye level. "'Darling Amber'— Who's Amber?"

Amber. Of course, the note wasn't written to me. Deep down I'd known that, but I was still disappointed.

"Hand that here," Francesca said, holding out her hand.

While Ann gave her the note, Gillian caught my eye. She wasn't happy that I hadn't told her about it. Francesca glanced at the paper.

"It looks ancient," she said. "Where'd you get this?"

"It's a note from my great-great-grandfather to his daughter," I said, flashing Kate a glare. "*Not* a love letter."

"Bo-ring," Ann said.

"Who'd send love letters to *Darling*?" one of the Girls asked.

The room rocked with laughter. Dulcie burned bright

red; I could tell she was just about to volunteer a name, so I poked her.

"Can I have my letter back?" I asked Francesca. "I need to get to work."

Francesca handed me the paper without bothering to unfold it. I stuffed it in my apron pocket.

"It smells musty; don't leave that under the pillow," she told me. Then she clapped her hands. "Let's get moving, Girls!"

I left immediately. Gillian followed so closely she almost trod on my heels.

Once we were on our own, she nudged me. "So tell me about it," she said.

"I found it in the armoire," I said.

She rolled her eyes. "I figured out that much. What does it say?"

"I haven't had time to read it," I said, digging the note out of my pocket.

Underneath *Darling Amber*, the paper was creased and water-stained. It was folded twice. I opened it. *My dear*, the note began—

As my life comes to a close, I have only two regrets: leaving you and leaving the magic unattended. You must take a message to Her Highness—

—and stopped, only to be furiously scribbled over with charcoal. I could only pick out a few more phrases:

I regret pouring the magic into the slippers.
I hadn't realized what—
    —agic unleashed, powerful—
    —threaten the foundations—
    —starlight unlocks the opals—

                                  Father

At the bottom, the words *Father's last letter* appeared in another person's handwriting. Lady Amber's, I assumed.

"That's useless," Gillian said. She kept talking, but I didn't hear a word.

Starlight unlocks the opals stood out in bold strokes. I swallowed. That had to refer to the slippers, but what did it mean? What was about to be unlocked?

I felt ill. Marci had been right; those slippers were dangerous. I remembered Magnificent Wray's letter to Queen Candace—*shoes that embody something new, different, strange, and wonderful. Shoes that can truly be appreciated only when seen by starlight.*

They'd changed my hair—they'd made it quite lovely, so I wasn't upset. But what *else* could they do?

Threaten the foundations—

And what would they do to the Princess? She planned to dance in them at her wedding ball! At night! When the stars were out! A vision of the ballroom sprang up before me: the patterned marble floor, the velvet curtains, the gilded carvings, the chandeliers—and the doors leading to the terrace. I could see the Prince whirling the Princess across the floor and straight into a waiting patch of starlight!

This was terrible. I had to stop the Princess from wearing those slippers!

"Darling," Gillian groused, "you haven't heard a word I've said."

I blinked; we were standing right outside the wardrobe hall.

"I think those slippers are dangerous," I said.

"Don't be silly," Gillian said, pushing open the door. "The Princess has worn them several times already."

"Good morning, girls," Marci sang out as we walked in. She had a pair of beige shoes in one hand and a pair of lace gloves in the other.

"Look at you!" Gillian exclaimed.

Marci beamed. Not only was she wearing her new mauve dress, but she had a gold-and-pearl pin atop the jabot and a mauve ribbon woven through her coronet of braids! Her silver chatelaine swung from its clip on her new mauve belt.

"Do you like it?" she asked, sashaying her skirt back and forth.

"I love it," Gillian said. "Did you sew it yourself?"

"No," Marci said, practically giddy with glee. "The Royal Dress Designer had it made—especially for me!"

"Oooh," Gillian said. "Aren't you lucky?"

Marci glowed, looking prettier than I'd ever thought possible. But then she eyed me. "Have you done something to your hair?" she asked.

I shrugged without answering.

"Be careful with those cooked-up rinses," Marci warned. "They can make your hair fall out."

The dressing room door opened. Princess Mariposa floated out on tiptoe, stocking-footed, holding her bluish-lilac gown up in one hand. Her other hand patted the jeweled lace butterfly in her upswept curls. Lady Kaye walked behind her.

"Look," Princess Mariposa said. "The courier just brought it. Isn't it beautiful?"

"Gorgeous," Gillian said.

"It is," I agreed.

"That was quick," Marci said. "Madame must have stayed up late creating it."

"It's very charming," Lady Kaye said, grinding her cane into the carpet. "But, Marci, don't you think that a princess ought to marry in a tiara?"

"What do you think, Marci?" The Princess's eyes danced.

Marci fiddled with her jabot, stalling. I was glad not to be in her shoes. Which was worse: getting on the wrong side of the Baroness or crushing Her Highness's enthusiasm?

"Generally, I would agree with Her Ladyship. A princess ought to wear a tiara. *But*," Marci emphasized before Lady Kaye could interrupt, "the hairpiece *is* perfect, charming and lovely, and it completely suits you."

"It does," Gillian said.

Lady Kaye pursed her lips; she didn't take kindly to being contradicted. Princess Mariposa cast a questioning look my way.

"You'll look just like an enchanted princess in that butterfly and your dress," I said.

"And your slippers!" Gillian added.

Which was the worst possible thing she could have said. Because it caused all of us to glance at Marci's desk, where the starlight slippers balanced on their satin pillow.

"My dear Mariposa," Lady Kaye said. "Have these slippers with their priceless gems been left sitting here unguarded? Why, anyone at all could walk right in and steal those opals out from under your nose. Marci, I believed better of you than this!"

A blush stung Marci's cheeks.

Princess Mariposa gasped. "You don't think that would happen?"

"Cherice is locked up," I said. "Nobody else would dare—"

"Are you the authority of who dares do what?" Lady Kaye demanded.

I shook my head.

Marci put down the shoes and gloves she'd been holding. "I don't believe there is any danger that the slippers might be stolen," she said, picking up the pillow. "But I shall lock them in the closet at once!"

She marched stiffly to closet two and unlocked the door. Then she took the pillow with the starlight slippers into the closet and left them there. She made a show of relocking the door.

"They are safe now, Your Highness," she said, throwing a hurt look at the Baroness and patting her chatelaine. "These keys never leave my side. The only way anyone will get in that closet is over my dead body!"

24

After lunch, Rose appeared with several of the sky-blue silk dresses to be hemmed. This time she didn't ask; she told me that she had to have help or several Girls wouldn't be attending the wedding.

I sewed, more aware of the jangling of Marci's chatelaine than ever before. Her keys rattled and clanged together as if they were hammers and tongs. Marci was the most conscientious person I knew. As the Wardrobe Mistress, she held the keys to all the Princess's valuable clothes and personal jewelry. She was responsible for their safety, maintenance, and preservation. In her former position as the Head Scrubber, she'd spent long, dull years in the castle's under-cellar, toiling in the soggy heat. She treated her promotion as a special sign of the Princess's favor.

The silver keys on her chatelaine were proof positive

of Her Highness's trust. Marci never forgot to clip her chatelaine to her belt, never left her keys lying around, and *never* lent them to another person. She personally unlocked and locked each door and drawer that was opened by those keys. They lay under her pillow when she slept. Another servant might have said *"Over my dead body"* as a casual oath, one they meant to break as soon as the sound of their words died away. But not Marci; she meant them with all her heart.

And the key to closet two, where the starlight slippers were, swung on her chatelaine. It might just as well have hung from the corner of the crescent moon, as far as I was concerned.

Thinking of chatelaines made my hand gravitate to my apron pocket to caress the starburst key. I could have sworn that the tiny buzz of magic in its bow had seeped throughout the key, making the whole of it tingle. For all the good it was going to do me. My inheritance felt so close that I could almost taste it. But I'd probably never know what it was, because the wedding was only days away. Princess Mariposa would don those shoes and dance at her ball. The starlight would unlock the opals and . . .

Imagination failed me. I didn't know what would happen after that. I only knew that whatever it was would change everything. Because every time Magnificent Wray used magic, it was for something big: chaining dragons, filling the castle, or bringing the dresses to life. I didn't expect the opals to be any different; otherwise why would he have written to his daughter about them just hours before his death?

Threaten the foundations—buildings had foundations.

This wasn't just about the Princess. The castle itself was in danger!

I needed a distraction! As soon as I finished my work for the day, I tromped down to the kitchens, where a frenzy of dinner preparations was under way. I eyed the locked drawers in the spice cabinet as Under-choppers and Under-slicers zipped past with aprons full of fruits and vegetables. There was no way the Head Cook had left one of them unopened in all her years there.

Extra tables had been hauled into the central kitchen, where wedding preparations had begun. The Head Icer, the Head Cook, and the Pastry Chef were each working on a different project.

"Can I help?" I said to the Pastry Chef.

"What do you know about the art of pastry?" he exclaimed, looking up from crimping a piecrust.

"Not much," I said. "But I can measure stuff—"

"Stuff!" He slapped his chef's hat, sending a puff of white powder through the air.

"She can count," said the Soup Chef, who walked past lugging a tureen.

"She can read," Esperanza, the Head Icer, chimed in from her station, where she was piping icing onto a sheet of petit fours.

"She can taste," the Head Cook said, measuring a pungent spice into a pot. "And if you don't need help, I do."

At that, the Pastry Chef became indignant. "She doesn't want to cook," he said, brandishing his crimping fork. "She wants to create!"

The Head Cook dusted her hand on her apron. "Does she?"

"Of course she does," he said. "Apron! Now!" He snapped his fingers at me.

I fetched a clean chef's apron out of the kitchen closets and tied it over my own. Then I went back to the pastry counter and found a cloth pastry frame, a crock of flour, a rolling pin, and a ball of dough waiting for me.

"Begin!" the Pastry Chef ordered, sprinkling his own pastry cloth with flour. "We will create the galette!"

I figured rolling out dough couldn't be any harder than pressing. But I was wrong. My dough was too thick or too thin or too sticky. And the more mistakes I made, the more I had to flour the pastry cloth, and the stiffer my dough became.

The Pastry Chef surveyed my mess. "Go help someone else," he said.

I decided that distraction wasn't a remedy for what

227

ailed me. What I really needed was comforting. So I went and found Jane knitting by the hearth. A pile of finished stockings sat by her side. The rapid clicking of her needles kept pace with the harried mixing, chopping, slicing, and stirring of the kitchens.

"Good afternoon," I said, sitting beside her.

"Hello," Jane said, pausing her knitting long enough to pat my arm. "Excited for the wedding?"

"I guess," I said.

I had been. All the Girls were to wear their new sky-blue silk dresses and scatter rose petals for the Princess to walk on. But the threat of the starlight opals had blunted the thrill.

"You don't sound happy," Jane said, peering at me with her blurry gaze. "Are you nervous?"

"No," I said. "I think I can walk and scatter petals at the same time."

"There'll be such a lot of guests," Jane continued. "All those eyes following you—you mustn't mind them. Just remember that you are a Princess's Girl. That means something." She pinked with pride at the thought.

"Thanks," I said, squirming.

Jane meant well, but the thought of a cathedral full of staring people wasn't comforting.

Dulcie bounced on the bench next to me, rattling the dishes.

"We get to go to the city," she said, "and see everything!"

"Not everything," Roger said, salting his food. "Just what's along the way."

"But I've never been to a city," Dulcie replied. "So that's the same as everything to me."

"She has a point," Gillian said, stirring her soup. She had a new book, *A Short History of the White Mountain*, propped up behind her bowl. "Listen to this: 'In ancient times, clans ruled the mountain, chief among them the Wrays.' Did you get that?"

"Figures," I said. "They're supposed to be one of the oldest families in the kingdom."

"*Mountain*, goose, not *kingdom*," Gillian said. "It goes on: 'While the other clans referred to it as the White Mountain, Eliora was the name the Wrays bestowed on the mountain, long before the land dreamed of becoming a kingdom.'"

"Huh," I said. "So the Wrays are older than the kingdom."

I thought of the face in the portrait; he'd looked like a king, even if he was just an architect.

"Maybe that's what Cherice meant when she said she

was royalty." Gillian scooped up a spoonful of soup and blew on it. "She thought she was because the Wrays were here first."

"I've been thinking," Roger said. "Maybe that key unlocks something at that Wray fellow's house."

"What key?" Dulcie asked.

Gillian and I shot Roger dirty looks.

"It's an old key Darling found," Roger told Dulcie. "It's a game we play: What will it open?"

"What does it open?" Dulcie asked.

"See, it could be anything—or nothing," Roger said. "Don't worry about it."

"Okay," Dulcie said, smiling at him. "I won't."

"Magnificent Wray had a house?" Gillian said.

"Darling said he had one," Roger replied.

Gillian cast a quizzical look at me.

"Lady Amber talked about it in her book. But if the key unlocked something there, then why was Cherice hunting through the castle?" I asked.

"I say we forget about this house and keep looking," Gillian said.

Not to mention that if the house was still standing, it was probably in the city.

"Agreed," I said.

"I'm goin' *poofing* this evening," Roger said. "Dulcie, you can come along, but no questions."

I eyed the Freckle-Faced Wonder in amazement. Had he gone soft or something?

"Yes, sir," Dulcie said, sitting up straight.

"Where are you going?" I asked, annoyed that he hadn't invited me.

"Gonna do a little *looking around*," he replied.

He was taking Dulcie to chart the passages!

"Fine," I said. "I'm busy tonight."

"Where are you going next?" Gillian asked, turning a page.

"Oh," I said, acting as if I had lots of options, "I haven't decided yet."

"Let us know if you find anything," Gillian replied, already lost in her book.

Lyric sang to me as I sat cross-legged on the rose-patterned carpet, key in hand. The dresses oscillated around me, vying for my attention. But I was fresh out of ideas. I'd tried every lock I knew about, every lock I could reach. Not that there weren't lots of locks in rooms I'd never been in, but I didn't know which rooms to try.

I sank back against the stone wall under the great peaked-arch window. One Hundred hung close by, wrapped in its train, ignoring me.

"What does it open?" I asked One Hundred, holding up the key. "Will you tell me?"

The dress didn't even so much as flash a crystal at me.

"Not talking?" I said, closing my eyes and letting the magic ripple across my back.

It splashed into me, filling me with wonder, joy, laughter, and calm. Whatever happened, the magic wasn't worried. I sank a little deeper into its flow. It was a comforting escape—tempting, even. I could do like the mice and fall behind its curtain. No one could find me then. Well, there would probably be a stone Darling sitting here in the closet, and *that* was bound to raise questions.

Under the trilling buzz of magic, the dragons snarled hungrily. At the Princess's orders, the King's regalia had been brought out for polishing and cleaning. Not that it needed any, but Her Highness wanted nothing left to chance.

Now, the dragons hissed in my mind, *we will have the regalia; we will break free.*

Their claws raked my back as if they meant to reach through the magic and compel me to fetch it for them. But I, Darling the Undaunted, was no dragon minion! I lurched forward, snapping free.

Besides, if I didn't figure out what to do about the slippers, the dragons might be the least of my problems.

A furry paw touched my hand.

I jumped. Iago sat next to me, nose twitching.

"Hi," I said. "How is your family?"

He dived at my hand, kissing it with a whiskery peck.

"Happy?" I said.

He spun around, arms flung wide.

"Really happy!" I said.

He chattered at me; he was so excited that he forgot I didn't understand Mouse. I pretended to listen. No doubt he was telling me all about his family's reunion.

"That's wonderful," I said as he wound down. "I would have rescued your wife sooner if I'd realized she was there."

Iago put his paws over his heart and then held them out to me.

"You wish you could repay me?" I guessed.

He nodded.

"Oh, that's not necessary," I said.

But his tiny brow furrowed in concentration.

My heart warmed at his loyal friendship. If only *he* could get the key to closet two . . .

"If you could sneak into Marci's room—" I began.

He squeaked indignantly; it was Marci who'd put out the mousetraps.

"Of course, you can't do that," I said quickly. "If only there were some way I could stop the Princess from wearing those starlight slippers."

Iago tipped his head to one side, considering.

Even if he did get the key for me, what would I do with the slippers? Hide them?

No, the Princess would turn the castle upside down looking for them. But she wouldn't find them if I put them in a hidden passage.... An image of the Princess's tear-streaked face flashed into my mind. I was torn. She wanted so badly to wear those slippers. There had to be another way. If only the magic hadn't gotten into them in the first place!

25

The day Father bound the dragons to the castle's magic, the earth shook. The stones rumbled. The trees quaked. At the tumult, the Queen ran out on the terrace. She saw where the starburst had formed in the stones. She knelt down and grazed it with her fingers.

"Wonderful," she said, amazed.

Squinting, I could see the tiny figure of the King on the castle roof. His men were with him. And writhing in anger, the chained dragons screamed. Their golden collars flashed in the sun, atop the glorious white castle they'd built and were now imprisoned by.

I marveled. Father had poured a magic into those collars that allowed the King to subdue the dragons. My father had seen the castle he'd drawn become substance. He'd sealed the magic into the very stones of that castle. He'd safeguarded the kingdom and the King and Queen. And he'd done all of it to protect the future.

I sat under the rosebush, reading about the history of the Wrays. The world spun beneath me. Dizziness whirled in my head. I felt myself thinner, weaker, colder. The page before me blurred as the words changed.

I gasped, rereading what I'd already read. Only now, the page no longer said what it had before.

The past was altered. The Wrays, once so proud and mighty, were diminished. And I knew then that the future Father had sought to protect would ever pay the price for his plunder of the past.

Rose, the Head Seamstress, lined us Girls up, inspecting the fit of our new sky-blue dresses and lace pinafores. She tweaked a sleeve here, a collar there, smoothing ruffles and double-checking buttons. Not that there was time to alter them; the wedding was two days away.

I flounced my skirt. The dress had been beautiful by itself, but the delicate lace pinafore with its heart-shaped pocket transformed it into a work of art.

"Hold still, please," Rose told Dulcie.

"Do I have to wear a petticoat?" Dulcie asked.

"Certainly," Rose replied. "That skirt is designed to stand out."

Kate rolled her eyes.

"Maybe we *all* should forget our petticoats," Ann sniped. "That way we can all look silly together!"

"*Everyone* will wear a petticoat," Francesca said, straining to catch her reflection in the Seamstress's mirror. "The Royal Dress Designer created these dresses. It's a privilege to wear them."

"Did she?" Ann said.

"Ooh," Kate breathed, fingering the ruffle on her lace pinafore.

"You have Darling to thank as well," Rose said. "She did much of the sewing."

All the Girls turned to gape at me, except for Dulcie, who was too busy scratching at her waistband. And Gillian, who smiled in my direction.

"You let her sew on my dress?" Gloria said. "She—she's just a—a—a—"

"Excellent Under-assistant to the Wardrobe Mistress," Marci said, walking into the Seamstress's workroom.

Gloria turned a funny shade of green.

"Her Highness wants to know if the Girls' dresses are finished," Marci told Rose. "I can see that they are. You all look lovely."

"Maybe we should check the mirror and see for ourselves?" Kate suggested, pushing Ann out of her way.

"Good idea. Girls, line up single file," Rose said. "And once you've admired yourselves, please hang your dresses and pinafores back on the hangers." She pointed to a rack of hangers off to the side of the room.

As Girl after Girl primped before the mirror, several Seamstresses glanced up from their work to watch. Their hands flew over the buttonholes they were sewing into the Messenger Boys' vests. They looked tired but pleased with their efforts. I was glad I'd helped them.

"I wonder if you could punch another hole in this," Marci asked Rose, tugging on her new mauve belt.

"It doesn't seem too tight," Rose replied.

"No," Marci said. "It's a little too loose."

Rose studied Marci's waist.

"That chatelaine is a bit heavy for it," she agreed at last. "Another hole might not hurt."

"If you're not too busy—" Marci began.

"Calling in your favor?" Rose grinned. "Take it off, and I shall punch a quick hole for you."

"Oh, thank you," Marci said, unclipping her chatelaine. She stood a moment, holding it, as if she were not sure what she should do with it.

"I'll hold that for you," I said.

"Thank you, dear," Marci said. She handed me the chatelaine and began unbuckling her belt.

The weight of the silver chatelaine pulled on my hand—and my conscience. I eyed the keys, all silvery and tempting. Stealing was wrong; I knew that. But if I borrowed a key—just for the afternoon—

I felt my free hand drift toward the key to closet two.

"Darling," Francesca said.

My hand froze.

"Good work." She stood at my elbow, once again wearing her everyday uniform.

"Um, thanks," I said.

"I mean it," Francesca said. "I didn't think you'd make it as a Princess's Girl, but you've done all right."

My mouth fell open. Francesca Pepperwhistle, Bestower of Sneers, was complimenting my work?

"I'll take that back now, Darling," Marci said.

Numb, I handed over the chatelaine with all its keys still attached.

"You haven't told me a story in ages," Gillian said, lounging against one of the bronze lions guarding the stairs to the east lawn.

It was late spring, and warm enough that the Underservants had strolled outside to enjoy the evening. Gillian and I stood at the top of the stairs, watching the others gathered into clusters, chatting.

"Huh." I'd been too worried over the starlight slippers to daydream.

"Don't tell me *you've* run out of them," she said. "Not Darling the Great Storyteller!"

That needled me. I didn't have a made-up story to tell her, but I had the next best thing: the tragic tale of me, Darling, Shoe Despoiler. And maybe if I told it to her, she'd come up with a solution for me. Because I was willing to try almost anything to save the castle—and everyone in it.

"So, once upon a time there was this girl—a servant—who . . . mended potholders," I said, improvising.

"This doesn't sound like one of your usual stories," Gillian remarked.

"It gets better," I replied. Actually, it got worse, but I was building up to that. "So, one day this girl found a magic—er—potholder, and she—"

"Darling," Gillian said, "you're a great storyteller, but a terrible liar."

"No, I'm not," I said.

"No, you're not a great storyteller, or no, you're not lying?"

"Um, well, it's not that I'm *lying*, exactly."

Gillian folded her hands; the evening breeze ruffled her curls. "Go on," she said.

"I'm in trouble," I blurted out.

"With who?" Gillian's brow wrinkled. "You haven't done anything lately."

"Not that kind of trouble," I said. "You know how overnight my hair got prettier?"

"That's not trouble," Gillian said. "*That* was a miracle."

"That's the starlight slippers," I said.

Gillian's eyes widened. "Tell me everything," she commanded.

I told her, whispering so that the milling Underservants wouldn't hear.

"Do you really think the castle is in danger?" she asked.

"Those slippers are loaded with magic—the kind that chained the dragons and fills the dresses. It's potent stuff."

"But the dresses aren't mean," Gillian argued. "They wouldn't hurt the Princess."

"No, but the slippers are different," I said. "The dresses protect the castle. We don't know what Magnificent made the slippers *for*. Or what the starlight *unlocks*."

Gillian thought about that.

"So the slippers weren't a problem before they got filled up with magic," she said. "Those opals were just gems to start with."

"True, but—"

"Listen," she said. "The Princess wore those slippers, and so did you, and nothing happened."

"At first, yes, but—"

Gillian smacked my shoulder. "Pay attention, I'm telling you what to do," she said. "But when you wore one of the dresses *and* the shoes, the magic behaved differently. Didn't it?"

"Y-yes."

"And you can only wear a dress and shoes once, right?"

"Uh-huh." I watched Marci and Lindy walking, looking chummy and conspiring. I wondered what they were up to.

"So just get the shoes and *wear* them with the wedding dress! That should put the slippers and their opals back to sleep." She snapped her fingers. "Problem solved."

"That's a great idea!" I said, relieved. Why hadn't I thought of that?

And then it came crashing back to me.

"Marci locked the slippers up in one of the Princess's closets," I said. "And the key is on her chatelaine. She never takes it off."

"Never?" Gillian asked.

"She sleeps with it under her pillow."

"Does she wear it in the bathtub?" Gillian asked with a naughty grin.

I polished the crown that Princess Mariposa would wear to her coronation, which would be held the day after the wedding. The royal robes had been brought out from the treasury, along with the Queen's regalia. And now the regalia lay about the Princess's rooms in jeweled chests, waiting to be brushed, polished, shined, and whatever else Marci determined ought to be done with it.

If I hadn't been so busy plotting how I would *borrow*

the key while Marci bathed, I would have been impressed. Because there I was, Darling Wray Fortune, Nobody, handling one of the great treasures of the kingdom.

Had Francesca ever held a crown in *her* hands?

I didn't think so. Not many people had. And this was gorgeous: a delicate gold filigree encrusted with diamonds and circled at the base with sapphires. A great pear-shaped diamond surrounded by rubies decorated the front, and a huge pearl dangled below it.

"How are you coming along?" Marci asked.

"It's looking very shiny," I said, holding up the crown. "It's kind of heavy, though."

"Hmm, yes, that's why Princess Mariposa wears tiaras most of the time," Marci said. "Just think, long ago Queens wore their crowns every day."

"I bet they had headaches," I said.

"No doubt," Marci replied.

Where did she hang the chatelaine when she was in the bathtub? In the other room? On the rim of the tub itself? How long did she soak? Long enough for me to dash to the wardrobe hall, open the closet, put on the dress *and* the shoes, and then take them off, lock up the slippers—and dash back to replace the key?

It made me dizzy contemplating it.

And how was I supposed to get in? Surely, she locked

the door first. I needed more information if I was going to pull this off.

Marci took a nearly invisible stitch, mending a loose tie on the Queen's purple velvet robe. Its long train was trimmed in ermine and pearls and embroidered in gold. Marci had changed back into her charcoal Wardrobe Mistress's dress to keep the mauve dress clean for the wedding. Marci and other important servants would be attending—sitting in the choir loft.

That gave me an idea.

"Dulcie won't be very happy," I said.

"Oh?" Marci replied. "Another underclothes issue?"

"No," I said. "She'll have to take a bath before the wedding."

"I see," Marci said. "It can't be helped."

"I suppose everyone will take one," I said, thinking I could ease my way around to the topic of *when* people were taking their baths.

"I hope so," Marci said. "I've been saving a vial of rosewater just for the occasion."

"You'll smell nice," I said. "And you'll look really pretty."

"Darling," Marci said, suddenly steely-eyed, "whatever it is you're angling for—forget it."

"W-what do you mean?" I asked.

"I mean business," Marci said. "That's what I mean. If

you or any of the others do *anything* to spoil the Princess's wedding, you'll have me to answer to."

"Um . . . ," I said.

"Remember the large wooden-handled sponge I used when I was Head Scrubber?" she asked.

"Y-yes, ma'am." My backside twitched as I recalled the powerful swats she used to admonish less-than-zealous Under-scrubbers with in the under-cellar.

"I still have it," she said.

26

That evening after supper, I gave Roger the starburst key for safe-keeping.

"What are you givin' me this for?" he asked, raising his eyebrows.

"We're wearing lace pinafores to the wedding," I said. "And they have see-through lace pockets."

"Heart-shaped lace pockets," Gillian chimed in.

Roger snorted, unimpressed. "I'll keep it for you," he said, "but are you sure you don't have some place to hide it?"

I thought about my crate stamped ARTICHOKES. I could have given it to Iago, but the wedding ball loomed before me. I didn't know what was going to happen, and I *still* didn't have a plan to get inside closet two. I knew I'd feel better—safer—if Roger had the starburst key.

"Oh, I don't know. I thought maybe it was your turn," I said.

Gillian shot me a glance; she wasn't fooled.

"Okay." Roger grinned and slipped the key into his pocket.

"Just don't let your girlfriend, Dulcie, get her hands on it," Gillian said, poking Roger in the shoulder.

"She's not m-my—" Roger sputtered to a stop. Then a sly smile creased his freckles. "Say hi to your boyfriend for me, Gil."

Gillian colored up. "Boys," she said, laughing. "No sense of humor."

But if she thought I hadn't seen her blush, she was mistaken.

"That's where you get the toffee," I said. "From your boyfriend."

"It ain't a Stable Boy," Roger rejoined. "That leaves—"

"A Messenger Boy!" Roger and I crowed together.

Gillian burned a dark shade of crimson.

"Whoo-ee," Roger whistled. "It's true." He nudged me. "Whatcha think, Darling, is it Ben or Dyson or Sergio?"

"If you think I would tell you," Gillian said crisply, "then you have another think coming."

She turned on her heel and stalked away.

Roger laughed. "That'll shut her up," he said. "Right, Darling?"

He smiled at me: a warm, melting smile that made my toes curl.

"R-right," I said.

And then, before he could say anything else, I took off running after Gillian.

"Go on," she said, flouncing up the stairs, "make fun."

"Be fair," I said. "You've teased me plenty."

She mulled that over for a while. "Truce," she said, holding out her hand.

"Truce," I agreed, shaking it.

We climbed the stairs to the wardrobe hall. She didn't say any more. It hurt me a little, her not telling me that she had a boyfriend. And it made me wonder how I'd missed seeing it all that time. I guess Roger was right: I didn't pay enough attention to what was going on around me. I'd have to do better in the future. Especially if I was going to scout out who Gillian's mysterious Messenger Boyfriend was. Because I *had* to know.

We reached the corridor that led to the Princess's suite and found Prince Sterling talking to a Painter.

"Thank you," Prince Sterling told the man. "It's even better than I expected."

The man bowed, picked up the pail of brushes at his feet, and walked toward us.

The Prince smiled at him as he went. Then he spied Gillian and me.

"Girls!" Prince Sterling said. "If it isn't my art lovers, here in the nick of time."

"Nick of time for what?" Gillian asked.

"To see my mural in all its finished glory," the Prince replied.

Before I could make an excuse and drag Gillian off, she answered.

"We'd love to," she cried.

"We would," I said, less enthusiastically. "But we don't want to keep you from Her Highness."

"Ladies, I am at your service," Prince Sterling said. "The Princess is out in the greenhouses. Some crisis over flowers. Shall we?"

He led us down the corridor and into the King's suite. The King's bedroom had been luxuriously furnished in walnut and cherry, gilding, and royal-blue silk. But we scarcely had time to admire it. The Prince strolled straight into his lounge, where he gestured at the walls.

"A feast for the eyes," he said.

And it was. The mural was a glorious riot of color. Waterfalls. Pools. Leafy trees. Flowers. Mountains. And in the distance, a palace.

"Wonderful," Gillian exclaimed, turning around to see what lay on every side. "Trumpet oil, for sure!"

"Trompe l'oeil," the Prince said with a trace of amusement.

"The Baroness said that it would be like standing on the lake, seeing the kingdom from every direction!" Gillian breathed.

"What lake?" I asked.

"Lake Teor in Tamzin," Gillian replied. "That," she said, pointing, "is the royal palace."

"You are well informed, young lady," Prince Sterling said.

"Oh, the Baroness told me," she replied. "She said it was her wedding gift to you. So you wouldn't be homesick."

Prince Sterling laughed.

"You won't be, will you?" Gillian asked.

"I am sure that the Princess won't permit it," he replied.

"Tamzin is a beautiful country," I said.

"It is," he agreed, and launched into a story about his homeland.

Gillian listened, enraptured. I kept twisting my hands together. The evening was passing, and I was no closer to getting into closet two.

At last the Prince said, "Ladies, the evening wanes. And as a busy day awaits you tomorrow, you should get a good night's rest."

Then he insisted on escorting us as far as the stairs to the Girls' dormitory.

"Now what?" I asked Gillian, seething with frustration.

"Marci is bathing tomorrow night," she said with a wink. "We'll think of something by then."

"How do you know that's when?" I demanded.

"I have my sources," she said, and skipped into the dormitory.

27

The next morning, when Gillian and I reached the wardrobe hall, we found Marci, Lindy, and Selma, the Head Laundress, clustered around Princess Mariposa.

"Oh," Princess Mariposa sobbed, "the white roses—gone! Blighted by beetles. There aren't enough to decorate the cathedral. There aren't even enough left for a—a—a bouquet!"

"There, there," Marci said, patting her hand.

Selma dabbed her own eyes, and Lindy wrung her hands in agitation.

"What were those Gardeners thinking, letting beetles in?" Lindy said.

"Beetles don't usually wait for an invitation," Marci replied.

"Now, now, Your Highness," Selma said. "Don't cry. I'm sure there are lots of other flowers in the greenhouses. Why, a nice posy of—"

"I su-suppose I'll make do with carnations or—or *daisies!*" Princess Mariposa hiccuped.

"Nonsense," Lady Kaye thundered, sweeping into the dressing room. "I have already rallied the court! Everyone's servants have been dispatched to the closest estates. Every greenhouse's flowers will be picked, packed on wagons, and driven straight to the city."

"They will?" Princess Mariposa asked, brightening. "By morning?"

"Indeed, they will," Lady Kaye said. "Your subjects are eager to throw their best blooms at Your Majesty's feet. I'm sure there will be plenty of white roses for the cathedral *and* the bouquet."

"But what will you all do without your servants?" the Princess said. "How will you get ready for the wedding?"

"If I have to," Lady Kaye said with a twinkle in her eye, "I can dress myself."

"My gals can lace and button," Selma exclaimed. "Happy to help!"

"Thank you, Selma, you're a prize." Lady Kaye turned back to the Princess. "Now, dear, you just come right along and change. Madame Zerlina will be here for your final fitting."

With that, the Baroness took Princess Mariposa by the elbow and steered her to the dressing room. Marci followed after them.

"Well," Lindy said after they left, flipping her long, straight hair over her shoulder. "Good thing it'll all be over tomorrow."

"And we can all be back to normal," Selma agreed.

The two women eyed each other. For a moment, I thought the old feud between them would reignite, but the door to the wardrobe hall flew open and Madame Zerlina blew in.

"Ladies!" she exclaimed. "Such a glorious day!"

Immediately, Lindy and Selma stood at attention, patting their hair and adjusting their collars.

"And here we have Her Highness's lovely servants," Madame Zerlina said. "Such cheekbones," she said to Lindy. "You should wear your hair up." Then to Selma, "Such expressive eyes. You should wear a *little* powder."

Lindy blushed and Selma simpered. And then, curtsying, they went off to work—Lindy to the pressing room with Gillian, and Selma to the under-cellar. Which left me staring at Madame Zerlina, indignant for my fellow servants.

"Something?" she said, gazing at me. "A question?"

"How can you say those things? Expressive eyes!" I harrumphed, indignant on Selma's behalf.

"You think I am insincere?" Madame Zerlina said, astounded.

I shrugged.

"When you look in the mirror, what do you see?" she demanded.

I thought about that for a minute. "A stubby nose—" I began.

"Flaws!" she exclaimed. "And do you know what *I* see?"

"G-good bones?" I said, remembering the first time I'd met her.

"Exactly," she said, clapping her hands.

"Then why don't I see them?" I asked, annoyed by her enthusiasm.

"Because when you look in the mirror, you don't see yourself," she said.

"Sure I do," I said.

"No. You don't." She shook her head. "Is the Princess beautiful?"

"Of course."

"She is for her," Madame Zerlina replied. "But she is not your standard."

"Well, I don't look like her—"

"You look like you," she continued. "You don't see what I am saying. Let me put it this way: when I look at a woman I *see* her. *Only* her. I do not compare her to another. But you measure *yourself* against the Princess and always find that *you* are lacking. Because you do not *see* yourself at all."

"Huh," I said.

"So I am entirely sincere!" Madame Zerlina said. "I see each lady's own beauty and discern what will best enhance it. I never compare one to another."

"Oh."

"Never," she said, poking me. "And neither should you."

With that, she took herself off to the dressing room.

I stewed all morning, plotting how I could stop the starlight slippers. And then, just before lunch, it seemed that my opportunity had arrived.

Marci swept out of the dressing room, headed to closet two, produced the key, and unlocked the door. I put down the shoes I'd been polishing. I stood up.

I couldn't snatch the slippers out of Marci's hand, but I could follow her back into the dressing room and bide my time. Sooner or later, they would finish trying them on. And I would be right there! Marci looked exhausted. I'd be persuasive. Eager. Helpful. I'd say, "I'll put them on the desk and keep watch over them. You can lock them back in the closet later." For once, she'd just hand them to me.

It was a spectacular plan.

But then a *scream* tore the air. The closet door blasted

open. And out bounded Marci, slippers in hand, white-faced with horror.

"What is it?" I asked, running to her.

Wordlessly, she held them up.

Someone had chewed a hole in the toe of one of the lace slippers!

Iago! I was saved!

"Ruined," Marci gasped. "Ruined!"

The dressing room door burst open; Madame Zerlina, Princess Mariposa in her wedding gown, and Lady Kaye galloped into the room.

"Are you ill?" the Princess cried. "Are you injured?"

Marci shook her head.

"Oh my goodness!" Lady Kaye exclaimed, spotting the hole.

And then Princess Mariposa saw it too. She took the slippers from Marci, pressing them close and caressing them as if they were wounded. "My shoes!" she cried. "Oh, Marci! What happened?"

"Mice," Marci said, chin quivering. "I've set out traps—"

"That Pepperwhistle," Lady Kaye growled. "I ought to give her a piece of my mind!"

"I'm sure it isn't her fault." The Princess sighed, welling up. "She's the most conscientious housekeeper a princess could have." A tear ran down her cheek; she dashed it aside. "What do I have that I could wear in their place?"

"Well . . ." Marci bit her lip, thinking.

I twisted back and forth—between delight that my problem was solved and remorse over the Princess's unhappiness. I was just deciding that as upset as she was, it was all for the best, when Madame Zerlina spoke.

"I will take the slippers back to the city with me," Madame exclaimed with a grand gesture. "I will have them repaired—as good as new—by tomorrow!"

"You can do that?" I said, fighting the urge to frown.

"I can and I will," Madame declared.

"But will you be able to come all the way back up the mountain in time for me to dress?" Princess Mariposa asked.

"No, but you can wear any shoes to the cathedral," Madame said. "I will meet you there with your lace slippers, in plenty of time for you to slip them on and walk down the aisle."

"Oh, Madame," Princess Mariposa exclaimed, "it would be wonderful."

Madame Zerlina scooped up the slippers and packed them in her basket.

28

Queen Candace cradled the bundle in her arms. The sunlight played on the scattered silver strands in her hair. She smiled warmly at me.

"A princess," she said. "Come see."

I leaned over as she pulled the blanket aside to reveal a tiny pink face and a curled pink fist the size of a button. I felt a pang in my heart. Here was the Queen's first child, born when we had all lost hope that there would ever be an heir.

"She's beautiful, Your Highness," I said.

"Here, hold her." Queen Candace held her out to me.

I took the child in my arms. Grief struck me. The arms that held this beautiful baby had never held a child of their own. Noble had a grown son and twin grandsons. My husband's stepbrother had a daughter. But I had none. Deep in my heart, I knew Father's meddling with magic was to blame.

"I've named her Paloma," Queen Candace said.

"She's precious," I murmured. "I'm sure she's destined to be a great queen."

Paloma would grow up safe and secure, happy. All because the magic surrounded, shielded, and treasured her.

As long as the seals held. As long as the dragons were bound.

The wedding day arrived with a sweet-smelling breeze, a luscious lemon-colored sun, and a robin's-egg-blue sky. Dew sparkled on the brilliant green lawns below. In short, it was a perfect spring day.

And yet I felt perfectly rotten.

I woke to find a parcel at the foot of my bed. When I opened it, I found a silk camisole and petticoat, trimmed with lace and pink silk ribbons. And a note:

Dear Darling,
We found a good use for that ripped petticoat!
Marci and Lindy

My eyes welled up.

"I don't like wearing them either," Dulcie said. "But that one is sort of pretty."

Marci and Lindy had made them for me out of a petticoat of the Princess's that Cherice had savaged. I, Darling Wray Fortune, Failure, was off to the royal wedding wearing the most luxurious, beautiful, and expensive clothes I'd ever owned. And I wasn't enjoying any of it. The weight of the day hung around my neck. The ball was coming, the starlight was coming—disaster was coming! I had done nothing to stop it.

Once we had all tied on our lace pinafores and buckled our patent-leather shoes, Mrs. Pepperwhistle arrived, bearing a velvet-lined tray.

"Her Highness has a special gift for her Girls," she said. "There's one for each of you." And she passed out little gold pins, each with a garnet heart glistening in the center.

We pinned them on under our collars. Ann beat everyone else to the mirror to admire hers. I helped Dulcie fasten her pin.

"You look beautiful," I told her.

She did. Her red hair had been brushed until it shone. And free from its braids, it fell down her back in a gleaming ruby cascade. The sky blue suited her perfectly.

"You too," I told Gillian.

Gillian looked almost like a fairy-tale princess, with her heart-shaped face, dark ringlets, dimple, and fancy clothes.

"You look nice," Ann told me, overhearing. "Almost . . . cute," she added. "Doesn't she, Kate?"

"She does," Kate agreed.

"You look wonderful," Gloria said.

I glanced at the mirror; there I was, Darling Wray Fortune, Princess's Girl. If I overlooked my stubby nose, I did look *almost* pretty. Spiffy, certainly. Like I belonged with the rest of them.

"Thank you," I told Gloria.

"Breakfast time," Francesca called as the Maids arrived with trays.

We weren't served our usual breakfast. No sticky, gooey, jam-laden selections this morning. Breakfast consisted of bowls of thick oatmeal garnished with cream and strawberries. Mrs. Pepperwhistle insisted that we eat with napkins tied around our necks to protect our new clothes. Dulcie spooned up her oatmeal with a grim expression while Francesca kept an eye on her. Dulcie would arrive at the wedding spotless, whether she wanted to or not.

Then we all walked down to the stable yard for our wagon ride to the city. Jane and the Head Cook were waiting there to see us off.

"Darling," Jane called.

"Here I am," I said, walking over to her.

"Let me look at you," she said, taking hold of my arms.

She smiled so proudly that it pained me, even though I knew she couldn't see me properly. What she saw in her mind's eye I couldn't say, but *that* Darling was the apple of her eye.

"I always knew you'd grow up to be a beauty," she said.

"Everyone looks good in fancy clothes," I replied, embarrassed that the other Girls could hear.

"Don't you believe it," the Head Cook said. "Clothes don't make the lady; it's the other way around."

"Load up, Girls," the Stable Master called.

We Girls received special treatment. The wagon had been swept clean, and all the fittings shone. The benches that lined the sides were covered with clean blankets. A Groom drove the team of steady horses, and a Footman rode along—just to help us in and out of the wagon!

The mountain scenery rolled past us as we rode along. Dulcie was so eager to see everything that I had to keep a hand on her to stop her from tumbling over the side at every jolt.

I slumped in my seat; what had I been thinking when I tampered with those slippers?

"Cheer up," Gillian said.

That was easy for her to say; the threat of impending disaster didn't seem to trouble her a bit.

"Tell a story." Gillian nudged me. "That one about the Heart of the Forest."

"What story?" Francesca asked. "I've never heard about any heart in the forest."

"Oh," Gillian exclaimed, "Darling is the world's best storyteller."

Now every Girl stared at me, waiting.

"Prove it," Kate said.

So I told them the story I had made up for Gillian over the winter. A tale about a great enchantress who pours her love for the Mountain King into an emerald. The Girls sat on the edge of their seats, drinking in every word. The wagon slowed as even the Groom and the Footman leaned back to hear my tale. It was such an exciting story—with a wonderful, happy ending when the little goat girl discovers the gem—that I forgot to be miserable.

And we had arrived at the tall, gleaming-white cathedral in the center of the city before we knew it. Men and women dressed in splendid clothes streamed up the front stair to the gold-bound, arched double doors. The Girls oohed and aahed over the sight.

"My great-great-grandfather built that," I couldn't resist telling them.

They eyed me with a new respect.

The Groom drove us around to the side of the building, where we were helped out and sent in through a side door. Lady Kaye, wearing royal-blue satin and a spectacular diamond necklace, was waiting for us.

"Girls," she said, "pay strict attention to my instructions. You will take a basket, line up as the Footman directs

you, and wait *quietly* until called for. Then you will proceed up the aisle in two lines, scattering your petals—on
the floor, Girls, *not* on the guests. At the steps to the altar,
you will divide, one group to the right and one to the left.
You will walk along the side front, out into the transepts,
where you will stand in complete silence and be permit-
ted to view the wedding."

The Girls buzzed with excitement.

"We get to watch!" Kate said, practically swooning.

"Is this all perfectly clear?" Lady Kaye demanded. "Are
there any questions?"

We shook our heads in unison.

"Then fetch your baskets," she said.

We clutched our ribbon-bedecked baskets and
soaked in the scent of the rose petals. Behind us,
two bridesmaids in ice-blue gowns and crowns woven of
pink roses waited. I recognized one of them as Lady Teresa,
who looked so frightened I thought she might be sick. In
the back, Princess Mariposa glowed like a candle flame,
from the twinkle of the jeweled lace butterfly in her dark
hair, to the sapphire sparkle in her eyes, to the gleam of
the white satin gown, to the shimmer of the starlight opals
on her toes. In her hands, an enormous bouquet of white
roses, gardenias, peonies, and lilies-of-the-valley quivered
with her excitement.

Music swelled in the narthex, where we waited, and the Footman assigned to us signaled to us to begin. We walked down the aisle in two parallel rows; Francesca headed one, and Ann headed the other. There had been a bit of grousing over Ann's being singled out, but it had died down when Lady Kaye glared at us.

Now we stepped out of the shade of the narthex into the sanctuary. Every surface gleamed with marble, porcelain, and gold. A dazzling-bright light rained down from the stained-glass windows that rose to dizzying heights on either side. Overhead, an enormous vault floated, seemingly on air.

I thought about Lady Amber's charcoal line that spilled off her father's paper and took shape. This cathedral was my great-great-grandfather's imagination brought to glass-and-stone reality. My heart throbbed with pride as I cast my petals along the main aisle of his great achievement.

A delighted gasp ran through the guests as the Princess appeared behind us. The scent of roses perfumed the air as the Princess trod on the petals. At the altar, which was piled high with flowers, Prince Sterling stood, smiling.

My heart skipped a beat; he was the picture of a storybook prince! Warm brown eyes. Wavy brown hair. Regal bearing. Blue velvet coat heavy with gold embroidery. Gold satin sash. Diamond buttons. Gleaming sword at his side. And underneath it all, a kind heart. I couldn't help contrasting him with the phony Prince Baltazar the Princess had nearly married. The fake prince might have been taller, broader of shoulder, and blond, but he couldn't compare with Prince Sterling.

Why, if I'd been a princess, I'd have married Prince Sterling myself!

As it was, I followed Lady Kaye's instructions exactly, and ended up—in all too brief a time—out in the transept on the side of the cathedral. There, we Girls watched breathlessly as Princess Mariposa arrived at the altar, the lace butterflies on her dress and in her hair fluttering delicately.

The ceremony began, and after the choir sang and the priest droned on and on, my attention began to wander. The transept was lined with great wood doors. I noticed that the door closest to us had a sheaf of wheat carved on it and a plaque that read CHAPEL OF THE SMALLHOLDERS. What were smallholders? Very tiny pockets? As Ann, Gillian, and the others in my group hovered closer to the sanctuary to catch every word, I wandered down the transept.

I saw chapels dedicated to Glaziers, Wheelwrights, and Carpenters. And then I found a door with an anchor on it and a plaque: MARITIME CHAPEL. I turned the doorknob, and the heavy door creaked open.

Inside, a room lined in sea-green tiles and decorated with painted porcelain fish awaited me. Brass tablets covered the walls. A podium with a big brassbound book stood in the center. I glanced in the book; lists of ships and names filled the pages. I quickly realized that the lists were alphabetical, and I flipped to the *F*s. There, on the thin onionskin page, was this inscription:

FORTUNE'S FOLLY; CAPTAIN JAMES FORTUNE G47

I put a finger on the inked writing, the only proof I had that my father had existed as more than a story told to me by Jane. As I studied the wall, I saw that the tablets were labeled. In a matter of minutes, I located *G47*. It was the only tombstone my lost-at-sea father would ever have. I gazed it at for a long time, trying to feel something.

A lingering emptiness was all I felt.

I left the chapel to return to the Girls, and as I did, a heavy iron gate caught my eye. It sat at the end of the transept, hunkered in a dark corner, with a great iron lock clutching its center. I went over to it, wondering what required such a lock.

I peered through the iron bars. Worn steps melted down into a deeper darkness. Whatever was down there was lost in shadows. I stepped back and saw the starburst engraved in the iron.

My hand darted to my pocket before I remembered that I'd left the key back at the castle with Roger.

"Psst," Gillian hissed. She waved at me from down the way. *Get back here, before you get caught,* she mouthed, pointing at Ann, who had her back to us.

I patted my empty lace pocket and went back to watch the wedding.

A flash of gold shone as the Prince held out his hand. The wedding ring! The Princess presented her hand to receive it—and just as she did, a bright blue butterfly floated down to perch on her wrist. I'd never been one to set much store in signs, but this *had* to be an omen! The Princess and her Prince would live happily ever after for sure.

Well, I thought miserably, at least they would until the ball.

29

The rest of the day passed in a blur. As a special treat, we Girls were taken to an inn and fed an enormous lunch. Then our Footman took us on a walking tour of the city, pointing out houses and buildings he thought would interest us. Lady Kaye's stately beige town house was among these. We visited a park and fed the birds. Finally, footsore but happy, we piled into our wagon for the ride home.

It was suppertime when we arrived back at the castle. The kitchens broiled with activity while we ate; the wedding feast was under way, and a squadron of Footmen dashed in and out, ferrying platters to and from the banquet hall.

I had forgotten my troubles over the course of the

afternoon, but they came crashing back now. I nibbled on cold chicken and stewed on the inside. Once the feast ended, the court would withdraw to change into their evening clothes and attend the ball. Only a handful of starlight-free hours remained. Soon starlight would strike the opals and rock the castle's foundations.

And it would all be my fault!

There was nothing else left to do; I'd have to attend the ball.

"Are you okay?" Gillian asked after dinner.

"No," I said.

"What's wrong?" Dulcie asked, tagging along. The day's excitement had been too much for her hair, which frizzed out behind her like a red comet. "Is it your tummy?"

"It's worse than that," I said.

Dulcie frowned as if trying to decide what could be worse than a stomachache.

"Is it a headache?" she wondered. "Do you need some chamomile tea?"

"No," I said. "There's only one cure for what ails me."

"Does it lie in a closet?" Gillian asked archly.

"Nope," I said. "It's Marci."

Gillian blinked in surprise.

"Do you think it's that desperate?" she asked.

"Yes. Are you in?" I asked her. "Or are you out?"

She hesitated for a moment, and then she nodded. "I'm in," she said.

"Me too!" Dulcie said, without any idea of what she was agreeing to.

I told Marci what I'd done with the slippers; Gillian and Dulcie went along for moral support.

"You did *what*?" Marci cried, aghast. "Darling, what were you thinking?"

"Never mind that now," Gillian said. "She knows it was really, *really* stupid, but she can't undo it."

I frowned at Gillian; *stupid* was a strong word. I preferred *misguided*.

"Yeah," Dulcie said. "Stupid."

"We have to keep those slippers out of the starlight," I said. "Whatever it takes."

"And what *exactly* might it take?" Marci demanded.

I told her my plan. She didn't like any part of it, but lacking any better plan of her own, she agreed to help me. Not happily. Not eagerly. Not even sympathetically, as she explained. Because she didn't feel one little bit sorry for me. But if that's what was needed to protect the Princess, she'd do it.

We'd talk about my punishment later.

Outside the great peaked-arch window, night fell over the castle.

"The fate of the kingdom is at stake," I told the dresses. "I am going to the ball!"

The dresses roiled in excitement, jangling their hangers and swaying as if they moved in time with music. One Hundred alone hung like a glittering icicle in its dark corner. Lyric stirred on his perch, chirruping. He flicked his tail; his tiny black eyes shone. *Do it,* they seemed to say; *go to the ball.*

"I need to protect the Princess," I said. "Who's going with me?"

Twenty, a black gown twinkling with jewels caught in sheer black net and trimmed in gold lace, dipped a shoulder at me.

"It could be dangerous," I warned it. "We could get caught; you might not make it back to the closet."

Twenty shook out its skirts as if preparing for battle.

"That's the stuff I need," I said, pulling the dress off the hanger. "The rest of you, stand by. There's a long night ahead of us. I might have to change. So be ready."

The dresses shivered in a tizzy of delight as I stepped into Twenty. Their enthusiasm warmed my heart; at least they were behind me, even if One Hundred wasn't.

Twenty embraced me, leaving me momentarily

breathless, and then it settled around me like a shield. In the mirror, a pretty brown-haired lady wearing a diamond-and-topaz necklace and an armful of diamond, topaz, and gold bracelets greeted me. From her jewels and apparel, she was obviously someone important. Her smile was kind, if uncertain, as though her stunning dark topaz gown with its turquoise ribbons and snowdrift's worth of lace was grand even for her.

"Wonderful," I said, clapping my hands. "She'll be perfect."

There was no time to waste. I turned to leave, but Twenty held me back.

A pair of brocade shoes sat under its hanger.

"Well, okay," I said, untying my boots. I wasn't eager to experience the weird stretchy feeling that occupied the last dress-and-shoes combination, but I trusted Twenty. It acted like a dress that knew its mettle.

I pulled off my boots, held my breath, and stepped into the shoes. This time when my ears rang, my vision blurred, and I felt myself thinning and stretching, it was less unsettling because I was prepared for it. But it took me a moment to adjust.

And then I was off and out the door.

"Darling, those jewels!" Gillian said. She'd planted herself at Marci's desk with a fistful of toffees and a book, ready to stand guard in the wardrobe hall. "Who are you?"

"I don't know," I said, "but she's off to the ball."

"Have fun," Gillian said.

I hurried past her to the hidden door in the dressing room that we'd had propped open. Dulcie stood ready, an oil lamp in each hand, to light my way. She jiggled her foot impatiently; she was so thrilled to be included that she wouldn't sleep for a week.

"Let's go," she said, and pounded down the hidden stair.

The plan was simple: run down the hidden passage to the servants' entrances at the back of the ballroom and then sneak into the ball. I had to keep an eye on the Princess *and* watch out for the lady in the topaz dress. I'd gotten off easy that night in the corridor with Aster; I doubted I'd get away with that again.

A simple plan, yes. But easy? My nerves were as tangled as Dulcie's red hair.

Dulcie planted one of the oil lamps at the bottom of the spiral stair, well away from anything wooden, as Marci had instructed. The other she'd take back upstairs. No one knew how late the ball would last. And it'd be nearly impossible to find the right path back through the passages in the dark. So it was Dulcie's job to keep the lamps lit. For that, she had to stay awake. Gillian had promised to keep her company.

"Are you excited?" Dulcie asked.

"Yes," I said, although *terrified* was more like it. "Be careful going back."

"I will," she said, and headed up the stair.

I took a deep breath and rapped very softly on the panel.

The wall slid aside. Marci was waiting for me. I'd hated to tell her about the passages, but there was no help for it. I needed someone there to help me slip in and out without being caught by a Musician or a Footman. And neither Gillian nor Dulcie nor Roger had an excuse to be there.

Marci pushed the baseboard lever with her shoe, and the wall shut. We stood in the space behind the twisting stair that led up to the Musicians' gallery. The sound of music tripped gaily down the steps.

"Are you sure about this?" Marci asked.

I nodded.

"All right, then," she said. "You're Lady Diane, Duchess of Vermilion. Your estate is some distance to the south; you rarely come to court. You garden—prize hyacinths. So don't talk to anyone about flowers. Lady Diane knows her stuff; just change the subject. Better yet, don't talk to *anybody*."

"I've done this before," I pointed out.

"Don't remind me," Marci said drily. "Get going."

She peeked out the door and signaled that the coast was clear.

I slipped out past the gilded screen and into the ballroom, a dazzling, whirling sea of dancers. At first, all I could do was gape at the dresses the ladies wore. Every color, every shade, in a wealth of styles and fashions. Full skirts. Trains. Skirts draped over skirts. Skirts caught up behind in squished bundles of fabric. And the trims! Jewels, embroidery, lace, ribbons, crystals, sequins—one gown even sported feathers.

And then I saw Madame Zerlina off to one side, a champagne glass in her hand. Her dress caught my eye in a way the others didn't. Closely fitted to her form, the dress was sewn of alternating horizontal stripes of black satin and black velvet. Pink silk roses wreathed the hem, almost as if she stood knee-deep in a field of flowers. She wore one pink silk rose in her hair and a single diamond bracelet on her dark arm.

She was stunning. And clever. She didn't have to convince anyone she was a genius with fabric; she was living proof.

Outside the ballroom's windows, stars winked in the dark blue night sky, mocking me. But their light couldn't penetrate the brightly lit ballroom. As long as the Princess stayed inside, she was safe.

"Oh, Diane," a voice said as a hand took hold of my elbow. "I thought you'd gone out to see the gardens."

I could have told Marci her advice was wasted. People always talked about the most obvious things. The woman who'd accosted me was Lorna, the Duchess of Umber. She smiled as though she knew Diane well, and she probably did.

"It's a little cool out this evening," I said, shying away from the topic of flowers. "But you should see the stars."

She laughed. "My dear, the stars are on the dance floor!" she said. "Twinkling away in Mariposa's eyes."

"He's a very nice Prince," I said.

"I think he's a great catch," Lady Lorna said, and steered me toward the dancers.

Marci had explained how the wedding ball would go. It had begun with the Princess and Prince dancing the first dance alone as the court watched. Then the music changed, a signal for the others to join in. The evening would proceed with several dances, followed by a pause for refreshments, and then the dancing would resume. The pauses were intended to give the Musicians a rest. And to allow the guests time to nibble the cheeses and fruits on the buffet table. Footmen circled the room with trays full of champagne glasses. Marci had threatened to wallop me if I touched one of those.

She needn't have worried. I wasn't looking to get into

more trouble. I was in enough already. I was there to act as a sentinel by the doors leading out to the terrace. Although, what I'd say or do to keep the Princess from going outside was beyond me. I would have to make this up as I went along.

Lady Lorna whisked aside onlookers like a Sweeper with a broom. Everyone stepped out of her way. We arrived at the edge of the dance floor in time to see the Princess waltz past, enraptured in the Prince's arms. Her wedding dress had an underskirt and train that Marci had removed after the wedding, making the dress lighter and easier for the Princess to dance in. It flowed around her like a river of satin as she danced. The remaining butterflies fluttered as she moved, creating the beautiful illusion that they danced with her.

"What did I tell you?" Lady Lorna said. "We could all go out on the lawns and she'd never notice."

"It's a beautiful dress," I said.

"Mmm," Lady Lorna replied, spying someone else of interest to her. "Look at what Lady Cardiddle has on! Can you believe it?"

"Oh," I said, as if I knew who she meant. In fact, I was wondering how to skirt around the dance floor and park myself by the doors.

"Stripes," Lady Lorna said. "They're fine for day, but evening? Too much."

"I think Madame Zerlina's gown is striking," I said, keeping an eye on the Princess, who was between me and the doors.

"Zerlina's stripes are all the same color, but *that* gown." Lady Lorna sighed. "It makes me dizzy."

And that's when I spied Mrs. Pepperwhistle's slight form off to one side. I almost didn't recognize her. Now, when I'd heard that she would be at the ball, I'd expected to see her in a sedate charcoal satin or perhaps a nice navy-blue taffeta, with her hair in its tasteful coil of ebony braids. So I nearly bit my tongue when I saw her. She wore a gleaming scarlet satin dress with a black velvet band around the hem and a black velvet *V* topping the bodice. Her hair cascaded down to her tiny waist in gleaming waves.

Francesca and Faustine stood with her, wearing identical dresses of powder pink with matching hair bows. I would have thought I was seeing double had it not been for the downward curl of Faustine's mouth.

Mrs. Pepperwhistle saw me. She smiled and nodded her deference to the Duchess of Vermilion. But the way she studied me made my skin crawl. Her gray eyes darkened. I remembered the eerie sensation I'd felt in the passage behind the Princess's bedroom; she had that same expression on her face now. That *I will find you* look. I had to resist the urge to shiver.

Of course, she had no idea that it was me, not the Duchess, but I added another goal to the evening's list: stay away from Mrs. Pepperwhistle.

At that moment the music ceased, and the dancers bowed and curtsied to each other.

"Ooh, now it's your turn," Lady Lorna said. "Your Highness, over here!" she sang out, waving.

"My turn?" I said.

Now, I'd expected the Princess and Prince to dance together all evening, but I'd been wrong. They both turned to choose new partners. And as Lady Lorna called, Prince Sterling headed straight in our direction.

30

"I can't dance," I squeaked, forgetting who I was supposed to be.

But the Prince was already offering me his hand. "If you would do me the honor," he said.

Lady Lorna nudged me. What could I do? I took his hand and walked with him out onto the dance floor. Twenty swished at my knees, reminding me *whose* idea it had been to wear the matching shoes. Which was a good thing. I'd never have fooled the Prince if I'd felt my own size, not Lady Diane's.

My heart thudded in my chest. I'd never danced! I'd have to watch the others and stumble along.

"Mariposa told me that we had to set the wedding in the spring or we'd never drag you away from your geraniums," he said.

"Hyacinths," I said, before I realized I was correcting the Prince. I blushed.

"Hyacinths!" he said. "That's right."

He bowed, so I curtsied. And then he put one hand on my waist and held his other hand out to me. I set my now Diane-sized hand on his. The orchestra struck the first note and we were off. The Prince swirled me around the floor. I followed along, stepping when he stepped. It wasn't as hard as I'd thought it'd be.

Soon I was dancing—and enjoying myself.

Until I realized that I'd lost track of the Princess.

"You dance like a fawn, Lady Diane," he said.

I smiled, thrilled by the compliment until I caught his smile. He was being kind. Not that that was a bad thing; I knew I couldn't dance. Not really.

"Tell me about your gardens," he said, as if determined to talk.

Which puzzled me until I glanced around, trying to spot the Princess, and realized that all the other couples were talking while they danced.

"Everyone's tired of hearing me run on about my gardens," I replied with a forced laugh. "But I hear you have the most wonderful mural in your suite," I added, grasping for some subject that didn't involve flowers and would force *him* to do the talking.

"I do," he said, and described it in great detail.

So I murmured things like "oh, indeed" and "lovely" while I kept watch on Princess Mariposa's movements.

Finally, the music stopped. I curtsied, happy to escape. But just as I bid Prince Sterling farewell, another gentleman asked me to dance.

This time I made an excuse; I was tired, I said. The man gave me a startled look, as if this were not something Lady Diane would say. I hurried off to a safe place near the doors and tried to blend in with the paint.

"A little tiff, Lady Diane?" an older woman asked.

"Excuse me?" I said, hunting for Princess Mariposa and her next partner.

"You refused to dance with the Duke," the woman said. "In my experience, that only happens when wives are angry with their husbands."

I, Darling/Lady Diane, Duchess of Vermilion, had just told the Duke of Vermilion *no*. I wished that Twenty had come with a matching fan so that I could cool my burning face. Twenty lapped my ankles sympathetically.

"I'm just tired," I said, and turned away to avoid further conversation.

What would the Duke say to the Duchess later? And what would she say in return? This whole ball thing was trickier than I'd thought. Not only did I have to avoid Mrs. Pepperwhistle and keep track of the Princess, but I had to avoid the person I was pretending to be *and* her husband or beau or whoever had accompanied her to the ball. Because it belatedly occurred to me that *nobody* had come here alone.

Except me.

As the ball went on, I watched from my post by the wall, speaking only when spoken to and then giving brief, vague answers. Finally, the music stopped and the dancers made their way to the refreshments. At that moment, the outside doors opened and the real Lady Diane walked in. Her hair was slightly mussed and her cheeks were pink, but she glowed as if she'd had a better evening than anyone else so far. She probably had, given that she'd been out in the gardens the whole time.

Before I could blink, someone had asked after her hyacinths, and she was regaling them in rapturous tones about mulch. This was my cue; it was time to get out of there before anyone noticed me. Coughing politely into my fist to partially conceal my face, I wiggled my way through the throng. The area before the servants' entrances was deserted, so—with a quick look around—I dashed behind the last screen and through the door.

"What were you thinking?" Marci said. "I told you not to talk to anyone, and there you are on the dance floor, of all places, talking to the Prince!"

"It wasn't my fault," I said. "It was the Duchess of Umber's."

"Oh," Marci said. "She's hard to say no to. Well, hurry up and go change."

She let me through the wall. I grabbed the still-burning lamp and skedaddled up the stairs, through the passages, and back into the dressing room. In the wardrobe hall, Dulcie and Gillian were playing a game of cat's cradle with a string.

"I kept the lamps lit," Dulcie announced.

"You did a good job," I said.

"Is the ball wonderful?" Gillian asked.

I stopped with my hand on the closet doorknob.

"I'll tell you about it in the morning," I said. *If I survive that long,* I thought as I flung open the door.

The dresses were astir as if they *all* expected to go to the ball. I hung Twenty up with my thanks and then looked around, trying to choose among the others. Two flared its apricot-colored skirt, and its gold underskirt winked at me.

"Are you next?" I asked. "Because this time I need someone who isn't married."

Two twisted on its hanger, ready to leap off.

"If you're sure," I said.

I took Two and slipped into it. Faster than I could catch my breath, it caught me in its folds. In the mirror, a pretty blond lady batted her lashes at me. Her gown was cream chiffon draped over icy-blue satin. Garlands of real flowers decked her bodice, twined her sleeves, and hung down her skirt. It was the most impractical dress I'd ever seen. I shrugged, slipping into the apricot-colored slippers. The real gown might shed petals like dandruff, but Two and I were in solid shape.

I was off, racing past Gillian and Dulcie, back down the passages, and knocking on the panel in a matter of minutes. When the wall opened and I stepped through, Marci stopped me.

"Lady Juliana?" she said. "She's the most popular young lady at court."

"Is she married?" I asked.

"No," Marci said. "But I think you'd be better off as someone else."

Just then, I heard Princess Mariposa cry out, "Open the doors!"

"I have to go!" I darted out into the ballroom.

The guests burst into applause as the Footmen threw open the doors. For a heartbeat, I thought everyone was going out onto the lawn. Last fall, after her ruined wedding, Princess Mariposa had held a fireworks display for her guests.

I squirmed through the crowd, bumping and pushing my way, gathering irate looks as I went. I mumbled apologies but kept going. Princess Mariposa and Prince Sterling stood on the threshold, inches from the terrace beyond. I wasn't going to make it! There were just too many people eager to see what Her Highness would do next.

And then a portly gentleman, whom I'd sat next to at Princess Mariposa's Ruby Luncheon the previous spring, captured His Highness's attention. I exhaled with relief, scrambling the last few steps to the Princess's side.

"Oh, Your Highness," I exclaimed as Princess Mariposa turned toward the terrace, fanning her face with her hand.

"Yes?" she said, turning back. "Lady Juliana! How delightfully bedecked in flowers you are!"

She gazed at me, waiting for me to say something. My heart skipped a beat. My face burned. The candlelight rippled across the jewels scattered on her skirt, unleashing my tongue.

"Your Highness, your dress is so lovely and—and your hair ornament, so beautiful," I babbled. "And the wedding! Oh, it was so, so—"

Princess Mariposa smiled patiently as I rattled on about the wedding, praising every little thing I could think of. And just when I'd run out of bridesmaids and flowers and whatnot, Prince Sterling took her by the elbow and whispered in her ear.

"Oh, indeed," she said. "Thank you, my dear," she told me, before addressing the room: "Let the dancing resume!"

The crowd applauded as the Prince led her back to the dance floor. I swayed, dizzy with relief. The orchestra struck up the next song. I sidled toward the open doors, where I intended to stand guard, when a young gentleman pounced.

"Lady Juliana," he crowed as if he'd won a prize. "I can't let you stand around without a partner!"

I opened my mouth to protest, but he'd already caught my arm and whirled me into the dancers. After that, one young gentleman after another demanded my attention, each more insistent than the last. Soon I was dizzy and confused. Which way were the doors? And what was the Princess doing now? After dancing with the umpteenth young gentleman, I tore myself away and stumbled into the crowd. That's when I saw the real Lady Juliana eating strawberries off a dainty china plate, surrounded by even more young gentlemen.

It wouldn't have been so bad if I could have traded places with her. As it was, I limped off in a hurry before anyone could notice me. Marci peeked through a crack in the door, shaking her head.

"I tried to warn you," she said, letting me inside.

I nodded, too breathless to speak.

She opened the wall, and I slid through like gravy sliding over mashed potatoes. I plopped down on the bottom stairstep. Stars swam before my eyes. I'd been awake since early morning, attended the wedding, walked all over the city, and stayed up so I could go to the ball. All that would have been enough to knock me out. But I'd spent the evening dodging ladies whose identity I wore, being whirled around the dance floor, and chasing the Princess.

I was exhausted.

The lamp on the floor sputtered as if it were about to go out.

"Are you okay?" Dulcie asked, coming down the stair with a refilled lamp in her hand. "You don't look too good."

Two caressed my shoulder with a concerned air.

I didn't have time to sit there; I needed to bound up those steps double-quick and get another dress. Now that the doors to the terrace were standing open, the Princess could waltz outside at any minute.

"I can't," I gasped out loud. "I'm so tired."

"It's late," Dulcie agreed, and broke into a yawn.

Which made me yawn—a cheek-splitting, jaw-cracking yawn that rolled my eyes back in my head. I tried to stand up, but my knees refused to cooperate. They were not climbing those stairs again, they let me know in no uncertain terms.

"I can't get up," I told Dulcie, panicked.

"I could get you a dress," she said. "I'll run real quick there and back."

She could; she was that fast. And having spent the evening playing games like cat's cradle, she wasn't as tired as I was. It was tempting; I reached up for the shoulder of Two—and stopped.

I had promised the dresses last summer that I'd never leave one off the hanger.

"I have to do it," I said, defeated. "The dresses need to either be worn or be on their hangers. Otherwise they ... die." *Die* came out in a thin whisper.

Two flinched. But then something unexpected happened. Something heroic. Two loosened its grip and began to return to its original size.

"No," I said, clutching its folds. "I can't let you do this. You'll be ruined!"

But Two squeezed my waist. Magic tingled in its touch, and deep down—somewhere I couldn't put a finger on—it was all right. The dress could be off the hanger briefly. Very briefly, but, still, it had happened before. Sixty-Eight had launched itself off its hanger onto the closet floor to get my attention. And I had to take the dresses off their hangers to put them on. And off myself again in order to hang them back up.

"Are you really, truly, absolutely sure about this?" I asked Two.

The magic in it buzzed faintly. Two would risk it. It had

been filled up with magic to guard the castle. And now, no matter what the cost, it would carry out its mission until the very end. Whatever that might be.

Tears welled up in my eyes as Two slithered off me.

"You have to run faster than you've ever run," I told Dulcie. "You have to hang this dress back on its hanger. And fetch me another."

"Okay," Dulcie said, gathering up the dress.

"Don't just grab any one," I said, catching her sleeve. "Tell the dresses who you are and what you've come for! Ask for someone who *won't* be dancing! Understand?"

"I can do it," Dulcie said, straightening her thin shoulders. "You can count on me!"

I nodded, knowing that I was putting the fate of Two— and whatever dress volunteered—in her hands.

"Run!" I started to say, but she was already off, shooting up the stairs like a pebble out of a slingshot.

31

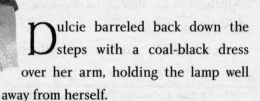 ulcie barreled back down the steps with a coal-black dress over her arm, holding the lamp well away from herself.

"I've got it! I've got it!" she announced, flushed.

"Is Two all right?" I stood up, knees still wobbly as I took the dress.

"Shipshape," she said, breaking into a big grin.

"You're faster than the Princess's horses," I told her. "Which number is this?"

"Seventy-Four," she said. "I like sevens and fours."

"Good, so do I," I said, and pulled on Seventy-Four.

Seventy-four was slashed on the skirt and sleeves to reveal an emerald velvet underdress. The thing weighed half as much as I did. I tugged it up over my shoulder, wondering how anyone could wear something so heavy all day. But Seventy-Four became as light as one of the Pastry Chef's piecrusts when it conformed to my size.

Dulcie stared at me, lamp bobbing in her shaking hand.

"Francesca?" she whispered. "Is that you?"

"No, silly, it's me, Darling," I said.

She swallowed hard. "If you say so."

"It's me, Dulcie," I assured her. "Besides, I can't be Francesca; I've already *been* her."

And then I realized that was true. I had. Which meant that I was Faustine.

I cringed; she was the very last person I wanted to be. I'd forgotten she was at the ball; I hadn't seen her since early in the evening. But I had asked for someone who wouldn't dance. Seventy-Four felt my disapproval and became a leaden weight hanging from my waist.

"I'm her sister Faustine," I told Dulcie. "Which is perfect," I added for the dress's benefit.

Marci laughed when she saw me.

"I always knew those dresses had a sense of humor," she said, escorting me out the door.

This time no one bothered me or spoke to me or even noticed that I was there. I was practically invisible. That suited me fine. I headed to the buffet table and helped myself to a plate of strawberries. Then I parked myself where I could watch the door and the Princess and eat without being bothered.

Music rolled through the ballroom. Dancers moved and shifted in complicated patterns. The candles on the candelabra burned low. I leaned back against the wall, tired and sore and stuffed with berries. My eyelids began to sag. My knees began to buckle.

"Whoa, missy," a voice said as a hand caught me. "Tumbling off to sleep?"

"Glug," I said, wrenching my eyes open and staring up into the Stable Master's face.

"Tina-bean," he said. "I thought your mother sent you to bed hours ago."

"Umm," I slurred, too sleepy to talk straight.

"Off we go," he said, and scooped me up in his arms.

The waves rolled as my father held a spyglass to his eye. He was tall and handsome in his blue coat and captain's hat.

"There's a storm blowing in, Darling," he said.

The wind howled. The ship pitched beneath me. A gigantic wave slapped at the deck. And swept my father clean away.

"Father!" I cried.

"Right here, Tina-bean," the Stable Master said.

The world around me was as dark as midnight. It took me a moment to realize that he was carrying me upstairs.

I was caught! I was in terrible trouble! I thrashed in his grip.

Seventy-Four gave me a sharp squeeze, bringing me to my senses. I wasn't me; I was Faustine.

"Hold still," the Stable Master said, "or I might drop you."

Perspiration rolled down my face. I'd been sound asleep. For how long? And where in the castle was I now?

And worse: *what* was going on back in the ballroom?

I squirmed uncomfortably; I wasn't used to being carried.

"I suppose you're going to tell me that you're too old for this?" the Stable Master said with a chuckle.

"I *am* too old," I said, latching on to the excuse. "I can walk all by myself."

"All right, Tina," he said, and set me on my feet. Then he reached to take my hand.

"I'm not a baby," I protested.

He looked sad.

"No, I suppose not," he said, sounding as if he wished I *were* a baby.

I felt a stab; I'd never had a father carry me to bed. Or take me riding on a pony. Or tell me a story.

"Thanks ... um, Father," I told him. "I can find my way from here. Good night."

"Kiss your old dad good night," he said, bending over.

I froze. *Kiss* the Stable Master?

He presented his cheek. The real Faustine would kiss her father; she wouldn't make a fuss. And I had to get out of there without arousing his suspicion. So I stretched up on tiptoe and kissed him *very* lightly on the cheek.

He grabbed me in a bear hug and kissed the top of my head. And for a moment, the warmth, the feel of his strong arms, and the scent of leather overwhelmed me. Then he whispered in my ear.

"I love you," he said.

"Love you," I echoed.

I tore myself away and bounded up the steps as hot tears coursed down my cheeks.

It wasn't fair! Not one little bit. Mean ol' Francesca and grumpy ol' Faustine had a real father. All I had was a plaque in the Maritime Chapel.

Seventy-Four stroked my arm with its velvet interior.

"It's okay," I said, dashing away my tears.

I might not have had a family or parents, but I had the Princess and the castle. And I was not about to let anything happen to either one.

By the time I circled back to the west wing and found my way to the ballroom, the crowd of dancers had thinned. The banquet table looked as if it had been ravaged by birds. And the music had died down to a single violin.

The ball was almost over! I'd done it! I, Darling Wray Fortune, Outsmarter of Opals, had kept those slippers out of the starlight! Any minute now, the Princess would bid everyone good night and go to bed.

And somehow I'd see to it that she never wore those shoes again!

Princess Mariposa and Prince Sterling lingered by the open terrace doors, gazing out. I hurried over to where they were—to be close to the slippers in my moment of triumph. A cooling breeze drifted in. Outside, the stars blazed in a brilliant display.

"It's such a beautiful night," Princess Mariposa said.

"Perfect weather," Prince Sterling agreed.

"It was the perfect day," she said.

"I know the perfect ending," Prince Sterling replied. "A dance on the terrace!"

My mouth dropped open.

"Maestro! A waltz!" Prince Sterling cried out across the ballroom.

"No!" I shrieked as the orchestra struck up.

Music rolled through the air, thick and rich and haunting.

And Prince Sterling and Princess Mariposa waltzed right out onto the terrace.

I scrambled to the doorway.

Around and around they whirled. Her skirt flared about her like a pool of moonlight as quicker and quicker they flew. The starlight kissed the jeweled butterfly in her hair and danced along her shoulders. The gems on her gown sparkled as they moved from shadow to shadow.

I tore my hair. What could I do? I raced out onto the terrace.

And then it happened.

Princess Mariposa stepped straight into a pool of milky starlight.

32

The starlight opals blazed with color, sending sparks into the darkness. Under the toe of the Princess's slipper, the ghostly outline of a starburst appeared. I rubbed my eyes. It hadn't been there a minute earlier.

Starlight unlocks the opals! I braced myself against the outside wall, waiting for the terrace to split open, the walls to crack, the ceilings to come tumbling down. Waiting for screaming and shouting and—

The Prince and Princess danced on, unaware. The starburst gleamed solid now, as if starlight had painted it there on the terrace. But nothing else happened. Maybe that was it. It might raise questions once someone noticed the starburst, but if the only thing the opals unlocked was a sparkly image on the terrace, well then—

A sensation started in the stones against my back, a rising tide of boiling *magic*, as if the wall itself shivered and shook. Caught by surprise, I stumbled backward, putting my full weight on the wall. Magic lapped over me and coursed through me and ran out to greet the shimmering starburst.

"Oh no!" I cried, but the magic paid no attention to me.

The magic hit the starburst, and—*whoosh!*—a surge of magic rocked the castle, and me with it. Every creature caught in the castle's web thrummed to life, straining against its hold. My insides wobbled. My head stretched sideways. My hair stood on end. Deep in the magic, the dragons stirred.

"No, oh no!" I gasped, my tongue as thick as a sausage.

With a roar of triumph, the dragons reared up and *pulled* with all their massive might.

In an instant, every creature in the castle's web panicked, each bird and beast scrambling to flee to safety. They created such a tumult in the magic that the castle stones themselves bobbled. The magic stretched paper-thin. With a ferocious growl, the dragons yanked all the harder. The other creatures grew frantic. The magic's hold wavered.

I gasped in horror. The magic couldn't *fail*! I couldn't let it!

I gripped the doorframe with my hands and reached through the magic, scrabbling for a hold on the dragons' collars. I slammed up against the fierceness of their hatred and the scorch of fire on their breaths. Determined, I flattened and thinned until I was half in the magic and half out, desperate to restrain those monsters.

Say it! the dragons commanded.

I knew what they meant: say the magic word, *Sarvinder.* If I broke down and spoke that word—the dragons would rip free.

"Never!" I told them.

They sank their teeth into my thoughts.

SAY IT!

"Not if I snap in two!" I sobbed.

They smacked against me with their spiky, scaly tails. *Whap!*

My vision blurred. My head spun.

Thousands of tiny cracks raced through the magic, plunging deep down to the base of the cellars and ripping all the way up to the roof.

The dragons licked their chops. They'd break free, and then—*then* they would consume the magic itself. Lap up every tasty drop. Because I understood what Magnificent Wray had been trying to tell Lady Amber in that letter. It wasn't the starlight slippers that had attracted the dragons so long ago. It was the magic *in* the slippers.

Magic pulled out of the Wrays and put there by her father. No wonder he'd lived to regret it. And I realized why she hadn't mentioned it in her book. He was her father; she'd wanted to protect his memory.

Not that finally figuring it out was going to help me any. My heart stopped. My breath died. My eyes glazed. I felt myself about to wink out like a snuffed candle. The dragons screamed in victory.

Then something deep, deep down in the magic awoke. It reared up like a great stallion tossing its head, champing its bit, and stamping its powerful hooves. The magic snapped those dragons back into its grip like a giant hand closing them in its fist.

And it held. The magic held!

Darling, the magic said, *breathe.*

My heart thumped. Air poured into my lungs.

A *boom-crack* sounded through the night. Overhead, streaks of light blossomed into gigantic flowers in the night sky. The Prince and Princess applauded. The remaining guests hurried out onto the terrace to view the fireworks.

Gently, like a hen gathering her chicks, the magic wrapped me in its folds.

Darling, the magic whispered, *stay strong.*

It released me into the cool evening breeze. I stood on the threshold, dazed and in one piece. Perspiration trickled down my sides. My knees wobbled, but I was still me.

Then I realized that the magic wasn't as unscathed as I—it had held, but at a cost. The thousands of tiny cracks were still there. But the dragons remained bound, and that was enough for the moment.

I turned and saw softly shimmering starbursts flower on the ballroom's floor and on its walls. Everywhere I looked, more appeared. I waited with bated breath and clenched fists for someone to notice and start screaming.

But no one did.

And nothing else happened.

I caught the threatening glare of a Footman. I, Darling Wray Fortune, Under-assistant to the Wardrobe Mistress, had no business watching the fireworks.

And then I remembered that I was Faustine. I smirked as if I had every right to attend the ball (which is what I thought a girl like Faustine was apt to do) and pranced back inside. Lady Kaye sat snoring in a nearby armchair, which she'd no doubt commanded be brought in for her. Footmen were clearing away debris from the banquet table. If anyone saw the starbursts glittering everywhere, they paid them no heed.

In a sense, I'd failed. The starlight had touched the opals. And if the starlight opals had unlocked something more than sparkly images, then they had. There was nothing more I could do. I swayed on my feet, worn to a frazzle.

Across the room, the eagle eye of Mrs. Pepperwhistle spotted me.

Me, Darling/Faustine, who'd been sent to bed hours earlier.

Her eyes narrowed. My heart pounded with terror. There was no way I could deceive *her.* The minute she caught up to me and I said *anything,* she'd realize I wasn't her daughter. Unlike Aster, Mrs. Pepperwhistle wouldn't let go once she had me in hand. She'd get the truth out of me whether I wanted to tell it to her or not.

She started toward me with a determined gleam in her eye.

I abandoned all ladylike pretense and bolted for the servants' entrances. Behind me I heard the quicksilver tattoo of her dancing slippers in pursuit. I dashed behind the screen and jumped through the door and right into a startled Marci.

"Come on, come on! Hurry!" I said, grabbing Marci and dragging her to the portal.

Startled, Marci hit the baseboard lever with her shoe. The wall slid open. I yanked her in and shut it just as the servants' door opened.

"What on—" Marci began.

I slapped a hand over her mouth. Her visage darkened

dangerously. She gripped my wrist with her hand and tried to tear it away.

"Faustine," Mrs. Pepperwhistle called on the other side of the wall. "Come down here at once!"

Understanding lit Marci's expression. I took my hand away. And we waited, listening to the click of her heels going up the spiral staircase to the Musicians' gallery. Behind us, Dulcie lay curled up, fast asleep on the bottom stairstep. We stood mute, barely breathing lest we wake Dulcie, and waited for Mrs. Pepperwhistle to climb back down the stairs. On the walls and floor, starbursts gleamed in the dark.

At long last, she did. We heard her open the servants' door—and leave.

"Do you see them?" I asked Marci.

"See what?"

"The starbursts on the walls," I said.

"Darling," Marci said, stifling a yawn, "I'm going to bed."

33

I woke up the next day, alone in the Girls' dormitory. Sun poured in through the open windows. The curtains sailed in the breeze. My head ached, and my mouth tasted like old socks. The room door opened and Marci peered in.

"Alive?" she asked.

"Barely," I said. And then I remembered the shining starbursts. I glanced around the dormitory, but if they were there, it was too bright to see them.

"I suppose so, after all that fuss over nothing," she said, unaware of the battle inside the magic. "But that punishment still stands."

"What time is it?"

"Late afternoon," she said. "Don't worry," she added as I was about to panic. "Everyone is too caught up in the festivities to worry about you. You've missed the wedding brunch and the coronation, and if you don't get dressed, you will miss the presentation."

"What's a presentation?" I asked.

"It's when the new King and Queen give gifts to all their faithful servants," Marci said, patting her coronet of braids. "I don't intend to miss it, whether you come or not."

I stood in a long line of servants waiting to enter the throne room. Faces were flushed, eyes bright. The air tingled with anticipation. A conversation about what gift each group of servants might expect to receive murmured around me.

I paid no attention; I was too busy staring at the glistening starbursts that nobody else noticed. What did they mean? Were they important? Or dangerous? I touched one.

Nothing. No sizzle of magic. No lightning. No thunder. Just nothing.

Why had the opals unlocked a bunch of . . . nothing?

My head began to hurt.

Eventually, the line moved into the throne room. Normally, I'd have enjoyed the chance to study the rich trappings. But I could scarcely see the tapestries or columns or arches or banners for the glistening trace of starbursts. As the line crawled across the inlaid tiles of the marble floor, I tipped my head back and stared at the sparkling starburst on the painted ceiling.

Could nobody but me see them?

The portrait of King Richard smiled at me from the wall behind the thrones. Queen Mariposa and King Sterling stood at the edge of the dais and spoke to each servant, one at a time. Next, Lady Kaye handed a small bag to the servant, who then went back across the room.

The bags jingled.

I noticed that the size of the bag differed from one class of servant to another.

I crept closer and closer until I stood on the great crest of Eliora inlaid on the marble floor.

Queen Mariposa glowed in her jeweled crown, her royal robe, her chain of office, and her rings. King Sterling— I broke out in a cold sweat. He was wearing the regalia! I'd forgotten all about it. I stared at the sleeve of his jacket, seeking the gleam of the gold cuffs under them. But as he moved, I saw that he wasn't wearing them.

Were they gone? Had they been stolen?

Then I remembered what I'd whispered to Queen Mariposa the previous fall. *The talisman,* I'd told her, and she knew I meant the heavy gold cuffs. I sagged in relief. She'd not forgotten my warning. The talisman was still safely tucked in its chest. Those dragons would have to wait for some other opportunity.

Since the threat from the dragons was nil, and the starbursts didn't seem to be doing anything particularly dangerous at the moment, I took time to enjoy where I was.

The great crest of Eliora was formed from a myriad of glass tiles that outlined a swan on a starburst, behind which were two crossed swords. Polished marble tiles surrounded it. The crest was fourteen tiles wide. Six tiles ran from the tips of the sword points at the top to the steps leading up the dais. I counted fourteen tiles across the top of the steps.

And then I saw it—a glittering *starburst* like those that dotted the castle walls. It was sparkling smack-dab in the gilded base that the thrones rested upon! And twinkling right there in the center of it was a keyhole!

Six and seven, Cherice had said.

And there it was! Six up and seven over. And it didn't matter which side of the crest you counted from: the number was the same.

I'd found it! I shoved my fist into my pocket, but the key wasn't there. I'd forgotten to get it back from Roger. I ground my teeth. Every fiber of my being wanted to use that key!

The Upper-servant ahead of me curtsied to Their Highnesses and turned to leave.

And then I stepped up to the dais. Queen Mariposa smiled at me.

"Thank you for your service, Darling," she said.

"Thank you," King Sterling said, "for being Her Highness's friend."

Her Highness's friend. She'd called me that once herself. My eyes welled with tears. I had tried as hard as possible to be her friend, even if I hadn't stopped the starburst opals.

"My privilege," I choked out, curtsying.

The Queen touched my hand. "It's *my* privilege," she said.

I turned to go before I started crying right there in front of everyone, but Lady Kaye stopped me.

"Don't forget this," she said.

She handed me a gold coin.

"Well deserved," she observed with a smile.

I closed my fist around my new treasure. And vowed to myself to return for my inheritance the first chance I got.

The next day the guests took their leave. And the new Queen and King climbed into the royal carriage and rode off on their honeymoon with a retinue of handpicked nobles. The castle servants stayed behind; the Queen and King would be served by others stationed at castles and lodges along the way.

Marci and I spent the day tidying up the wardrobe hall. With the wedding festivities past, the castle was quiet. All the Upper-servants dallied over their chores.

"I'm rich," Dulcie told me that evening, flashing her gold coin.

The Under-servants were out enjoying the peace and quiet on the east lawn. I'd been telling Gillian, Roger, and Dulcie the saga of my ball adventure. Jane and Marci sat by the bronze lions, out of earshot.

"You'd better find a safe place to keep your money," Gillian said, squeezing Dulcie.

"What are you doing with yours?" I asked Gillian.

"Saving it for something really special," Gillian replied.

"What?" Dulcie asked.

"I'll know it when I see it," she said.

"I'm sending mine to my mother," Roger offered. "Darling, what are you gonna do?"

I shrugged. I'd never had money in my entire life. And now I had a whole gold coin!

"I guess I intend to keep it and look at it for a while," I said. "Dulcie, you'd better go see the Baroness. I bet she'd keep that safe for you until you need it."

"That's a good idea," Roger said. "That's not something you want to lose."

As soon as Dulcie was gone, I told Roger and Gillian about seeing the keyhole in the base of the thrones.

"That's wonderful," Gillian said. But then she grimaced. "Not only are there gobs of Guards posted in that part of the castle, but it's not a place we have any excuse to be."

"I've got a way in," Roger said. "Remember that I told you there were lots of passages to places you shouldn't go?" He jabbed the air. "That bit that branched off from the passage to the ballroom and into the west wing? Gold mine! It opens straight into the throne room."

"Ooh," Gillian said. "We can walk right in and no one will know we're in there!"

"Are you sure the Guards don't check inside that room during their shifts?" I asked, so excited my stomach hurt.

"I'm sure," Roger said. "Just another empty room these days."

Gillian gripped my hand. "This is it!" she said. "A magic invisible keyhole, a special key—your inheritance is just a twist of a wrist away!"

Roger and Gillian grinned like fiends. They couldn't have been more thrilled if it were *their* inheritance we were after.

"Great!" I said, afraid to say any more lest I bawl like a baby.

Just then, a tall shadow fell over us.

"Good evening, ladies, Roger," the Stable Master said. He had Roger's folded map in his hand.

The three of us sat round-eyed like three fat mice cornered by a cat.

The Stable Master sat down next to us as if he meant to keep us company.

"Um . . . ," I said.

"This map has intrigued me," the Stable Master said. "At first, I thought it was just what Miss Dimple here claimed it was—a map of the castle."

"Huh," Roger said.

"Yeah?" Gillian breathed.

"But it isn't," the Stable Master replied.

I felt sick to my stomach.

"I know that castle inside and out. So you can see why my curiosity was piqued," the Stable Master continued, ignoring our discomfort. "I wondered how and *why* you three ambitious youngsters created this. And then a reason occurred to me."

"It did?" Gillian asked, looking as if she just might pass out.

"It did. These lines"—he pointed to the map—"aren't corridors; they're passages behind the corridors."

"Oh," Roger groaned.

"Very enterprising of you three." The Stable Master chuckled. "All these years and no one else ever suspected they were there. So why don't you explain to me how you found them."

"It was an accident," I said, hoping that excuse would exonerate us somehow. "We weren't looking for it; we just fell into it."

"That explains it," the Stable Master said, slapping Roger on the knee. "Just lucky."

"That's us," Gillian chimed in. "Lucky."

"It also occurs to me that mapping hidden passages could be dangerous," the Stable Master said in that ominous tone adults use just before they forbid something.

"We found the skeleton of that ghost in the south tower, only it wasn't a ghost, just a dead lady. Well, not a whole dead lady, just clothes and a skeleton," Roger babbled.

I poked him. There was no reason to volunteer details.

"You don't say," the Stable Master said. "That solves that mystery."

"My, my, it's getting late," Gillian said, starting to rise.

"Not so fast, missy." The Stable Master caught her arm. "Sit down." She sat. "Now then, I could order you three to cease exploring, and you'd probably all solemnly swear to stop."

Our heads began to bob in unison.

"But in a few weeks, the temptation would get the better of you."

None of us spoke.

"So here's what I'm going to do," the Stable Master continued. "I will leave lanterns and candles in the tack room cupboard for you to use. *You* will *never,* at any time or for any reason, go exploring without leaving me a note of when you left, where you went, and what time you expect to return. And none of you will ever, *ever* go alone. Do I make myself clear?"

Once again our heads bobbed in unison.

"Good." The Stable Master smiled. "Because I'd hate to have to tell Mrs. Pepperwhistle about this. She's not always as agreeable as I am."

You can say that again, I almost replied. And then I thought better of it and held my peace.

"See you bright and early, Roger." The Stable Master rose, dusted off his pants, and loped away into the evening.

We sat in silence for a few minutes, stunned.

"Whew!" Gillian said at last. "He makes Lindy seem like a regular old pussycat."

"We'd better follow his rules if we know what's good for us," Roger agreed.

"Of course," I said glumly, my hopes of obtaining my inheritance anytime soon dwindling.

"Right after we sneak into the throne room this evening," Roger added with a grin.

That night, when everyone but the Guards was asleep, Roger, Gillian, and I wormed our way through the passages. Roger opened the portal into the throne room and, with a bow, handed me back my key. Then we snuck inside.

It was dark, but shards of light from the high side windows cast a ghostly light over the marble tiles. We tiptoed to the dais and crept up the steps. The starburst in the base of the dais gleamed fitfully, as if it couldn't rest easy.

"Do you see it?" I asked.

"See what?" Roger said.

"The starburst—there—shining away!"

"I see lots of dark," Roger said.

"I see the outline of the thrones," Gillian offered. "Are you sure there's really a keyhole?"

"Yep," I said. I stepped forward, bent over, and pointed. "Right there."

"Oh-kay," Roger said, scratching his head. "Unlock it."

"Go on," Gillian urged.

And then, feeling as if generations of Wrays were looking over my shoulder, I put the starburst key into the lock.

"Gosh, I see the keyhole now!" Roger gasped.

"Turn it, turn it," Gillian squealed, forgetting to be quiet.

"Go on," Roger said. "Let's see this thing. If it's been kept at the foot of the thrones all these years, it's gotta *be* somethin'."

Magic surged through my fingers, murmuring in agreement. Anticipation boiled in me like a pan on a stovetop.

The key turned with an audible *click*. A drawer slid out, its bottom invisible in the shadows.

"Ooh, I can't wait!" Gillian breathed.

"What is it?" Roger whispered.

"I can't see," I said, squinting.

He dug a candle stub out of his pocket and struck a match. Then he lit the wick and held the candle over the drawer. Black velvet lined the bottom, and in it were two oval depressions.

"Is this the right lock?" Gillian said. "This can't be!"

I stared. This was it. This was what I'd been searching for. But nothing was there!

Roger waved the candle over the two hollows, and its flame lit the darkness between them. And then I saw.

The light hit something between the two oval depressions, something that sparkled brilliantly against the velvet. I reached down and picked it up.

"Hold it here," Roger said.

"Oh my goodness," Gillian sobbed. "It's a diamond!"

"It's a crystal," I said, squinting at it.

And it was. I scooped it up and held it in my palm, a beautifully beveled stone.

"That's pretty, but . . . ," Roger trailed off.

"Wait," I said, eyeing the shapes in the velvet.

I took off my starburst-engraved silver locket, which was inscribed with the name *Wray*. I pinched it open and laid the crystal inside. It clicked into place. Then I closed the locket and carefully fit it into the oval on the right side of the drawer. A buzz of magic tingled under my fingertip. And the locket lapped up the magic like a thirsty dog.

"It fits," Roger said.

"That's it? That's your inheritance? A crystal for your locket?" Gillian asked, sounding disappointed.

But I wasn't. It was right somehow. It had been passed down to me through my mother. It had been in our family since the time of Magnificent Wray. And I knew now that it wasn't *just* a locket; it was something *more*. I didn't know just what yet. But I'd find out.

And I realized something else. The first chance I got, I was going to seek out One Hundred. Because if it *hadn't* filled the slippers with magic, the starburst wouldn't have been unlocked, and I'd never have found the keyhole. *The dress had done it on purpose.* I'd asked One Hundred for help, and it had helped me.

I owed that dress an apology. And my thanks.

I picked the locket up and polished it on my sleeve.

"Who would have thought that I was carrying around my inheritance the whole time?" I asked.

Gillian shrugged; her visions of jewels and deeds to castles had evaporated.

"The real mystery," Roger said, poking his finger in the empty depression to the left, "is what goes here."

"Hmm," Gillian said, perking up. "Maybe it's an emerald—like the Heart of the Forest?"

"You girls," Roger said, shaking his head. "All you think about is jewels."

"I thought you said that all we think about is the Prince?" I said. "Er—King," I corrected myself with a laugh.

"That too," he replied.

"Hand me the candle," I said.

Roger held it out to me and I took it. Then I crouched down to study the other depression in the velvet. That size! That shape!

"I've seen this before," I told them, tracing the shape with my finger.

"Where?" Gillian asked, plopping down next to me.

"Cherice wore that shape every day," I said, "swinging around her neck!"

They both eyed me like I was as crazy as Cherice.

"She said she was the last Wray," I reminded them. "And she always wore"—I thumped the depression—"her magnifying glass around a chain."

Gillian screwed up her face in thought. Roger chewed his bottom lip.

"Do you think it's valuable?" Gillian asked doubtfully.

"No, but I'll bet it's *magic*," I said, remembering how easily she'd spotted the talisman.

At that, their eyes lit up.

"She's locked up in that asylum," Roger pointed out.

"Do you think she still has it?" Gillian asked.

"She did when they took her away," I said. "So it's probably there with her."

"For now," Roger said.

"For *now*," Gillian agreed.

"But not for long," I said, rubbing the engraving on my locket.

The magic flared under my thumb. Magnificent Wray had gone to a lot of trouble to conceal that drawer. He'd made hiding spots for the locket, the crystal, and the magnifying glass for a reason. Had they all been in there to begin with? If so, who'd taken them out? And when? And why?

Maybe I just needed to collect them together again.

One thing I was certain of: he'd had a purpose in creating them, whatever it might be. And whatever *that* was would be his legacy. *And my true inheritance.*

I intended to find out what it was, even if I had to break Cherice out of that asylum.

B irds sang outside the open kitchen window. A beautiful spring day beckoned. The white stones of the Star Castle sparkled in the bright light. A ghostly starburst glimmered on the wall beside me. My locket gleamed on my crisp white apron front. My new sky-blue cotton Queen's Girl's dress rustled as I sliced the peel off my nine millionth potato—Marci's idea of a suitable punishment.

"It's generous of you to offer to help, Darling," the Soup Chef said. "After the recent furor, the Kitchen Maids are frazzled. And supper must still be served."

"I'm happy to help," I said, tossing the potato into a basket.

The Soup Chef pursed his lips as if he didn't believe me. The other Girls were enjoying a day in the gardens.

But it was true; saving the castle was worth a few potatoes.

Acknowledgments

In 1973, I came home from school to find a letter in my mailbox—from Madeleine L'Engle! At the time, I felt lost in the cold, lonely world of junior high, sort of like I was living on the dark side of the moon. But Madeleine answered my rather impertinent questions as though she were speaking to a fellow writer. Her words were warm and personal, and that letter meant more to me than I can say. She inspired me to keep writing. I've endeavored to pay that forward to other writers.

In some ways, writing is a lot like a chain letter. You send it to five of your friends, who send it to their friends, who send it to theirs. And on and on. A good book gets passed around. People tell me about their favorite book, the one they've never forgotten. It might be an old book, something few people bought, but it meant something special to them. Writing is personal, and so are books.

Thank you to everyone who has taken my books personally,

from booklovers and bloggers to librarians and booksellers. Thank you to every student who has written to me, whether by email or snail mail. I read your letters. I relish every word. And I do my best to respond. Parents and teachers, thank you as well; I read your notes just as thoughtfully.

Thank you to my editor, Diane Landolf, who pushes me to write better novels. And to everyone at Random House who labors over my books, from copyeditors to book designers, typesetters, publicity, marketing, and foreign rights: **thank you so much!**

Thank you to my agent, Sara Crowe, for her continuing support and enthusiasm.

Thank you to my family: Jon, Sara, and Rebecca. My critique partners, Rachel Martin and Kaye Bair. The Ames group: Ann Green, Kate Sharp, Christine Robinson, and Jane Metcalf, for all your wit and insight; and especially to Sarvinder Naberhaus, for making me think deeper. My friend Faye Wade. And to my great-nephew and great-nieces: yes, you are getting books for Christmas! Count on it. Because books are personal.

And thanks to God for creating words and enduing them with power.

Cast of Characters

(in order of appearance)

Darling Dimple: Under-scrubber, Under-presser, Under-assistant to the Wardrobe Mistress, Dress Warrior and Dragon-Thwarter, secret weapon of Princess Mariposa

Princess Mariposa Celesta Regina Valentina: butterfly-loving ruler of Eliora

Jane: Under-slicer and later Picker, Darling's very nearsighted adoptive mother

Marsdon: Head Steward, mustached overseer of the castle servants

Cherice: Wardrobe Mistress, scheming inheritance-hunter who claims to be the last Wray

Lindy: Head Presser, Darling's lovestruck boss

Gillian: Under-dryer, later Under-presser, enamored of stories

Roger: Second Stable Boy, later First Stable Boy, freckled wonder of the world

Marci: Supreme Scrubstress, later Wardrobe Mistress, Darling's nemesis and champion

Francesca Pepperwhistle: Head Girl, Darling's contender for the Princess's approval

Lyric: canary, magical bird that once belonged to Queen Candace

Iago: Darling's mouse friend, father to Bonbon, Éclair, Flan, and Anise

Dragons on the Roof: pair of creatures too vile to describe

The Dresses: one hundred in number, bursting at the seams with *magic*

Lady Teresa: Princess Mariposa's shy cousin

Prince Sterling: seemingly impoverished prince who comes to woo the Princess

Prince Baltazar (Dudley): charming imposter

Queen Candace and King Richard: Princess Mariposa's late grandparents

Mrs. Irene Pepperwhistle: Head Housekeeper, soft-spoken, rules the Upper-servants with a knee-melting gaze

Charlotte: Head Cook, good-natured monarch of the kitchens

Pastry Chef: believes food can cure all ills

Bryce: Captain of the Guards, Lindy's not-so-secret boyfriend

gryphon: sarcastic monster, formerly part of the tower masonry

Lady Kaye, Baroness Azure: wealthiest peer in the realm, never without an opinion

Selma: Head Laundress, Lindy's feisty archrival

Warden Graves: caretaker of the Royal Cemetery, never speaks ill of the dead

Magnificent Wray: architect, Darling's ancestor, and the man behind the *magic*

Dulcie: Princess's Girl, the fastest Girl, believes that petticoats slow her down

Ann and Kate: Princess's Girls, the oldest and the tallest, respectively

Master Varick: Royal Librarian, guardian of the King's library, despises children

Lady Sara Mallory: reader

Marie: Princess Mariposa's confidant and friend to the Princess's late mother, Queen Paloma

Lady Amber DeVere: Magnificent Wray's daughter and the author of his biography

Rose: Head Seamstress, owes Darling a favor

Madame Zerlina Trinket: Royal Dress Designer, exuberant fashion maven

Gloria: Princess's Girl, hides peppermints in her pillowcase

Derek Pepperwhistle: Stable Master, strict with Stable Boys, easy on horses, not readily fooled

Faustine Pepperwhistle: Francesca's twin, formerly a Princess's Girl

Aster: Lady Kaye's personal Maid, has a high opinion of herself

One Hundred: Queen Candace's wedding gown, mysterious prima donna of the 100 Dresses

Try on a little magic with the 100 Dresses series!

Can Darling Dimple and 100 magical dresses save Princess Mariposa?

The magical adventure continues in the second book!

Is there a ghost haunting the castle?

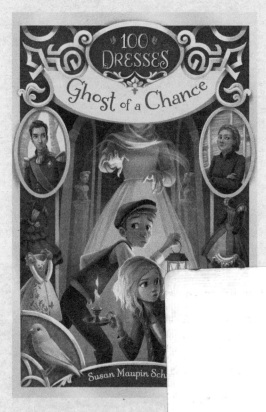

"The charming, persistent, and
fluff-haired Darling . . . rema[...]
to cheer for." —*Kirkus Reviews*